# J.A. ROCK
# MINOTAUR

RIPTIDE
PUBLISHING

Riptide Publishing
PO Box 6652
Hillsborough, NJ 08844
www.riptidepublishing.com

Minotaur
Copyright © 2015 by J.A. Rock

Cover art: Imaliea, imaliea.deviantart.com/gallery
Editor: Delphine Dryden, delphinedryden.com/editing
Layout: L.C. Chase, http://lcchase.com/design.htm

ISBN: 978-1-62649-313-1

First edition
October, 2015

Also available in ebook:
ISBN: 978-1-62649-312-4

# J.A. ROCK
# MINOTAUR

*For my sister.*

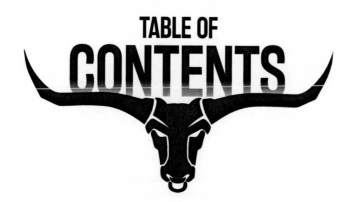

# TABLE OF CONTENTS

Book Three: Twenty Years

# PROLOGUE

**K**now this: I am not a warrior.

I am a disease.

If I go down in history a hero, it will be someone scraping half-truths off the floor and the undersides of desks, sculpting something ugly and defiantly off-center. It will be a careful rearrangement of facts, and it will involve so many lies of omission that the truth will end up amputated from me like a limb. I'll stagger around, a lopsided idea of who I was, everyone too polite to discuss what I'm missing.

I don't trust heroes; I don't think I should. At Rock Point, many of the girls liked stories that ended happily, or at least offered a sense of closure. But I liked tales with abstruse people screwing and killing their way toward ambiguous outcomes. I liked *shadows*. And I liked *gore*.

And secretly, I liked redemption. I liked monsters who regretted and heroes who mustered a revolted sort of compassion for their enemies. Even better were the heroes who saw villains as a mirror—not one that reflected the world precisely as it was, but one that showed the hero what she might become. Like when you and someone else are staring through the same window, and you shift to make your reflection line up with hers. You become an awkward mutt—eyes in the wrong places, too many mouths, but you can almost fit yourself to her outline.

We are all a step away from goodness cracking under our feet and collapsing us into villainy. There are few unbreakable things in the world, and I have cataloged people's stress points with the same earnest vigor with which little Rina once cataloged Rock Point's fauna. Loss, violence, bullying, starvation, boredom, the promise of beauty or fame or sex—chances are there is something somewhere you'd turn wicked for. Innocence starts to look haggard with age, same as skin. I once knew a man who murdered his wife because he couldn't stand that one of her eyebrows was higher than the other. Some people will turn wicked for nothing.

Me, I was born ready to break. I had so many soft places. My tantrums, my rotten words, the joy my fists took in meeting flesh— those were to distract others from seeing all the spots the spear could go.

Until one woman stripped me truly bare, and together we built an armor that rendered me both powerful and humble. It looked so right on me that seeing myself in it for the first time was, I imagine, much like those women who search for the perfect wedding dress and finally find it—they look in the mirror and see that their breasts are high, their stomach cinched, their hips arched like the sides of tombstones.

My sister felt that way about the dress she got married in. In fact, I thought at first the best place to start this story would be at her wedding, at the ceremony I ruined. But I have since discarded that possibility. I then thought of beginning the moment I entered the labyrinth. But there are things you need to understand first. I don't care so much whether the story is appealing, whether my actions make sense to you—my reasons *why* are thin and pale and will flee at the sound of footsteps. But I want you to meet the beast I went up against, in a place that, long ago, people called both palace and dungeon, fortress and ruin. Because I so prefer antagonists to heroes, and because the story you will hear from others likely casts me as the latter, I want to do something kind but ultimately self-serving. I want to make you see *her*.

You may not believe me when I say I owe her a debt. You'll claim I was deluded by a powerful witch whose spells were haphazard and crude. And you're half right. Her magic was often as ugly as its consequences. When she attempted to control the weather, for example, she grew to an ashy and shapeless enormity, swollen with her own storm. The rain she conjured came in burbling sheets, as if the clouds had been sword-swiped across their bellies and were bleeding out. Her thunder was clumsy and overdone, knocking you down and then kicking like a bully.

But sometimes, she was precise. And when she thought—truly *thought*—about what she wanted and how to get it, her magic retreated and her power became real. She seduced me, but she did not delude me. She manipulated, but I could have followed the thread back to the truth anytime. I *wanted* to be under her spell. And for making room for me under that vast overhang of power and agony, secret torment and bold skill, love and whatever preys on love—reason, perhaps—for that, I am grateful to her.

But I am already making a hash of this. I should have started with the wedding. Instead I'll start with the day I arrived at Rock Point Girls' Home. You will think I have gone back on my word, that I am telling you all about me and nothing of her. But to understand her, you must look at my incomplete idea of myself. Because I have very much fitted my reflection to her outline.

Enough.

I do, indeed, have too many mouths.

# BOOK ONE

# ROCK POINT

# CHAPTER 1

**ROCK POINT GIRLS' HOME**
**Logbook**

*New Intake Form*

*Name: Thera Ballard*
*FID #: 11305094*
*Age: 16*
*Height: 5'8"*
*Weight: 145*
*Hair: Dark*
*Eyes: Brown*
*Distinguishing features: 1-inch scar behind right shoulder blade.*

*Intake Processed By: Darla Ling*

*T was admitted last night around 11 p.m. She was uncooperative and could not be trusted to shower on her own, so she was cold hosed and then strapped down for a medical check. She kept yelling things like "I'm a queen where I come from," and just generally deriding the staff's appearance but also not making a lot of sense, so I do think this kid was snowed. As we are not permitted to discipline new intakes (ahem, Rollins—ha-ha!), the whole process was quite frustrating. A good slap would have settled her right down. I told her Rock Point provides tributes to the Beasty. That got her quiet. We finished examining her, gave her the grays, and put her in a solitary room for the night. I heard her stomping around in there till morning.*

## Morning Report: Bessie Holmes

*T didn't have woke up when i entered her room. Lissen, if you give a kid a tranqilizer, you have to document it. No mention of T been doped & yet it was clear she was. i'll also say, whatever she was gave, it worked, because she didn't fight like she supposably did last night. She was very compliant & leaned against me while i led her from the room. She got more lively when we reached the bathroom & she didn't want me to stay in there with her. i explained it was necessary for me to make sure she has regular bowel movements. She screamed that i was a bowel movement. Urinated but did not defacate. I was took her to the breakfast hall.*

## Breakfast Monitor's Report: Darla Ling

*I was alerted to a disturbance in the breakfast hall around 7:15 at the older kids' table. I went to investigate. P Farmer had a bloody nose. T Ballard, the new intake, was sitting beside her. T asked me if she could leave the grounds this afternoon, "just for a little bit," to meet a friend. I ignored her, and that was when she spit at me. I was furious and may have socked her; I don't remember. This possible socking may account for the bruise I'm told she has now under her eye. Anyway, security staff took her out of the hall. She ate nothing but her eggs.*

## Security Staff Report: Officer Molly Grenwat

*Rose Van Narr and me shut the new girl up in her room because CLEARLY she is not fit yet for decent company. Now I'm sure Dr. DuMorg will talk to her and go on about her FEELINGS and other New Theory puppyshit. But if you ask me, this is simply a waste of time because this kid needs a tanning to kingdom come. You should hear what she said about Van Narr's upper LIP HAIR, and now Van Narr is hurt, and I hate working with Van Narr when she's in a pissy mood because she takes it out on me. One more thing: I've been saying for a long time we shouldn't take JUNKIES. I'm telling you, this facility is not equipped for that. Of course we have Riley Denson, and now Riley's taken a special interest in this hophead.*

**Rollins's Note:** *Please remember this log is not a place for your personal opinions. Stick to factual information about the new intake, please. Rock Point has dealt with many problem children in the past, and we will deal with T Ballard with patience and compassion. End of discussion.*

**Darla Ling's Note:** *Ha-ha, actually, it's good if Riley's interested, because she's got a way with the girls. P.S. Learn to spell, Holmes. It's "defecate."*

**Officer Grenwat's Note:** *Also, it's "supposedly."*

Think of that place: not a prison, yet still a trap, with its narrow halls and its water-stained plaster ceilings. The rooms were small. You were a ballerina in a music box, waiting for a lid to open, waiting for the chance to do one fixed performance and be shut away again. You could be drugged to the gills—past the gills; drugs were leaking out your fucking gills—when you arrived, and still realize that this place housed a trophy room of sorrows. That girls suffered here, not in the routinely beaten, chimney-sweeping way I'd always imagined orphans suffered, but deeply. Rivulets of grief sliding down their bones, blushes of it in their cheeks. They suffered because they were lonely in a way people seldom talk about, a way that affects grace and movement and dreams and memory.

If you have seen a dog in a cage—and you know that dogs are all love, that they were born to scavenge and to love and to quarrel over bones and to keep loving even in sleep and in sickness—then you have seen this loneliness. It is frightening because it is not hopeless. Just as a caged dog will wake at every sound, wag its tail, and wait—the girls at Rock Point Girls' Home hoped. They tempered that hope with jokes and anger and their fists, and while I was treated like an especially wretched specimen, in a sense I fit right in.

I met Riley Denson my first morning at Rock Point. She entered the solitary room with caution, though she didn't seem afraid of me.

I wanted to make her afraid. I was lolling, my mind cotton, my eyes burning, and my mouth dry. I wanted something to swallow. Something to inject or lick or chew or *anything*. Anything that would make me feel different.

I sat on the bed, staring out the small window, and watched her approach out of the corner of my eye.

"Hi, Thera." Her voice was sweet. I remember even now, she always sounded like she was inviting you on a fucking picnic.

I wanted something that would thump my heart like a fist, something that would leave ruts in my brain. I glanced at her and tried to imagine she was lickable, drinkable. Her skin was pale—a rarity in the town of Rock Hill and its outlying lands. Mine was brown with washed-out spots, like a fucked-up watercolor. She wore glasses and had hair colored like the crud you'd scrape off the bottom of a pan after dinner. Her eyes were too small, her glasses too thick, her hair pushed flat on the sides so it looked like the cap of a mushroom. I was thrilled by her plainness. Pretty girls never did much for me. Goddamn, but I'd rather look like a killer than a princess.

The only lovely thing about her was that, from the side, her features slid neatly into one another. Her profile looked drawn by a skilled master, while mine, I knew, looked scrawled by a child—bulgy forehead, upturned nose, wide lips with clumsy edges, chin round and sagging slightly.

"Riley Denson. Afternoon staff. I brought lunch." She set the plastic container on a small night table that was bolted to the floor. All the furniture was bolted—the cot and the narrow dresser. I supposed if it hadn't been, I'd have loaded it all into my damn hot air balloon and sailed off toward whatever clouds the sky was farting out that morning.

My arms itched. I sat on my hands and waited. She'd introduced herself by her full name, not "Miss Denson." Maybe that was why I didn't mind her so much. I'd arrived here blown out of my fucking mind by various shit I'd found in Auntie Bletch's bathroom cabinet, but the hosing last night had sobered me, as had my terror at the way people here were so quick to grab at my body, pull me where they wanted me to go. I needed to believe in Denson's calm.

I went back to looking out the window. After a moment, she crouched near me. She wore a dress, but she crouched anyway. She had long stockings on, so I didn't get a glimpse of leg or anything. She gazed at me. "That's quite a shiner you've got."

She was ready in case I lashed out; I could see it in her shoulders and in her gaze. My cot was low enough that even crouching, she was almost at eye level. I tried to hurl all my hate into her eyes—stuff it down those black centers. Behind those unfashionable slabs of glass, her pupils contracted slightly, fans of gold and green around them.

There was something odd in her expression, the look you might get if you'd spent a particularly pleasant day at the seaside and were now driving away, toward nightfall and work the next day, peering back at the vanishing ocean and the setting sun. I stared at her hand. Small and pale with cracked nails. "I gotta leave here," I told her conspiratorially, as though she might be grateful to know this secret of mine. I didn't really know where I'd go, but I figured anywhere but here would do.

She stood slowly. "Rec's in half an hour. Soccer today. Think you can play nice with the other girls?"

"I can go outside?" I was genuinely surprised. Despite Auntie Bletch's assurance that this was a place where I'd be "cared for," I'd been convinced it was one of those asylums I'd heard tales about—ghost children leaving bloody footprints in the bathroom; lobotomized women lurching through corridors, oblivious to the screams echoing behind steel doors. Rock Point didn't have steel doors, from what I'd seen. It wasn't a homey place, but it wasn't a white-walled institution either. It was more like a very large house with long halls and high ceilings and dirty corners. But I hadn't forgotten the wretched feeling I'd had last night as I was dragged through those halls and up the wooden staircases. The wide eyes watching me as I'd screamed and struggled. Those suffering girls with their waiting hearts.

"If you can behave." Denson coughed suddenly, and pulled out a handkerchief to dab at her mouth.

I nodded.

"No leaving the playing field."

"Okay." My voice sounded gruff and strained, like an old woman's.

She sat on the end of the bed, far enough away that I relaxed a little. I'd had fun last night making furious mockery of every face I saw. But I couldn't think of a nasty thing to say to or about Denson. Even her glasses had, over the past few minutes, become admirable.

"Can I ever leave?" I asked.

"When you find a home or you turn eighteen."

I showed her my teeth—not a smile, and I hoped she knew it. "I don't like this place."

"You've only been here a few hours."

"Well, it's been a lousy few hours."

"Try to eat some lunch."

"I don't want to."

Denson got up. "Half. Just half of it by rec time. I'll come get you in twenty minutes."

"Fuck," I muttered. Back at Auntie's, I'd have been slapped for that. Denson only smiled.

## Rec Time
## Report By: Glenna Formas

*Today is soccer. Girls line up to receive jerseys. One girl missing: #76510228. New intake, #11305094, demands to play barefoot. I permit this. Things going well, red team winning despite being a bunch of scrimshankers, and suddenly new intake bolts toward the west gate. I leave #44990033 in charge of game and pursue. I am not the fastest runner, but new intake seems not very strong, exhausted, etc. But adrenaline must be working overtime for her, because as soon as I get close, she finds another gear and tries to scale the gate. I catch her and pull her down. She fights better than I'm expecting, but she gets tired pretty quick. Then she acts like she can't hear anything I say. I drag her to admin. When I get back to the field, I discover #38812096 has sprained her ankle, which I regret from a liability standpoint but personally I find her to be kind of a wiener and anyway it seemed more important to catch new intake than to babysit wieners.*

*And I mean serious wieners.*

*Admin Log*
*Date: 12 March*
*Event: Disciplinary Hearing*
*Report By: Christine Rollins*
*Present: Kennedy DuMorg, psychologist. Christine Rollins, co-owner/ overseer.*
*Child: 11305094*

*T Ballard was brought before me following an escape attempt at rec time. I discussed the nature of her transgression with her, but she appeared uninterested. Her breathing was labored—I assumed from her flight attempt—and she had difficulty focusing. I asked if she understood that she is in Rock Point's custody now and must follow our rules until she is placed in care, adopted out, or comes of age.*

*T said she needed to meet a friend off RP grounds. I told her this was the sort of privilege afforded to well-behaved children, and I pointed out she had caused nothing but trouble since arriving here. I placed a hand on her shoulder to indicate I understood how hard this adjustment period must be, and she grabbed my arm and twisted it. I required considerable assistance to fight her off. She did not respond to any of my statements or questions thereafter. I informed her she was banned from rec for the next three days.*

**Rollins's Note:** *Darla Ling is no longer with Rock Point. The new weekday breakfast monitor will be Bessie Holmes. Please note it is never acceptable to strike a child in anger.*

## Psychological Evaluation: T Ballard
## Report By: Dr. Kennedy DuMorg

*T claims a history of physical and verbal abuse. However, she refuses to elaborate just yet. I thought it best not to push her at our first meeting. She also claims her mother murdered her father with an ax. Can anyone confirm this?*

**Rollins's Note:** *Untrue. Her parents died in a car accident. T claims no memory of the tragedy, though she was present.*

## Medical Report: Dr. Brenda LiPordo

*T Ballard is being treated for opioid withdrawal. Staff, please expect early symptoms—anxiety, muscle aches, sweating, runny nose, etc. Clonidine administered for treatment of symptoms. T is to report to the health room each day at 2 p.m. She has not eaten a full meal since arriving here three days ago.*

## Morning Staff Report: Bessie Holmes

*So aparenntly i get the duty of now giving this fucked-up new kid her meds every morning. Yippee. Tried this morning & she has slapped the pill cup out of my hands. i picked up the pills & pinched her nose shut, & she hit me in the throat. Dr. LiPordo says it will be a while before my voice fulheartedly returns, which is terrible news. As many of you know i sing in a divorced women's choir & we are having our anual autumn concert in just 3 weeks. See me for tickets.*

*i couldn't get ahold of T after that because I was been in to much pain, so i called Riley Denson in. T fought Riley too, & T was screaming so loud we couldn't talk sense to her, so i drew my arm back, preparing to give her a good slap. Denson asked me to refrain from hitting.*

*i composed myself & left her to Denson.*

**Rollins's Note:** *This log is not the place for solicitations, unless those solicitations are relevant to a child's accomplishment. i.e. When little Rosie, #3592801, played the wise man in the town Christmas pageant.*

I've chosen to tell this part of the story through what I've reassembled from Rock Point's logbooks because, to be honest, I do not remember this period well enough to recount it properly. I was a wreck, sweaty day and night and behaving like a true beast. Paranoid, angry, and deeply, wildly alone.

I have a vague sense of Riley Denson as my savior. Growing up, I never had a high opinion of women who devoted their lives to caring for others. I considered them dull and feeble. To have any real fun in the world, you needed power. And to gain power, you had to wound others—not coo over the wounded. But Denson never cooed. Her scuffed, simple wisdom was comforting. *This is how things are, Thera. If you try to change them you may fail. But that doesn't mean you shouldn't try.*

Rock Point's logbooks came into my possession when Rock Point was dismantled years ago. I like "was dismantled" better than "closed." Forces acted upon it. Construction workers stripped the building for parts and then blasted its skeleton to dust. The town wants to build something new there, and I approve. I'm not one of those people who's in love with what was.

# CHAPTER 2

I was vastly unpopular at Rock Point. The staff, the other girls, the teachers all loathed me. I preferred it that way. To draw lines and dare others to cross them was an enjoyable game, a villain-lounging-on-a-tower-of-cakes sort of feeling. I taunted my enemies, and when they charged, I whisked my cape away and stuck spears into their shoulders. There was one little girl who cried at the sight of me. She was my medal of honor.

The girls' home was fairly large. There were four wards of eight rooms each—two wards upstairs for girls ages five and above, one downstairs for infants and staff, and another downstairs which consisted of a large parlor, two classrooms, a small library known as the reading room, a dining area, and a cramped kitchen. The décor was simple: wood paneling, faded pink and beige wallpaper, and framed paintings of flowers. The home sat on a cliffside acre; it was bordered on the front by a browning lawn, and on the back side by a scraggly wood.

When I wasn't plotting my escape, I was tossing, sweaty and terrified in my narrow cot—pitched from the cart of my own nightmares into an empty road. Or else snapping pencils in class and spitting on the desk until I had a large clear pool in front of me through which to rub my chewed erasers. In my mind, over and over, I picked the lock on Auntie Bletch's medicine cabinet. I found the things I needed, swallowed, and went hurtling somewhere no pain could touch me.

I suppose it was Miss Ridges who changed things.

One afternoon, Riley Denson came into my room. She had taken over my medication routines. She always spoke softly and had even, once, made me laugh. I wouldn't say I trusted her, but that day I did not fight her when she led me, sweating and whimpering, down to the reading room. I'd eaten lunch, which felt like a dangerous accomplishment. I was dressed, not in Rock Point grays, but in a sweater and jeans. The sweater was too big, old and ragged, and had cheap, glittery gold thread woven through it. I kept looking down, following the shining, broken strands with my gaze.

The reading room had a wooden floor covered by a thick oriental rug. There were three small tables along the back wall with a green lamp on each one. A painting on the wall showed a meadow on an overcast day, a single bare tree in its center.

I stopped in the doorway, Denson just behind me. At least ten girls were sitting on the floor. So far, I'd hardly paid attention to the other kids here, except to lash out at them in the cafeteria or during rec time. But now I was expected to sit with them, and they were all staring at me. Their faces were different shapes and ages, but they all held, it seemed, the same expression of sly disgust.

Miss Ridges sat on a stool beside a low table, her gray-streaked hair in a neat little bun, her brown skin soft looking and wrinkled. She smiled at me. "Welcome, Thera."

Denson nudged me, which made me want to snap at her. "Go on," she whispered.

I stepped into the room. One foot in front of the other. Took a seat next to a girl who looked about my age, and who wore a black blouse and spangled jeans. I picked at my sweater as I felt her turn to study me.

Miss Ridges picked up a book. I was too far away to see the title. But as soon as she began to read, I stopped caring what the title was or who was around me. The only storytellers I'd known before were grade-school teachers, with their sick-sweet voices and their big faces telling me how I should feel about what I was hearing. Miss Ridges didn't make faces. Her voice was low, and it slipped even lower when she started to feel the words she was reading. She read like she was singing in a jazz bar, closing her eyes, shaking her head slowly, getting lost in the music. I listened to every word of the trite tale, and when she was finished I hugged my knees, reluctant to move. It had been a foolish story, but Miss Ridges seemed anything but foolish.

The girl next to me shifted. Her knee bumped mine. I saw she had painted nails. "I thought the ending was stupid," she said aloud. "Just . . . stupid."

The girl's name was Bitsy, and she had long blond hair tied in a messy ponytail, ragged bumps along her scalp. She talked constantly about other people's shortcomings in a husky voice that sounded like she was suppressing a laugh—the sort of strained, defensive laugh you'd give someone who has just hurt your feelings, deeply and publicly. A *What's* your *problem?* laugh.

She had little interest in tales of woe. When I explained I'd come to Rock Point addicted to drugs, she only laughed and told a story about the time her cocaine addict mother had tried to strangle the milkman. She recounted to me just about every story Miss Ridges had read aloud over the last year. She had an opinion on why each one was silly, and yet she remembered them in such detail it was hard to believe she felt only disdain for them. Most were fairy tales—secret princesses rescued from slavery by true love, children lost in the woods, a beanstalk leading to a kingdom in the sky.

I told her Bitsy was a dumb name, and she glared at me. "My mother's idea."

"Is your name Elizabeth?" I asked.

"Yes."

"So why not go by that?"

"Because you're a gummed-up box."

"Box" was one of Bitsy's favorite words, and I was embarrassed when I finally had to ask her what she meant by it, since she didn't seem to be referring to cartons. She rolled her eyes and slapped my shoulder affectionately. "You've got one between your legs, waddy brain."

Bitsy, I decided, was wonderfully disgusting.

The weeks went by, and I sweated less. I stopped waking at night with cravings so deep I had to kick the wall and dig my nails into my hips to find some release. I attended classes, and while I was generally disruptive and a poor student, I learned tricks for controlling myself. If I stared out a window, I felt less combative. Some teachers were okay with this, and I got along well with them. Others said things like, "Eyes up here," or, "Pay attention, Thera," and I wanted to spit at them, but I spat on my desk instead.

It also helped to go around the room and imagine how each girl had come to Rock Point. There was a very thin girl with a distant gaze whose parents could only have died tragically in some bloodless accident—like a joint drowning or mutual consumption of sleeping pills. Another girl was the sort who'd been given up, I reckoned. She was a terrier with a pant leg—grabbing an idea and shaking it and not letting go until she was kicked. I didn't see how the teachers could stand her. She tried to make meat of the history of some long-ago revolution, all because she believed cannons hadn't been around at the time.

"I assure you"—Miss Tophitt, the history tutor, looked as though important blood vessels might be close to bursting—"that cannons existed and were used."

"But no," the terrier insisted. "That's a tale we're told. In fact there were only swords and catapults."

After lessons I often found myself in Bitsy's room, half listening to her tirades, which generally focused on her roommate Liz, the dining hall food, or Riley Denson, whom Bitsy hated. One day, we were sitting on her floor. I had a pack of cigarettes Bitsy had snagged from Bessie Holmes's dress pocket. In the absence of a lighter, I was breaking them in half and rolling the tobacco between my fingers. Bitsy was painting her nails with oil paints she'd nicked during craft time.

"So then—" Bitsy held out her hand and carefully painted a green stripe on her middle nail "—Lizzie says, 'Well, it'd be *nice* if your side of the room wasn't always a pigsty.' And I say, '*Okay*.' I mean, isn't it my business what I do with my side of the room? I don't tell her to trash that awful pink unicorn."

I glanced over at the stuffed pink unicorn on Liz's bed. It had purple eyes and a dopey smile and a horn made of yellow pipe cleaners.

I shrugged, a cigarette dangling from my lips. "She's just being an ass." I didn't tell Bitsy that her side of the room really was disgusting.

I liked the messiness of it. At Auntie Bletch's I'd been made to keep my room clean. I'd gotten very used to having almost nothing, and to keeping what I did have out of sight. But Bitsy let everything she'd collected—clothes, toys, books, hairbrushes, stolen markers and paints—mountain up beside her bed.

Bitsy rubbed at some paint she'd gotten on the skin beside her thumbnail. "I end up feeling like *I'm* the crazy one for expecting people to behave like adults."

Everyone in the world had done Bitsy an injustice, and I was the one she confided in. I never had to say much. I could go on chewing the ends of cigarettes, staring at the scuffs on the wall, as long as I nodded every now and then and said, "Uh-huh," or "That's a shame," or "You should tell her how you feel."

"And then that *lousy* bitch, Denson," Bitsy was saying. "God, I'd like to putt a nut into that box."

I'd long since grown used to Bitsy saying she wanted to putt a nut into people's boxes or assholes or mouths or ears. She liked golf and the prospect of damaged orifices. "What's so bad about Denson?"

"The way she *looks* at me."

"Looks at you?"

Bitsy was also more than a bit paranoid. She shook her head. "She hates me. I don't know what I ever did to her." She leaned back and studied the sloppily painted nails of her left foot. "She loves you and hates me."

I had come to be on decent terms with Denson. I couldn't think of a time in my life where any adult had preferred me to another child, and I felt a small, guilty satisfaction, a hope that Bitsy was right.

Bitsy held out her hand. Her nails were painted alternating red and green. "What do you think?"

I leaned over and put my fingertip on the middle nail of her left hand. The wet paint came off on my skin.

"You ass!" Bitsy jerked away. "It's not dry."

"Miss Alpern said during crafts yesterday that oil paint takes years to dry." Sometimes it was little things like that—stupid facts that drew my attention and fascinated me for unknown reasons—that made life here bearable.

"To be honest . . ." Bitsy blew on her nails and glanced at me. "I think Denson likes you more than is entirely proper."

I'd been playing with Liz's unicorn, making it ram its horn into the edge of the bed. I stopped. "What are you talking about?"

"You have to know she's a BD."

"What's that?"

Bitsy rolled her eyes and shook her head. "You're really hopeless. I can't say it out loud. She's just . . . She *likes* you. You know."

I thought about how Denson often put a hand on my shoulder, or combed my hair with her fingers. The way she looked at me for long moments before speaking, as though I was something quite fascinating. "You're mentally ill."

Bitsy laughed.

"I'm serious. Just quit talking about it, okay?"

Bitsy shrugged and pulled herself to her feet using the edge of the bed. She left oil paint stains all over the gray sheet. "Just watch your box, is all I'm saying."

The town of Rock Hill sits on an isolated stretch of knobby land. I didn't think the solitude strange growing up, but now that I've seen more of the world I wonder how Rock Hill survived, forgotten and miserly as it was. Perhaps it would have been a mercy had the beast, the Minotaur, destroyed it.

The sea surrounds the area on three sides, and the air is always gray. A feeble mist clings to the cliffs, and the clouds are low and swollen, moving gracelessly. In winter, the leafless trees look like black prongs thrust into the sky. The sea collects a layer of frost, and as spring nears the waves seem to hatch as though from an egg, spilling across the shore. In summer, the sun is like a pathetic rag hung out to dry, badly stained and dripping weak light.

To the south of Rock Hill is a headland called Rock Point. For years there was nothing on it but the girls' home and the prison. On another cliff north of the town—one obscured by fog and simply known as the promontory—was the labyrinth.

When I was a child, my family lived in a landlocked neighborhood full of slung-up houses and street prowlers with their hardened slouches, long strides, and pockets full of knives. I envied those toughs for what I believed at the time was an elegant attempt at anarchy. I too wanted people to fear me, to cross the street when I approached. To hold tighter to the worthless things they valued in case I made a lunge.

My parents never took my sister and me to the ocean. They told few stories, and those they did tell were told blandly. I knew from a young age a bare-bones legend of the Minotaur—a beast who was half woman and half bull, who, forty years before I was born, had terrorized Rock Hill, killing indiscriminately, kidnapping children and whisking them to her lair. She had taken only wicked children, according to my parents.

So *be good, Thera.*

And *pay attention.* And *don't hit.*

And *eat everything on your plate.*

But I didn't know the *story.* I had seen paintings of the labyrinth, and they looked like fairy-tale illustrations of a castle. Draped red silk below the windows; a vast exterior of stone and wood. A massive clock tower and a ceiling made of glass. And yet it was a prison. It had kept the beast contained for decades. On the only long drive my family ever took, we had a view of the promontory, and I stared up at the black cliff and its mask of fog and imagined I could see that labyrinth through the mist. Tried to visualize what lay inside. Oddly, no matter how generously I offered evil a place in my fantasy, my vision was one of beauty. Fountains and ancient trees and rib-thin cats finding holes in green hedges.

The town still bears scars you might not notice unless you set out to look for them. There are places where grass doesn't grow, rooms with rusty stains on their walls. Houses where half the bricks are old and half are new. Piles of debris behind crumbling buildings. A mass grave in the town center, simple white stones around two water-filled ditches dug into the earth to form a cross. Every year, on Unity Day, people throw white flowers into the cross, until it looks full of drowned Ophelias.

The children I played with growing up were terrified of the beast. Abby Serona said the creature was sure to escape the labyrinth someday and return to Rock Hill. Sara Reed asked me once what church my family went to, and when I said we didn't go to church, she told me the beast had my soul. She said I'd be dragged into the labyrinth and would never leave, even in the afterlife. I knocked Sara into a puddle and clobbered her blond head with a handful of mud, but deep down, I was scared she was right.

The beast was shadowy in my mind. I pretended I was living during her reign, and that each day she galloped through the town on cloven hooves. She ate victims slowly. She tore pregnant women open with her claws and whipped men's faces to pulp with her tail. How she could, in stories, be both hooved and clawed puzzled me—until I heard from other children that she was magic, that she could transform at will.

I imagined we were tangled, the beast and I. She pulled my dreams down like curtains and stuck her laughing head into the empty space. And instead of cowering, I laughed back. I began to have fantasies where I tamed her. Slipped a golden bridle over her horrible head and became her master.

# CHAPTER 3

**A**fter three weeks, I was moved out of the solitary room and into a small bedroom with sticky floorboards and twin narrow cots. I was assured I would have a cellmate soon, but days went by and the other half of the room remained unoccupied.

Some nights I would jump on one bed for a while before leaping the small chasm to the other bed and curling up there. I could be quite childish, was prone to acting younger than my years. We all were, even the seventeen-year-olds—the girls who would be leaving Rock Point in a few months' time. It was a place that, despite its sporadic strictness, gave us all the illusion of not being alone, and perhaps we believed that if we never acted like adults, we'd never be forced out into the wider world to confront the magnitude of our desolation.

I was allowed to stop wearing the Rock Point grays and request regular clothes in addition to the gold sweater and jeans I'd worn to story time. Denson searched the secondhand shops in town and found me some black trousers a size too small that squeezed my waist and rode up my ass. She also brought me a few sweaters, a couple of skirts I swore I'd never wear—though after an hour in the trousers I was rethinking that vow. And a variety of hair clips, which I named and set up in various army formations on my tiny desk, and guided them through battles with the Minotaur.

I had to take pills each morning—pills that would apparently help rid my body of its dependence on other pills. I didn't like how they made me feel—sluggish and sad—and so I took to hiding them under my tongue and spitting them into the back of a dresser drawer once Denson was gone.

Bitsy and I began to request the same chores. We had lessons together, but we wanted more time to talk. Sometimes she fell asleep on the spare bed in my room, but the night monitor always came looking and hauled her back to her own room. One night, Bitsy rolled under my bed when Van Narr came looking. Van Narr seemed surprised not to find Bitsy in my room, and I think we would have gotten away with it if Bitsy hadn't giggled.

Van Narr damn near pulled Bitsy out by the hair. Bitsy was still giggling. I slapped her side as she was dragged past me—just to let her know she'd ruined things.

I wanted her to be my sister. I had a storybook understanding of sisters. They whispered secrets and held your hand, and you dug in the dirt together and went exploring. They had ribbons in their hair, and they were usually in some way tragic. Too shy and gentle to withstand the brute world's lashings, they coaxed fawns and sang sweetly and ended up vanishing in the woods or dying of some obscure fever. They were nauseating and lovely, a hindrance and a blessing.

I never wanted to *be* anyone's tragic, ribboned sister; I only wanted to have one. Someone I could protect and disdain and kiss goodnight. Bitsy was not tragic or sweet, but she was bitterly fun. Her scorn was almost buoyant, a sort of hobby that brought her a casual, infectious joy. And—I see it now; I didn't then—it was a veneer. She cared deeply about what others thought of her, and she was frightened of being on her own.

My real sister, Rachel, had been skilled at keeping her distance. She was three years older than I, but the gap seemed more like ten years. She was tall and thin and careful and grave. We engaged in minimal exploring as children, and after our parents died, she was unable to believe I remembered nothing of the accident. I became suspicious and creaturous to her—a dangerous thing that might entrap you in a murky place and toss you riddles until you earned your freedom or died trying.

Rachel and I lived ten years with Auntie Bletch, my mother's sister. In that time, Rachel grew taller, more elegant, until finally she became a matter of some interest to a diligent farmer's son named Marc who treated her like a prospective hire: *Can you cook? Can you lift? Can you pluck a chicken?*

Rachel spent hours at the shops in town, trying on dresses and finding private flaws. I was bored and told her all the dresses were unflattering even when they weren't. I was cruel, and I knew it, but I wanted her to hurt. She'd hounded me for years after the accident for details I couldn't give. She'd had her fingers in all my worst wounds. I was only fighting back.

Auntie Bletch was quite ill by that time, and I can only assume Rachel had envisioned a future spent as Auntie's nursemaid, or as a housekeeper in Rock Hill's dolorous inn, and had chosen instead a future with Marc—who could provide for both of them, and could contribute some money to Auntie's care as well.

Rachel went to live with Marc's parents until the wedding. I would have felt abandoned, had she not already abandoned me years before, and had I not become recently engrossed in two consuming hobbies: raiding Auntie Bletch's medicine cabinet, and fighting. Twice I was suspended from school for punching other girls. The second time the school included a note saying I was "no lady." Which felt like a relief, like being assured by a doctor that I did not have some terminal illness.

Auntie Bletch had a pharmaceutical bounty—pills of all colors and sizes in beautiful glass bottles, with lists of side effects and warnings as lovely as parade banners. *May cause drying of the throat. Take this medicine WITH or AFTER MEALS.*

I was careful at first about not taking what Auntie Bletch truly needed in order to manage her illness. I stole her indulgences—the biweekly painkillers that blunted smaller aches after the narcotics had done the heavy lifting. The muscle relaxants that were to be used only as needed. The sleeping pills that left me half awake, drifting and wetting the world around me into a dream.

But soon I grew careless and took no note of what I was stealing. Opioids, phenacetin, some strange potion Auntie Bletch had bought at a market stand . . . In school I sweated and daydreamed, and on the playground I snarled at anyone who came near. I said things I knew would make them come near—things about their noses, their mothers, their ripped tights and paltry lunches—and when they approached I lashed out, tangling fingers in their hair or punching them soundly on the mouth. I was detained, I was suspended, I was scolded, I was struck with a ruler, and in the end it was suggested to Auntie Bletch that I be homeschooled. But Auntie was barely in a state to walk, and I got the sense that if she had been able to move efficiently her choice would have been to strangle me, not educate me.

She had, for a time, put the disappearance of her medications down to her own delirium—*"I must've forgotten how many I took"*—and then later to the doctors. *"They're not giving me enough. I tell them I need more, and they do nothing, the uncharitable slobs. Nothing."*

But at some point she must have looked at me—foaming at the mouth, dazed into a bizarre ecstasy, squirming in graceless arcs just to feel the damage inside me—and figured it out. That wasn't the last straw. The last straw was the wedding. But she was furious. *"I am* frightened *of you, Thera. Truly frightened."* She put a padlock on the medicine cabinet, which I learned to pick with bobby pins. I believe she began to think then about sending me away.

The girls' home stood a few hundred feet from the cliff's edge. Girls in the east ward could see through the smeary windows to the precipice. There was iron fencing around the entire property, but rumor had it that years ago, two girls had escaped and wandered off into a fog. They'd gone over the cliff, their bodies discovered days later, broken on the rocks, the waves slipping salt into their hair.

Another legend had a girl climbing into the next-door prison yard and being torn apart by criminals. The prison was a solid, gloomy building, separated from the girls' home by both our iron fence and by its own chain-link barrier, topped with coils of barbed wire. There was much speculation among the girls that one day a killer would escape the prison and come make a mess of the prettiest girls here. I was, in odd moments, disappointed that I was not considered pretty enough to be the imagined killer's victim. That dubious honor went to Wendy Mabler, or little Rina Graham, or Samantha Bonner. These moments of envy came suddenly, and I loathed them. I didn't give a *shit* about being pretty. Yet it's hard sometimes, in a world that promises you the most basic treasures in exchange for being a looked-upon thing, not to wish your face had been a better construct.

Rock Point offered a dubious shelter to girls up to age eighteen. At eighteen, you were turned out, or you took a job at the home—cooking, cleaning, or taking care of the infants. About half the girls left, and half of those returned. Most who left got married, and group outings to town were considered by many girls to be opportunities for husband searching. Bessie Holmes, when she chaperoned, made sure each girl was as well-groomed as possible, and pointed out young men in the sort of clothes that suggested they wouldn't be above marrying an orphan.

To me, the most fascinating of Rock Point's dregs was the cook, Tamna Fen. She had been at Rock Point since the age of nine, and by the time I arrived she had stayed on for three years after her eighteenth birthday. She was a skinny white girl whose silver-blond hair looked like a bleached tree branch—so filthy that it had formed matted, crisscrossing rolls. Her eyes were too large and rimmed in purple. She moaned and hummed, like she was starting a song she couldn't quite remember. Her fingers were always moving, twisting her frayed hair or scratching at a raised mole on her neck.

She cooked so much corn. Corn casseroles and stews, over-roasted ears, and stir-fries that were primarily yellow kernels. Most girls barely noticed her, but I volunteered to work in the kitchen. Not cooking—I was hopeless there—but stocking shelves and carrying large pots to the sink to drain the water from them. I wanted to listen to Tamna moan and sing. What came out of her was mostly nonsense, and it did not occur to me for several months that she was perhaps genuinely crazy.

Couples would come to Rock Point sometimes for what Bitsy called "baby shopping." They all wanted babies. They'd take the leanest, squalliest infants—the ones whose wrists you could pinch and dent like a wet bar of soap—over the healthiest, sweetest girls. I grew to hate them, the couples who held hands and commented to each other in voices that sounded like roadside splats.

*"These are sweet girls, Mary. Aren't they sweet-looking girls?"*

*"Oh, yes, very sweet."*

But they kept their eyes down and looked at our holey shoes and dirty feet, and they waited to be led to the infants' ward.

*"Aw, Jonathan, doesn't she look like the Bakers' girl? We'll have to tell them their long-lost love child is here. You know, don't you, that before they were married . . ."*

I told myself I didn't care that no one glanced twice at me. I told myself I didn't want to be adopted. I'd had parents, and I wasn't looking for more.

One day, a man stumbled into the kitchen while I was working with Tamna. He had booze on his breath and flecks of food in his beard. He glanced around as though confused. I was startled to see a man—apparently unaccompanied by a wife—and didn't move or speak at first. His gaze fell on me.

"Well, well." He leaned back sloppily and stuck his hands in the pockets of his trousers. "How much is the doggie in the window?" He looked me up and down. Then glanced at Tamna, who was staring at him and moaning softly under her breath. "Is this one for sale?"

You'd think, given all the people I'd socked and shouted at over the course of my life, that I'd have been prepared to deal with someone like him. But I could only gaze at him, stunned. My shock increased when Tamna stepped forward. Tiny, ghostlike, she walked right up to him and jabbed him in the chest. "Girls are not for sale, sir, no, no."

His mouth opened in a small O, and then he grinned. "My mistake." He turned and walked back out the door, singing to himself, "'How much is that doggie in the window? The one with the bea-u-ti-ful tail?'"

I said nothing, just went back to scrubbing pans. For several minutes after he left, Tamna repeatedly reached between her legs and grabbed fistfuls of her skirt and what lay beneath it. She tipped her head back and gasped over and over, a moan as quick and hot as a spark behind each breath.

I didn't eat the corn casserole that night.

# CHAPTER 4

One day, Bitsy and I stood in the yard and watched the unloading of prisoners. Through the iron and the chain-link fences, we saw three men, two tall and one short, chained together at the ankles. They shuffled across the ridge toward the prison entrance, ushered by a guard with a club. The truck that had delivered them had a slatted trailer, as though for transporting animals. The back was open now, and I saw straw bales, jumpsuits, canvas bags, nets, and chains.

I nudged Bitsy. "Look at all the stuff in the prison truck. What's it for?"

She turned from the prisoners to look at the truck. "Well, the chains, it's obvious. The bags must be for carrying out dead bodies."

I felt sick and fascinated.

"A shame." Bitsy was back to watching the new prisoners. "They'll stay there until they start to rot, and then they'll be taken to the labyrinth."

"How do you know?"

"Most prisoners end up there if they've done something unforgivable."

"Well how do you know those men have?"

"You can tell just by looking at them."

"Have you ever seen the labyrinth?"

She shook her head. "My mother has been to the spot where the beast was found as a baby."

"What do you mean?"

Bitsy studied me with a chilly sort of pity I wished I could learn to imitate. "You don't *really* know the story, do you?"

I hated to let on when I didn't know things, especially to Bitsy. "No," I admitted finally. "Just that there's a beast who lives in a labyrinth. She's got the head of a bull. And the labyrinth is like a palace."

Scorn in Bitsy's gaze. "That's not even half of it." And so she sat with me on the grass and told me the story of the Minotaur. She told it well, as though she had rehearsed it many times. I tore blades in half, looked for clovers to mangle, and listened.

"Long ago," Bitsy began, "a master wood-carver had three daughters. The wood-carver was very ill—about to die—and she didn't know which daughter to leave the shop to. So she asked them each to make her something to demonstrate their prowess." Bitsy glanced at me, as though to make sure I was properly enraptured. "The eldest daughter carved a boat. Lavishly structured and grandly painted. Yet as soon as she set out to sea in it, a storm tipped it, and she drowned.

"The youngest daughter constructed a bracelet of the finest wooden beads. Each bead was intricately carved with the topography of a continent, so that the whole thing looked like the world pulled apart. It was a beautiful piece, but looking upon it caused an instant sadness, a sense of unfixable chaos."

She paused to glance at me again. I whipped her elbow with a clover. "Well, go on."

She cleared her throat and removed her arm from my reach. "And the middle daughter built a white wooden bull, set to lead the parade of animals her dying mother had been carving for a carousel. The bull was handsome and alarming, its shoulders broad, its head small, its eyes blank, and its horns curving like scythes. The middle daughter decorated it with scars and rips in its hide. It looked as if you might push aside its tattered flesh like curtains and find something beyond imagination inside."

I wished I could see the white bull.

"When the middle daughter finished, she loved her creation too much to give it to her mother. And so she crafted another beast for the carousel—this one made of cheap wood, painted dully—and presented it to her mother. But her mother had spies everywhere, and she'd heard about the beautiful white bull her daughter was hiding from her. She demanded the bull, and when her daughter refused to give it, she cursed her daughter to have eyes only for the bull."

"Have eyes?"

Bitsy leaned close and whispered, "Made her want to *hmm-hmm* the bull."

I burst out laughing so hard I choked.

Bitsy glared at me. "Listen! The daughter planned everything around the bull. She ate next to it, slept sprawled on top of it. And one day she got jabbed by a good-looking young trader, staring up at the bull's white underbelly and imagining the bull itself was giving it to her. She got pregnant, and her belly swelled much bigger than a pregnant belly ought. She swore she could feel two sharp points digging into the wall of her womb. Horns, she thought."

"Why would she think that?"

"I don't know." Bitsy sounded irritated. "She'd been dripping for a bull for months—she had bulls on the brain."

"Fine," I said. "Go on."

"At first the daughter was comforted. She believed the bull had indeed been her lover, and that she was going to have a miracle child— half human, half bovine. Several days before the birth, she began to bleed down there. She thought perhaps the baby was hurt, but it came out normal. Black, curly hair. A daughter."

"That's disgusting. The blood and everything."

"Shh. This is the best part. She cared for the child as she knew she ought to. But it kept changing. She'd look, and she'd see a baby. She'd look again, and it was a small black bull with red eyes and hooves and twisted horns as yellow as bone. She asked others to examine it, but nobody else saw anything unusual about the child. Afraid, she sought refuge with her carving. Night after night she lay in the woodshed with the bull, while inside the house, the baby wailed with hunger."

I began to feel sick, though I wasn't exactly sure why.

"Eventually, she came to realize this was part of the bull's curse. And so one day she bound the baby to the white bull's body, and she left both on the promontory."

Bitsy nudged my knee with her foot. "A man called Darwull found the baby. He was an architect, well loved in town for the beautiful church he'd built. He untied the child from the bull and raised her as his own. But the girl always had problems. She was forever being sent home from school. Her teachers called her a monster. Other children feared her. Darwull tried to love his adopted daughter, but she frightened even him."

I felt sicker.

"When she was fifteen, she tried to murder him with a pair of scissors. He managed to fight her off, but she ran away and was not heard from again until she returned to Rock Hill a full-grown woman. Different, though. A sorceress." Bitsy whispered the last word. "And a wicked one."

I'd always heard that magic existed in Rock Hill. There were rumors of old witches in bent houses, traveling men with potions under their cloaks. But magic was, for the most part, a stale idea. Rarely could those with power use it for anything of consequence. When the beast's reign of terror began, the town's police had apparently begged the help of those with "extraordinary" abilities. But no spell could quiet the beast; no potion could protect the people.

Bitsy reached out and took my hand. I was startled, but said nothing.

"She had transformed herself into a creature part bull and part woman—"

"Wouldn't she be a cow?" I interrupted. "Not a bull?"

"Thera, I'm going to putt a nut into your box in a minute. She's a goddamn sorceress; she can be whatever she wants."

"Okay. Fine." I still felt sick, and nagging Bitsy made it a little easier not to think about the abandoned baby, crying in the house day after day and then left to die on the cliff. I squeezed Bitsy's hand.

"She transformed herself and began to ravage the town."

"Killing indiscriminately," I supplied.

"Yes," Bitsy agreed. "And wrecking homes."

"Tearing children from their mothers' bellies."

"Eating the men sent to slay her. Slowly, in front of their wives."

"And then eating their wives."

Bitsy looked at me and grinned. "Darwull felt so guilty. If he'd never found the baby, the town would have remained safe. And so he agreed to build a prison for his own daughter. High on the promontory, he built the labyrinth. He constructed it around the white wooden bull, which had remained there all those years, unscathed by weather. There'd been a game in town where children dared each other to go to the promontory to touch it. Many reported they could feel a beating heart beneath the wooden chest. Many died—swept off the cliff by a gust of wind. Or, according to some reports, hooked suddenly on the white bull's horns and tossed over the ledge."

"That's some baloney right there."

"Hush up. Darwull lured his daughter to the promontory with a promise—she could take his life, as long as she vowed never to harm another townsperson. She met him on the cliff in her human form. He tried to run. She followed. He was faster, and so she transformed herself into a bull and galloped after him. He ran inside the labyrinth, and she followed. The door swung shut behind them.

"Nobody knows what happened in there. We can only assume Darwull was the Minotaur's first tribute. He left a blueprint in Rock Hill showing the labyrinth he'd built, and he'd told of his plan to trap the Minotaur inside. People came to the labyrinth in hopes of hunting the beast and slaying her once and for all.

"Only one person who ventured into the labyrinth ever returned—a man called Granz. He told of a maze unlike anything from Darwull's blueprint. A place full of danger, jungles, illusions. A place worse than nightmares. He said he had spoken to the beast herself, who had agreed to release him if he passed along these demands: She was to be provided, regularly, with tributes. At least nine per year, or she would escape her prison and destroy Rock Hill."

"And nobody thought she was lying? That she couldn't have gotten out of the labyrinth if she'd tried? Or that Granz was lying?"

"I suppose"—Bitsy let go of my hand—"nobody wanted to find out. Rock Hill has sent tributes ever since. And many people continue to volunteer. The tributes of the past often brought gold and jewels, hoping to soften the beast with bribes. It's said that there's now a massive room in the labyrinth full of treasure. And that many who vow to slay the beast are really going treasure hunting."

I was terribly intrigued by this. "Treasure?"

She stared at me. "Yes. Why? Do you think you'll be the one to find it?"

"Maybe so. Maybe I'll become the richest person in all of Rock Hill."

She snorted. "Good luck with that."

But I could not stop thinking, that night or in the days to come, about a room full of treasure. About that palace full of secrets. About the abandoned child and the monster everyone feared.

Perhaps a beast was what I was meant to be. A cast-off daughter, a dangerous sorceress. I might have done quite well at indiscriminate devouring, at creating a legend much larger than myself, and much more frightening. I wondered if the beast was lonely. If there were tributes she could not find; if she went to bed hungry.

# CHAPTER 5

**B**itsy and I became casual bullies. We told the other girls what we wanted—their spare change, sweaters, stuffed animals—and they were usually scared enough of us to give it over without us even needing to make threats. One of the worst things we did was take a rock from Rina. Little Rina wanted to be a biologist. She spent hours making notes on Rock Point's flora and fauna. She'd collect rocks, eggshells, dead rabbits, anything. This particular rock looked like any other rock to me, but she swore it held the fossil of some something-or-other. She begged us to let her keep it, but I took it from her hand and tossed it high over the gates and into the prison yard.

Then one day we made the mistake of telling Kenna Murphy to give over her small beaded purse, which she carried pinched between her fingers like a cigarette.

Kenna was our age, a spiky girl oafishly angry over everything. She moved like a top, like some invisible hand was spinning her until she wobbled and fell. She wore her hair close-cropped, which emphasized how narrow her skull was, how it didn't look much wider than her neck. She was always yelling at everyone on the rec field like she was the coach, and she dressed in faded rugby jerseys and pants with elastic in the waistbands.

She could also pull your goddamn leg like no one else. She'd stare right at you without a trace of a smirk and tell you about the time she was on that cargo ship that sank twenty years ago, even though she was only sixteen and had never been to sea in her life. Or she'd tell you she'd gone to the deserts and the jungles, slain a zebra with a bit of flint. Or that her brother was a contortionist in a circus, until he'd gotten stuck with his legs behind his head and now had to walk on his hands.

I might have been jealous of her, since my attempts to tell everyone my mother had done my father in with an ax had been met with derision, while Kenna's tales were taken with good humor and requests for more. I'd avoided challenging her up to that point, but Bitsy and I had grown bold.

Kenna laughed when I told her to give over the purse.

"Awf!" Kenna stepped back, baring her teeth like a dog. "D'you know where I got this? Off a rickshaw pedaler in the Far East. We played the shell game for thirty-six hours straight, and I finally won."

"You're fulla shit; now give it over." I hadn't been raised to speak like a tough, but I'd hung around enough of them in town that I knew how to mimic their voices, their speech. Usually girls quailed at it, but Kenna just frowned, breathing noisily through her nose.

When I tried to grab the purse, Kenna threw a punch. I threw one back, and she and I ended up grappling until she had her fingers in my mouth, and I was biting down on them while simultaneously trying to pull her left ear off by the lobe. A crowd of girls had gathered to cheer on the fight, and I was well prepared to do serious damage when somebody yanked me away, slapping my hand so sharply that I released Kenna's ear with a cry of pain.

Bessie Holmes.

Bessie Holmes, with tightly curled hair and her freckled cheeks and forehead. She was something of a joke among us girls, with her mixed-up way of speaking and her tendency to get flitty over nothing. But at this moment, she looked almost intimidating. I was breathing hard and so was Kenna. I wiped my hands on my jeans.

Bessie Holmes looked from me to Kenna and back. "Apologize." The word was a furious whisper. "Apologize to each other at once."

I stared, still wired from the fight, not at all ready to apologize, but afraid—all at once, *terrified*—that I might be sent to the labyrinth as punishment.

"Apologize!" Bessie repeated, and her voice echoed through the hall. She smoothed her skirt. Her jaw was quivering. She leaned close to Kenna and me, as if we were small children. "We are all we *have.*

You hear me? We are all we have ever *has*, and we are being *on* the *same side.*"

I stuck my hand out to Kenna grudgingly. She took it and nearly crushed my fingers, glaring at me. We shook. And in the days after that, through some odd muddle of necessity and rancorous admiration, we became something like friends.

I was sure I'd be dragged before Rollins and the psychologist for another disciplinary hearing. When that didn't happen, I worried that my trip to the labyrinth was a surprise the Rock Point staff intended to spring on me. I lay awake several nights, expecting my door to burst open and a crew of women to grab my limbs, haul me from my bed, and throw me into the back of a truck like the one that had unloaded the prisoners.

"Do you really provide tributes to the beast?" I asked Denson finally. A week had passed since the fight with Kenna, and still no one had disciplined me. Denson and I were in my room, and what I found to be an irritating gush of white-silver light poured steadily through the window.

Denson, who had been sorting my afternoon meds, looked up. I only took three pills now: one for nerves, one to help with a series of stomachaches I'd had lately, and one to balance my moods. I still spat them into my dresser.

I was used to instant, no-cowshit responses from Denson, so it made me suspicious, the way she seemed to consider her words. "Do I personally? I don't have that kind of time."

"Not *you*. Rock Point."

"No. We don't send any of our girls to that fate."

"But some orphanages do."

Denson plopped a pink pill into the cup. "Yes, some."

I sprawled backward on the bed. I had large breasts, especially compared to the other girls here, and I liked the sideways spill of them when I lay on my back.

I caught Denson looking. I thought, as I often did now, about what Bitsy had said. *"You have to know she's a BD."*

Maybe Denson was. I didn't mind. I liked the idea that Denson had a secret or two. She was old—at the time she seemed unimaginably old, though she was probably only in her midthirties—and the way she looked at me made me feel extraordinarily noticed.

"So why not do it?" I asked. "It would keep the girls' home from getting too crowded."

"Nonsense." There was a slight edge to her voice. "Would you do that to children?"

I shrugged and lolled my head toward her. "I would go into the labyrinth if I was sent there. And I'd club the dumb beast's head off."

Denson stopped moving. I could see her pinching the little pill cup until it looked like it might crack. "It is all right to have an imagination, Thera. But sometimes it's better not to comment on what you don't understand."

But what I didn't understand kept me anchored in my body. Otherwise my mind would have woven new truths and soared, unhumbled, through space and stars. It would have backstroked through the mulch of the earth, and I would have been a living doll, my body frozen and my dreams on stilts. As it was, I let the locked-away truth rap me sharply. Until I sat back, shaking my head, and began to circle it again. "Do you think the beast ever gets lonely? She's got no one but tributes for company, and she eats them."

"I really don't concern myself with that creature."

"I'm just saying, after my mother hacked my father's head off with an ax, she grew so lonely she poisoned herself."

When I finally looked at Denson, she said slowly, "Your mother did no such thing."

I felt a jab of fury. "How do you know?"

"Your parents died in an auto crash."

I sat up. "Is that what my Auntie Bletch told you?" I kept my voice hard and sly. I saw her waver for just a second.

"It's what the records say."

"Why would you believe Auntie Bletch and not me?"

"Be quiet, Thera."

"Why would you believe Auntie Bletch and not me?" I shouted again. "Why am I not worth listening to?"

"You are lying; now stop."

"Don't you like me? Don't you like me more than all the oth—"
"*Just stop it, you horrid brat!*"

I fell silent. It was the first time Denson had raised her voice to me. She closed her eyes and shook her head, breathing in soft huffs, as though she were crying.

When she offered me the pill cup, I touched her hand—deliberately, but with such casual clumsiness that she might think it was an accident. Something flared in her eyes, a desolate longing blunted by weariness. Some old demon of hers had been snagged from the sea, cranked up, and dangled before her. Now I credit myself with tidier thoughts than I could possibly have had at sixteen, but I felt I was seeing a dual reaction: Denson's soft, secret joy at my touch, and her loathing of whatever had been pulled out of the water. That blue-lipped, bloated mystery from her past, with its closed eyes and its smug, sleeping smile. She knew it wasn't dead. Knew it would wake and cough a stream into her face.

Maybe I realized then that I had ammunition. And perhaps I was ashamed, because I suddenly slapped the pill cup from her hand, and we both stared at the damned little things that skittered into the cracks between floorboards. Things that failed to improve me and turn me forgivable.

# CHAPTER 6

Allendara came to Rock Point on a Saturday, two months after my arrival. She'd been picked up in town by Dr. LiPordo and driven to the girls' home in the doctor's white car.

Allendara—Alle—was tall and as full figured as a grown woman. She had dark-brown skin and black, shiny curls. A wide nose and full lips, and enormous dark eyes that glistened just a bit too brightly, like they were always covered in a layer of tears. She entered Rock Point regally, as though she were being shown a new, grand home she was thinking of buying. Dr. LiPordo ushered her into a seat by the parlor window and left her while she went to find someone to complete the check-in process.

I watched from the stairs as the new girl folded her arms on the back of the chair and rested her chin on them, staring out the window. In tales, women are often soft, pensive, and trapped. They sit by windows, and where a starved dog in a pen is a sad thing, a maiden silent at a window is supposed to be a thing of beauty.

I never bought that shit, and I was unimpressed by Alle's lovely wistfulness. It seemed perverse, if you truly had a secret sadness, to advertise it as boldly as she did. I went upstairs to find Bitsy and complain. Instead, I ran into Denson.

"Thera," she said, as I tried to slip past her. I stopped and turned. "What?"

Denson took my face in her hands. I was too startled to say anything. She looked at me through her thick glasses, which slid down her nose a bit. "We've assigned Allendara to your room."

I went completely still. I didn't even feel anger so much as a quiet despair. For the next two years, my life would be told to me like a story. *This is your roommate. These are the classes you must attend. Here are your new clothes.* I couldn't stand it.

Denson continued: "Most of the staff members here don't trust you to be civil to a roommate. I have insisted they are wrong. I would very much like it if you would prove me correct. Do you hear me?"

I scowled, displeased at being spoken to like a child. "I hear you."

"And do you just hear me? Or do you also understand?"

Now I did pull away. "Why are you talking to me like I'm stupid?"

Her expression grew gentler. "It's not about thinking you're stupid. I know you're a good girl. Please—*please*—be kind to Alle."

"All right," I muttered.

When she ruffled my hair, I stood there glaring, even after she'd gone downstairs. I didn't want to find Bitsy anymore. I went to my room to wait.

"Are your parents dead, or did they give you up?" I asked as I lounged on my bed and watched Alle unpack.

She glanced at me but didn't answer. She had an alligator-patterned suitcase that held a few clothes and three books. She stacked the books on the tiny table by the bed.

"Mine are dead," I told her. "My mother split my father's head open with an ax." I yawned. "Then she—mmm, 'scuse me—poisoned herself."

Alle didn't look at me this time, but I was pretty sure I heard her mutter, "Uh-huh."

"You don't believe me?"

"I believe you."

I watched her fold a dress into a neat little square like a linen napkin and place it in the closet we shared, and I knew this was going to be a nightmare.

## New Intake: A Beadurinc
## Report By: Dr. Brenda LiPordo

*New intake, A Beadurinc, #00986773, was very quiet as she was introduced to Rock Point. By all accounts a lovely girl, nonetheless there are unpalatable elements to her past that indicate she must be watched. Rollins feels that the logbook is not the place to discuss this history, but full records are available to those who must know. Miss A was given a tour and shown to her room. She is to room with T Ballard, a decision many have protested and yet I and Rollins feel that if there is anyone T might get along with, it is a very quiet girl like Miss A.*

**Bessie Holmes's Note:** *That girl is bueatiful. & bueatiful often equalls trouble. Rollins, i will need to read all the files. i want to know what this girl have been up to that makes us untrust her.*

Alle was a mystery. She rarely spoke. She was full before dessert; she was lovely beyond words. I desired to impress her for reasons I couldn't understand, and I went about fulfilling that desire in the misguided way of suitors in stories, who, before growing up to be brave knights, are generally foolish and scorn-worthy.

I stamped on the centipedes that sometimes crawled on the dining room floor. Picked up their smashed bodies and leaned over Alle—she always sat beside me—to place them in Kenna's stew. Kenna was a good one to include in this act, as she would make the centipedes talk before she slurped a bite of stew and swallowed without chewing, creepy crawlers and all.

Alle smiled at the younger girls in such a way that they all worshipped her, but many of the older girls thought she was stuck up and a prude. I didn't know whether to agree. Alle also caught flak for her skin. She was darker than most of us, and in the same way I'd seen Bitsy, Tamna, and Denson whispered about for their paleness, and Franny Gammel teased for her extreme thinness, Alle became a target by virtue of being too noticeably different.

"You've got something right here," Kenna said to Alle, the way you'd point out food lingering at the corner of someone's mouth, except Kenna gestured to her whole face.

Alle stared right through her as if she didn't hear. I thought it a sign of weakness that she didn't fight back, but later I learned better.

"You shouldn't let her say things about you," I told her after a particularly brutal dinner during which Kenna had flung mashed potatoes into Alle's hair, and I in turn had put Kenna in a headlock and scrubbed my knuckles over her scalp until she squealed.

"I don't care." Alle sat rigidly on the parlor sofa. There was a depth to her expression that made clear she was neither weak nor stupid. Her eyes were very large. Her lashes were short and curled upward. I'd always thought I hated prettiness in girls. It seemed a useless trait, and too many girls used it as license to act like dimwits. But Alle . . . I wanted, not just to know her secrets, but for her to want to know mine. Her beauty seemed indicative of goodness, which was a dangerous correlation, but one I couldn't stop myself from making.

We arrived in our room that night to find that somebody had stolen the blanket off her bed. Alle stood by the bare cot under the flickering light, her black curls shaking almost imperceptibly. I couldn't see whether she was crying. I got to thinking how damned angry I was—not just on her behalf. Who the hell had come into our room? Had they taken anything of mine? I checked my paltry collection of old toys and sweaters, but found nothing missing.

I stared at my own blanket for a few minutes, then tossed it over Alle's head, turning her into a moth-eaten ghost. An hour later, both of us in our beds in the darkness, I heard her muffled whisper: "Thank you."

I smiled and lay shivering.

I didn't mind that Alle didn't speak to the others, but I wanted her to talk to me. I wasn't sure what interested her. She never seemed to listen when the others discussed boys. I had little invested in the subject either, but I at least knew lewd things to say to make the other girls laugh. Yet Alle never laughed at such jokes. She owned a dark-blue dress and a pale-yellow shawl. I sometimes thought about her when I shouldn't. I imagined adjusting the shawl around her shoulders and holding doors for her—all sorts of embarrassingly civilized things I'd never been inclined to do for anyone else.

Bitsy started treating me coldly. I barely noticed at first, I was so focused on Alle. But soon I realized how much I missed Bitsy's rants, her company. When I asked her to come to my room one night, she said, "You have *her* now. You don't need me."

And the sad thing was, she wasn't wrong.

Alle was gentler than Bitsy, and though she lacked Kenna's hardness, she was not soft, as I'd first thought. She was powerful in her silence, and she made me doubt my bullying ways and the wicked deeds I fantasized about. Her judgment hurt because I couldn't know the extent of it. I imagined a set of preferences and morals for Alle that may have had nothing to do with what she really felt and believed. A soldier-ish loyalty grew on me ivy-thick, and I started to feel less like an awkward, angry child, and more like a warrior, with followers and a destiny and a tortured soul.

I noticed things about her—the way she held her pencil between her fourth finger and pinkie, instead of between her third and fourth fingers, as I did. The way she swept her skirt underneath her with one hand when she stood. The way she listened during story time, but didn't gasp or laugh, or moan when Miss Ridges left off at the end of a suspenseful chapter. She carried herself with a gawky sort of confidence, her chin too far up, her strides too short. It was sometimes hard to decide whether she looked clownish or elegant. She did look *ready*, like she'd stoically outlasted many crises and would weather still more without protest.

I also noticed the way the Rock Point staff watched her—with a wariness that I at first believed was directed at me, because I was often by her side when I noticed it. But no, they were studying her. Alle did not participate in rec for her first week at Rock Point, and the monitors visited our table more frequently than the others during meals. But these oddities were eclipsed by my fascination with Rock Point's latest addition.

"Hey," I called to her in the hall one day after classes were done. When she turned, I felt a moment's panic. "Where are your chores at today?" I didn't need to ask. I knew she worked doing laundry.

"Laundry room." Her voice was gravelly, like she'd just woken.

"Can I come down and look at the towels? Tamna asked me to find an old one to keep around the kitchen to clean up spills."

It was all cow drippings, to be sure. But I went down with her to the laundry area in the basement, trying desperately to think of a topic of conversation. While I was there in that dank space, my chest grew tight. The shadow cast on the wall by the washbasin became sinister and seemed as if it might begin prowling at any moment. Alle headed for the towels, but I turned wordlessly and walked up the wooden steps.

She followed me to the top step, where I sat, clutching my knees and looking at all the lint my black trousers had accumulated. Being next to her gave me a merciful sense of quiet. I looked at the smooth skin of her hands. Smelled, in her hair, the cheap soap we all used. I nearly rested my head on her shoulder the way I sometimes did with Bitsy. She seemed, in that moment, familiar enough.

"I think we should be friends." I didn't look at her. "Really, I do. I think it would benefit both of us."

"Nobody here wants to be friends with me." She didn't sound bitter about it. Just tired.

"That's what I thought at first too. About myself, I mean. But now I'm friends with Bitsy, and Kenna—though she's unpleasant."

Alle pinched the hem of her skirt delicately between her thumb and forefinger and tugged it over her knees. My gaze flicked toward the movement, but I don't think her eyes ever left mine. "I've heard about you."

"Oh?" I couldn't figure out why that made me nervous. What did I care what she knew, what she thought?

"I've heard you're not nice."

The sting flooded me. This was the sort of comment that would once have made me proud. Now, for the first time, I felt mortified. Alle was the sort of person who admired niceness. Anyone could see that. She probably enjoyed birdsong and sunsets. She probably wished all people would cut their food into small bites. I didn't answer.

"I don't think it's true," she said after a while. "Not entirely."

I clutched my knees, digging my fingertips in. I was desperate to change the subject. "Do you know the story of the Minotaur?"

"Yes."

I didn't say anything else for a moment. "Do you think magic is common?"

"I don't know."

I was a cast-off daughter. What if there was a magic growing deep inside me—a magic that would cause me to crave blood and to loathe everyone, forever? And then to be shut away in a maze, where people would loathe and fear me in return?

If that were the case, why should I be afraid of my fate? I wanted magic. I wanted to be more powerful than anyone here. More powerful than my parents had been, more powerful than Auntie Bletch. I wanted people to fear me. And if, as appeasement, I was offered a palace, a grand world where my only job was to think up inventive traps for foolish tributes, then that was a good thing. Wasn't it?

"I'm getting better," I said softly. "At being nice."

Alle patted my knee. "You wanna help me wash clothes?"

No, but yes, perhaps, certainly—I did.

# CHAPTER 7

**Rec Report**
**Glenna Formas**

*Today was the first day #00986773 joined the other girls for rec. I have to say I do not see what we were so worried about. She plays well with the others. She manages to be gracious while also not being a wiener. This means a surprising amount to me.*

*I know it is not my business, but maybe we should put less stock in her past. Do you see what I'm saying? Sometimes people do intense things in self-defense. I have never seen a girl who seemed less capable of causing harm than #00986773.*

**Bessie Holmes's Note:** *Glenna, may i say something? Often those who's best suited to cause harm are being most efficient at concealing it. We disgust this the other day in my divorced women's choir. So many of those women had relationships of abuse and mistrust. That is because nearly any man can act the part of a gentleman. & so, i'm sure, can children deceive.*

**Van Narr's Note:** *I think it is no wonder the children don't like you, Bessie.*

I was staring just to the left of Dr. DuMorg, the psychologist. I'd stolen enough glances at her so far to know that her face was too serious and her spine too straight, her boots too stiff and her lips too red. Her bobbed hair was parted severely to one side, so that the bulk of it lay curved against her cheek like a massive hand was cupping her face.

We were in the reading room.

Dr. DuMorg believed in talking about our pasts. She had studied something called New Theory, which stated that children should be treated as adults, their feelings validated and their pasts thoroughly examined for clues about their futures.

Among us girls there was an unspoken rule that we did not talk about our lives before Rock Point. But in my sessions with DuMorg, she pushed me to remember things that made me feel like I was sitting on thorns. It was not that I'd had a bad childhood or disliked my family. But what I remembered of my parents was limited. And what I knew of my sister was colored by what I wanted her to be, rather than who she was. I had no interest in scratching at scabs until they balled up under my nails.

I pictured my family as insects caught in separate sections of a spider's web—all condemned to the same fate, but unable to face it together. Each of us struggling alone in a thread cocoon, waiting. My mother and father had been taken first, and Auntie Bletch was to be devoured next, if she hadn't been already. And Rachel and I . . . were we still trapped, or had we escaped?

"Your father." DuMorg spoke very quietly. "Was he close with you?"

"I don't remember. My parents died when I was six." I'd decided to give up on the ax bit for a while.

"You don't remember anything about them?" DuMorg pressed her red lips into a line. Rubbed them together until some of the lipstick faded.

Lizards. At our house in Rock Hill, there had been tiny geckos on the porch. I'd been obsessed with catching them, but they were too fast. My father had built a small mesh cage, and he'd helped me bait it with dead moths and spiders. I'd practiced lying perfectly still on the porch swing, a bit of fishing line tied from my finger to the cage's sliding door. I remember my dad smoking while he worked. I remember the wire mesh cut him and he had a thin red line on the back of his hand. I remember he sanded all the sharp edges off the wire so I wouldn't be cut too.

I didn't tell DuMorg this.

"What about your aunt?" DuMorg laced her fingers around her knee. "How is your relationship with her?"

"She doesn't like me." I shifted, wishing my trousers would magically be three sizes bigger. My sweater today was blue with tiny silver beads forming what looked like the crests of waves. "She sent me here. So obviously, I'm not her number one."

A trip to Main Street near Christmas time. Rachel, old enough not to want to be seen with Auntie and me, walked a few strides ahead, her back perfectly straight. I remembered thinking she looked like a bowling pin, like something I wanted to tip. In the distance, a train whistled. The crowds pushed against us like a tide and we were in danger of being separated, until Auntie grabbed my hand.

I remember feeling the soft, wrinkled skin, and thinking she wasn't so bad. That maybe she did care for me. She looked stooped, oily, sick. I squeezed her hand and kept squeezing it as the shoppers barreled past us. She squeezed back, and we stayed like that as we headed toward the car, as though we would each come to mean something to the other by virtue of how hard we held on.

DuMorg continued to press. "You told me before that your parents were abusive."

Had I said that? It wouldn't surprise me. "I was having some trouble with a lust for medication."

DuMorg nodded, not even cracking a smile. "If you tell me the truth about your life, about what you remember of your family, I may be able to help you make adjustments. Be a happier girl." I got the feeling that DuMorg didn't care about the adjustments as much as she cared about the secrets. She, like everyone else here, was bored. Waiting for a good story.

There is something that happens—even now—when I try to remember details from my childhood. A sense that whatever memory or feeling I'm seeking is just around a corner, and I'm chasing a bit of its shadow. Every way I turn, there is that sliver of darkness, and I don't know if I am playing a game or losing my mind.

DuMorg tipped her head, and her hair slid like fingers down her cheek. "Thera?"

I could have shouted, I supposed. Thrown something at her. But I thought of Denson asking me to prove her right by being kind to Alle. I thought of promising Alle I was getting better at being nice. I was chasing a shadow again, some long-ago feeling. I was warm, the sun on my hair. A cloud passed overhead, and I stopped and looked up, aware suddenly of how alone I was. That whatever I was seeking was hidden somewhere nearby, peering at me.

"I don't remember," I said again.

"Miss Rollins's hair looks like a hornets' nest." Alle offered the observation with a shy glance at me. They were some of the first words she'd offered to me unprompted, and I held still, as though afraid to spook her back into silence.

I had invited her outside with me to find fallen leaves for a sketching project we were doing in a class called Arts, Health, and Living. I'd never considered Rock Point's grounds particularly attractive, but today everything looked splendid—the leafless trees, the oozing patches of muddy yard, the old huddle of stones near the front porch that passed as landscaping. "What's a hornets' nest look like?"

"Have you never seen one?"

I looked away from her and tried to sort through my general tiredness at being reminded of what I didn't know. "No."

"Well, it looks like Miss Rollins's hair. You know how her hair's gray and sitting on her head in a sort of papery clump? And all those pins sticking out of it—those could be hornets buzzing around."

I thought it would be nice to have a mind that did that— observed the world carefully, came up with descriptions that could make someone else see things as you did. "Well. What's Bessie Holmes look like?"

"A sheep."

I snickered.

"She has curly white hair, and her mouth is very small. And her ears stick out."

"And she's always baahhh-ing about something. What's Dr. DuMorg look like?"

"Like a plastic person," Alle's reply came at once. "Like someone built a model of a person and then stuck a real person inside it. Perhaps the real DuMorg is trapped."

"Alle!"

She ducked her chin, grinning. She bent to pick up a leaf, but it crumbled as she pinched it.

"Do you like it here?" I asked.

She shook her head, but not like she was saying no. "It's not bad."

"The staff seems afraid of you."

She straightened and brushed bits of leaf from her hands. "Aren't they also afraid of you?"

"Yes."

"Then perhaps the staff here is just afraid. In general."

I shrugged. "Well, the owner of this bin has a head full of hornets."

"And the psychologist is a mannequin with a human trapped inside."

I threw my arms out and spun in a circle. "We are in a farce! Everyone is strange and afraid. Why, even Miss Van Narr's mustache curls up in fear of the goings-on at Rock Point."

Alle threw back her head and laughed. Her teeth flashed and her eyes scrunched up, and she stuck her tongue out just a little, pressing her front teeth into it as she continued her peals of laughter.

I'd never felt so good.

I mean never.

### Child Wellness Report: Officer Van Narr

*I guess we've heard by now that F Gammel got pushed at rec time and took a stick through her foot. I am thinking some of these girls need better shoes, but I understand we are on a limited budget. These sweet dears tug at me, they really do.*

*Anyway, the bloody details will be in the doctor's report, but I just wanted to note a strange thing. I was jogging over to where the girls were gathered around the fallen Miss Gammel, and when I got there I saw T Ballard, whom we all know is not God's finest work, crouched by the injured child. I was about to shoo her off, because I figured she could only make the situation worse, but she was talking very softly to Miss Gammel, and Miss Gammel stopped crying. I actually let T Ballard help me take Miss Gammel to the infirmary.*

*I would love if we could make the doctor's report public, because I'm curious about what was done to remove the stick from Miss Gammel's foot. I feel awful for her, just awful—that sweet thing.*

*I was once conscious for a damn painful tooth extraction. I mean, I had opiates, but the ripping sensation was terrible. Officer Grenwat knows what I mean. She got buckshot when she was a girl, and she received real primitive first aid. I'm talking brandy-and-the-tip-of-a-knife kind of doctoring. Sometimes being awake is a damn unfortunate thing.*

I once eavesdropped on a meeting about me. DuMorg was talking to Rollins and Bessie Holmes about my dead parents. DuMorg loved dead parents. I had, according to the report, been in the backseat when my parents' car crashed into an oncoming truck. I don't remember anything about that night. Not where we were going or what the sky looked like. I can't even remember the color of my parents' car.

I was listening at the meeting room door, which was open a crack, and I glimpsed the long, scored oak table and the ugly blue china tea set. Bessie Holmes held a folder and was speaking.

"...claims she does not remember her parents' death, though she has been witnessed it. I don't think we can rule out the possibility she had something to do with it."

"Something to *do* with it?" Denson's voice was sharp. "Auto accidents happen all the time."

"The driver of the other vehicle said Mrs. Ballard was driving. Said that in the instant before they collided, Mrs. Ballard was not having been facing the road, but was looking into the backseat."

"And this proves...?" Rollins asked.

"That perhaps the child was throwing a tantrum, or otherwise have been distracting her mother."

"Please," Denson snapped. "Even if that were true, the accident was not Thera's fault."

"Children's capable of treachery," Bessie said. "And this child has a history of violence."

Rollins gazed hard at Bessie. "She was only six."

"A history of violence?" Van Narr spoke up for the first time. "Miss Beadurinc, now that's a history of violence. What's Miss Ballard done but get a bit rough with the other girls?"

I didn't dare breathe, hoping they'd say something more about Alle's history.

"And she's a junkie," Bessie said. "Don't you forget."

"Thera no longer has any drug dependencies." DuMorg sounded forceful, eager to contribute. "She's doing quite well."

Denson took a sip of tea. I felt a sweltering tenderness for her tumbling over me like a shovelful of hot coals.

Bessie smacked the table with her folder. "She is still been a heathen, if you ask me."

They moved on to discussing things I already knew—that I was difficult, that I didn't pay attention in classes, that I was a bad influence on other girls, that I spent too much time with Bitsy. I shouldn't say "they." Denson and Rollins said nothing negative about me. Denson said I had been doing much better since Alle came to Rock Point. I felt no gratitude toward her in that moment—just churlish disdain.

But for days and years afterward, I thought about Bessie Holmes's accusation. What if I *had* done something that made my mother crash? I had been an unhappy child, I remembered that much. Cranky and obstinate. It wasn't a stretch to imagine I might have been demanding my mother's attention, distracting her at the moment she'd most needed to focus.

I grew to hate the smaller children at Rock Point. I loathed the sound of *needing*—complaints of hunger or thirst, tears over scraped knees. I began to worship Alle more fiercely, because she never cracked. Because Kenna could taunt her and Alle didn't weep.

Even now when I try to read Van Narr's report about the day I comforted Franny Gammel, I am mystified. I comforted her mainly for Alle's sake, so that Alle would see me doing something kind. But something about holding Franny moved me deeply. I can only think that there are moments when I pity the child I was. More often I hate her, but pity sometimes swims in the same river. And maybe on that day, with Franny quivering and clutching her mouth, I showed what I truly thought should happen to girls who cry. That they should be heard and loved and held.

# CHAPTER 8

At dinner one evening, Kenna was going on about some treasure-hunting expedition she'd been on in the southern jungles. Something about a one-eyed guide and a recalcitrant donkey.

Bitsy was working on a literature lesson across the table, next to Kenna. "Does this sound right?" she asked, without looking up. "'The novel utilizes vivid imagery and concise sentences, but fails to display a clarity of purpose. All in all a successful work of literature, but with some notable shortcomings.'"

"So what about *you*?" Kenna snapped her fingers in front of Alle. Alle jerked her head up. "You been anywhere?"

Alle shook her head. "Nowhere of note."

"Well, you could at least tell us a story," Kenna grumbled. "Who's gonna know if it's the truth?"

"But I really haven't done anything."

"Are you sure?" I turned to Alle. "Don't you have any good stories? Don't you have a *history*?"

"Yes, aren't you the long lost princess of some ice realm?" Kenna asked her.

I put down the roll I was about to bite into. "Knock it off, Kenna."

"Or you'll what?" she asked.

"Beat your face in, and you know it."

"Awf, yeah." Kenna glanced again at Alle, quick and shrewd. "That's Thera, a wannabe tough. But she's all soft for our dark friend."

A rage came over me that was just splendid. I slammed a fist on the table and stood so fast my plate tipped and corn scattered across the table. "You shut *up*! God, you're a bitch's box. She's hardly darker than you or I." I felt pleased with myself for rushing to Alle's defense.

I didn't realize Alle was angry until she stood. "And so what if I was?" she shouted. We all turned to stare at her. "So what if I was blacker than the devil's asshole?"

We froze.

"You're all children. All of you. You don't know what's important and you have never had to do anything difficult." She strode away.

Bitsy eventually went back to her lesson, scrawling something on her paper. "Miss Beadurinc makes use of vivid imagery. Concise sentences. Clarity of purpose. All in all, a successful retort." She leaned toward me and whispered, "And I applaud your use of 'box.'"

A week later—a week during which Alle and I were cold toward each other—Alle undressed in front of me. Normally she waited until I left the room, or else stepped into the narrow closet to put on her nightgown. But that night, she began undoing the buttons of her dress, right there in the narrow aisle between our cots.

I'd never seen a woman naked, except in paintings in the museum in town. Kenna changed beside me sometimes in the equipment shed before rec, so I'd seen her in a brassiere—a dreary gray garment with big flimsy cups her breasts couldn't fill. Seeing Alle was different. More real than a painting, and far more captivating than Kenna. She let her dress fall, then unhooked her white bra. She was turned to the side, so all I saw was the outline of one breast, rising a little as she leaned forward to grab her nightgown. Her body curved so perfectly—her breasts were not as large as mine, but they were high and round. Her belly was rounded too, the skin smooth and soft looking. Her ass pulled her cotton underwear taut, and I could just see the under curve of the flesh as she bent over.

"What?" she asked. I snapped my head up, surprised by how calm she sounded. I expected her to be embarrassed, angry, to find me staring like that.

"Nothing." I tried to focus on her face, but my gaze kept falling to her breasts, to the shadow between them, the curve of them against her ribs, the tiny peaks of her nipples. And then lower, to her wide hips and the slight ridges of muscle down each thigh. She watched me watching and made no move to cover herself.

I kept bypassing her underwear, even though I wanted to look. I was *scared*. I knew on some unspecific level what I'd like to see, what I'd like to do—and yet if I pressed myself for details, my desire pushed aside shame and became something nearly unmanageable.

She held her nightgown above her head and dropped it over her body. I rolled toward the wall and closed my eyes. As soon as I did, I saw her again—the curve of her breast, the arch of her spine, the glimpse of her ass under cotton. I listened to her cot squeak as she climbed on it. Heard the rustle of her sheet. I listened until her breathing slowed and evened. Placed my hand tentatively between my legs and didn't move it—just left it there. There was heat, and dampness, and I felt both wicked and uncertain.

"I don't like Kenna," she said eventually through the dark.

I pulled my hand up, my heart pounding as though I'd been caught. "She's just an idiot." I wasn't sure whether I should defend Kenna. I had few enough allies here that I would have liked for Alle and Kenna to get along. "She doesn't think before she opens her gob. And me either. I didn't mean to . . ." Apologizing didn't come naturally to me.

"I know." Her voice was soft.

I rubbed my cheek against the pillowcase to scratch an itch.

She shifted again. I glanced at the shadow of her covered body, then went back to looking at the ceiling.

"Do you think you'll stay here, once you're of age?" she asked. I could have lain there in the dark listening to her voice all night. "And teach, or take care of the babies, or anything?"

I felt inexplicably affronted. "No. I'm going to be a warrior."

"Oh. Can you . . . do that?"

"What do you mean?"

"Are there warriors anymore?"

I shrugged even though she couldn't see me. "There'll be at least one after I learn to fight. We still need them." I paused. "I'm not going to take care of anyone. But I might make the world safer."

"What sorts of people are you going to fight?"

"Villains." She didn't seem like she was mocking me, so I went on. "The Minotaur, maybe."

Alle sighed softly. "Is she still a threat? She's trapped now."

"She's a threat as long as the town has to give her tributes."

"I suppose so."

I didn't tell Alle about my dreams of the monster, about my visions of the maze or my thoughts of taming the creature. "Do you think the beast remembers what it was like before she was a beast?"

A pause. "I suppose, probably. You think about her a lot, don't you?"

"I just think the most pressing issue facing a modern warrior would be the beast's blood-drenched legacy. It wouldn't hurt for me to know all there is to know about her."

Alle didn't answer, and eventually I heard her breathing slow even more, and I knew she was asleep. I wanted to keep talking. I wanted to tell her she could let me know what she thought about. I'd listen.

I awoke suddenly in the night. Moonlight was spilling through the window, and I was shivering and gasping, still half-caught in a dream. Something was wrong—no deep breathing from Alle's side of the room. She was awake. Maybe she'd heard me whimpering. I couldn't even remember the dream.

It was so cold that my blanket was of little use. I silenced my gasping and stared across the darkness at her. I could see the glint of her eyes just before she asked, "Are you all right?"

"I'm cold."

"Me too."

I slipped out of my bed and knelt on the chilly tile next to hers. I folded my arms on the edge of her mattress and rested my chin on them. Tried to smile as I stared at her, shivering.

"Hi."

"Hi," she whispered back.

I was worried I'd have to ask, but she lifted up her blanket without another word, and I climbed in beside her. Her icy foot nudged my leg, and she giggled.

"Shh." I smiled. I wished I could be even closer to her, but I was afraid, and so I lay rigid on the very edge of the bed, and after a moment I rolled onto my back so I wouldn't have to look at her.

She placed a hand on my shoulder. I didn't dare breathe. My chest ached with the effort of being silent and still. Every few seconds I felt the subtle movement of her hand—the twitch of a finger, the scrape of a nail. My heart was going too fast, and I tried clenching and releasing my thighs in an effort to take my mind off the heat that curled deep inside me like a strange smoke, unfurling in lazy tendrils.

I rolled back toward her, keeping my eyes clenched shut, and pretended to fall asleep. Then I pretended my head had tilted forward of its own accord so that my lips were almost against hers. I prayed— prayed for maybe the first time since childhood—to be allowed to keep Alle this close to me, her hand wedged between our bellies, our chests touching. I shifted a little, pressing my legs closer together as though I could somehow protect myself from this want, this feverish hope.

She moved her foot until I felt the gentle scratch of her toenail against my ankle. I swallowed. When the actual moment came, it required almost no thinking. I simply put my lips to hers, and after only a second's hesitation, she kissed back, her mouth moving gently, rhythmically. I wished then that it could be more. That she would wrap my whole body in hers and run her hands over my skin and drown me in her.

I knew I was whatever Bitsy had called Riley Denson—a BD. I knew this was unnatural, but right then I wanted to care not a bit what was natural and what wasn't. We kissed until she broke away with a soft sound. She stared at me, breathing hard, the moonlight outlining her black curls where they spread on the pillow.

"It's all right," I whispered, more to reassure myself than her.

She nodded. We slept eventually, fitful and uncertain, our bodies not quite touching, but my mind opening in a thousand places, letting in so much light I felt blind.

We slept like that the next night too, and many nights after. Each day during lessons and chores, I told myself this would be the night I placed my hand somewhere other than her shoulder. The night I would have the courage to hold her, to touch her. And yet each night, one of us drew away in the middle of a kiss, and we both lay on our backs, staring at the ceiling. I began to whisper to myself that I was in love. That I was in love in the way of knights and poor young men who could not offer the princess riches but who had good hearts and trusty, knob-kneed horses. And suddenly I was furious with those tales, because love was not as simple as singing a song under a maid's window or breaking her up into poetry and spitting her at empty rooms.

Love had a current of shame running through it, and in a way it seemed lonelier than just about anything.

"Aren't you going to story time?" Denson asked.

"Not today." I lounged on my cot, my head on my arm. I'd skipped grammar that morning. Alle had promised she'd bring up a roll from the breakfast table, but she hadn't arrived yet. "I'm ill."

Denson placed the back of her hand against my forehead. I felt even more irritated by the gesture. "You don't feel feverish."

"Well, then maybe I'm in no mood for stories."

She sat on the edge of the bed and was quiet until I looked at her. "What's wrong with stories?"

"I don't know." I drew one leg up and sighed heavily. "I only wish they weren't such cow drippings. So full of lessons and people getting married."

"Miss Ridges tries to find stories that work for everybody, even the young children."

"I know that."

"But . . ." Denson's smile seemed private, just between her and herself. "Miss Ridges, you might be interested to know, is the author of many stories that would be far more . . . *suitable* to someone with your tastes."

I frowned. "What do you mean?"

Denson looked like she was trying not to laugh. She reached out and rubbed my shoulder. "Come down to the reading room tonight at nine. I'll write you a note, in case you get stopped."

And so Riley Denson was how I found out about the Dark Tales. Miss Ridges was their creator, and she'd populated her stories with girls who struggled and girls who lied. Girls whose goodness was not innocence, and whose beauty was not in their high cheekbones or their sweeping lashes, or even in their pluck and grit—as was the case with so many of the fairy tales she read during story time—but in their terrible humanness. In the sorrows they laid on themselves with their greed. In their fear of death and of fate—which, in Miss Ridges's tales, were often one and the same. These girls empathized with their enemies without pitying them, and often they spared a villain's life, telling the scoundrel at sword point to leave and never come back.

Each night, after the younger girls had gone to bed and the older girls were busy with games or schoolwork, we'd meet in the reading room—Riley Denson, Miss Ridges, and Bitsy, Kenna, and I. The deal was we girls had to have our lessons done first, and we'd never been so diligent about schoolwork in our lives. We'd listen to Miss Ridges read a Dark Tale, her low voice well suited to antagonists and their murmured cruelties, their vengeful cries. And to heroes—their pride and certainty, their private doubts. The stories contained so much gore and so many lost souls that Miss Ridges would glance up worriedly on occasion, glancing at each of us as if waiting for permission to continue.

A couple of times I'd invited Alle to attend these covert readings—I felt an aggressive need to share with her the mystery and terror of the Dark Tales. The first time she refused, but the second, she came down with me. I tried, from the corner of my eye, to watch her face as Miss Ridges read. I couldn't tell what she was thinking until, at a scary part, she took my hand, and I felt glad and brave and ready to defend her from anything.

Denson got caught up in the stories right along with us—she winced at decapitations and crowed when those who deserved to fall finally tumbled over a cliff. We all praised Miss Ridges incessantly for her genius. She took the compliments with a blush and a lowered head, but always you could see the smile—delighted and a little roguish—twitching at the corners of her mouth. You got the feeling she was quite talented, quite brilliant in her way.

Bitsy, in her more bitter moods, pretended to dislike the Dark Tales. "She gives her villains black hair, just like every other story," she said one night as we headed back upstairs.

I grabbed a lock of my own dark hair and whisked it across Bitsy's cheek. "It's common knowledge villains do have black hair."

"Uh-huh. And we fairer folk are all lambs?"

Conversations with her had become rare since I'd grown close with Alle, and I wanted to keep her talking. "Yes."

"So I'm not a villain. But you and Kenna . . ."

"And Miss Ridges."

"Miss Ridges, yes. And your roommate . . ."

"Dark magicians, all of us," I affirmed.

Bitsy snorted and trudged up the last couple of steps. "I just don't understand this obsession with black-haired and blackhearted. Anyway." She stood in the hall and pulled something from the waistband of her skirt. "I have a favor to ask you." She handed me Lizzie's pink unicorn. "I've taken it hostage until she stops hassling me to clean up my side of the room. I need you to hide it. If she asks you about it, say nothing."

I took the unicorn with a grin. "Who's the villain now?"

"Stuff it." She walked off toward her room.

"Who's the villain now?" I followed her down the hall. "Blondiekins? You like the Dark Tales, and we are still friends. Don't you deny it!"

"Good *night*, Thera," she called, without looking back. But I could tell she was trying not to laugh.

# CHAPTER 9

**B**essie Holmes had a dog named Walter—a Labrador mix whose tail had been docked in some accident. He mostly stayed in Bessie's room in the north ward, but every now and then she'd bring him out into the main yards for us to play with. He was friendly but scared of birds and garishly stupid.

At the start of spring, Walter fell in love with a stray that had been hanging around the prison. The prison workers called him Murdock. Murdock was a thick-coated shepherd mix with one ear that flopped and one that stuck straight up.

Murdock would slip onto the grounds when the front gate opened for the food delivery trucks, and then he'd wait in the courtyard until Bessie brought Walter out to do his business. Then he and Walter would run at each other, colliding in what looked like an embrace, licking each other's faces and under each other's tails. Bessie tried to shoo Murdock away, but he stayed just out of range of her hands and feet, darting in now and then to bestow as many caresses and kisses on Walter as he could manage before Bessie drove him away again.

Bessie was deeply troubled by the notion that Walter had such strong feelings for a male dog. Several times, Murdock mounted Walter, or vice versa, and poor Bessie was so disturbed by this she could only shriek and turn away and beg for one of us girls to turn the hose on Murdock.

Eventually the truck drivers were notified to look out for Murdock when they opened the gate, and to drive him back with rocks. This worked for a time, as poor Murdock was afraid of rocks.

But then Walter started slipping out Bessie's first-floor window when she left it open in the summer. He would wait until Bessie had gone off on her rounds, then shove the window up with his snout and squeeze through. He'd disappear for long stretches—days, sometimes. Bessie would search the grounds, unable to understand how he could have gotten past the fence.

But she would leave the window open for him, and always she'd return to her room one day to find him curled on her bed, burrs on his flanks and mud in his ears.

One night, I was staring out my window, unable to sleep. Alle was breathing noisily beside me, her arm against mine. I saw two shadows approaching the fence. Murdock and Walter. I watched them, determined to figure out how they got onto the grounds. But then Alle let out a massive snore, and I turned toward her and missed the dog's entrance. When I looked again, Murdock was standing outside the gate, staring through the bars as if to see Walter safely inside, before he turned and trotted up the drive and disappeared into the night.

## Staff Welfare Update: Bessie Holmes

*Many of you understand i am in a difficult situation with regards to my dog, with regards to homasexuality. He is a mixed bred & perhaps was been weened too late. Tainted bloodlines & a poor upbringing the veterinarian says. i'm having been tempted to love him all the same & also understanding this may be a phase. But it is hard to trust him as I once did. A member of my divorced women's choir says her German Shorthaired Pointer fell in love with a stuffed animal. i am not sure which is worse.*

**Officer Grenwat's Note:** *Dogs do not have homosexuality, they only have INSTINCTS. And their instincts are to hump anything that moves. You could replace Murdock with your own right LEG, and Walter would be in love.*

**Van Narr's Note:** *Homasexuality? For god's sake, Bessie.*

"Tell me a story." I said it like a dare.

Alle was on her stomach on her bed, looking over notes from our history lesson. "About what?" She didn't look up.

"About your parents."

Her shoulders grew rigid. I imagined Alle's story must be something wretched, something to build nightmares on. A real history of violence, as Van Narr had suggested. But when she turned and looked at me over her shoulder, her yellow shawl wrapped around her neck like a scarf, there was no pain in her eyes. She rolled slightly onto one hip, and the pull of her dress across her body distracted me.

Alle told me a story, but it wasn't about her parents. It was about the farm she'd grown up on. The work she'd done there. She described her parents—her mother practical and stoic, offering blunt plans for the horses, the crops, the household renovations. But in deed, she was looser, freer. If she said the chickens had to go to the Buckmans' for slaughter, she'd end up keeping a favorite hen or two.

And Alle's father—a quiet man, a dreamer who grew shy when asked what he wanted for himself. Bashful, as though he'd been asked to dance and didn't know the steps. A gambler, and sometimes a fool.

She described the seasons on the farm, and the work that needed to be done during each. I expected to be bored, once I realized there was no blood in this tale, but I wasn't. Eventually, though, I noticed her parents disappeared from the story, phased out so subtly I almost hadn't noticed. When she stopped after describing last year's threshing, I asked, "Was your dad upset that the crop was poor?"

She was silent for a moment. "My father is no longer living."

I wondered why people needed their secrets and their mysteries. Wouldn't it feel good to lay them out, entrust them to someone?

I only tucked my own closer to my heart.

"Do you ever wonder," I asked Denson, "what the beast does? When she's not devouring tributes, I mean."

"No." Denson was braiding my hair. I liked when she did it, though I looked stupid in braids. "I don't waste time wondering about a monster."

"But maybe she's not so bad as people think. Maybe she likes . . . cards, or knitting, or—"

"Thera, please. It's not wise to take such a dangerous creature lightly."

"She was once human," I insisted. "It was only magic that made her more beastlike, right?"

"I believe she always had the soul for it."

"But you don't know her."

"I have no need to." She tugged too hard on my hair, and I winced.

I recognized I had hit a nerve that grew like a weed, one that bled and jittered when it was cut. I turned, and Denson gave a smile like a grimace and shook her head. "I'm sorry," I offered.

She stared at my braid through her thick glasses. "My brother," she said after a long moment. "My brother was sent into the labyrinth. Years ago."

My jaw fell, and I tried to look at Denson in a way that suggested I was not frightened, but gruesomely fascinated. Bad things. Bad things, I thought, can't hurt you if you pursue them with devotion. If you try to pat snakes, if you coo at roaches and ghost hunt late at night. If you relish tales of murder. Then, perhaps, you are safe. "How'd he get to do that?"

She gave me a sharp look. "It was not a privilege!" She coughed.

"I didn't mean that it was!"

She continued the braid. "I'm sorry. It's just something that doesn't hurt any less with time."

I didn't dare speak again. Denson in distress was enthralling.

"He was convicted ten years ago of murdering his landlord. Spent five years in Rock Hill Prison, and then one day the truck came and took him and three other inmates away."

"And you know for sure he went to the labyrinth?" She nodded. "But you don't know if he survived?"

Her words came immediately and flatly. "No one survives."

I gazed out the window toward the prison. "Did you work at Rock Point back then?"

"I came here the month before he was taken."

I turned back to her, nearly yanking the braid from her grasp. "Did you come here to be near him?"

She glanced at me again, but there was no anger in her expression this time. "Goodness, Thera. You'd wear out a saint."

"You brought it up." I hoped, guiltily, to engage her in a spat.

"You're right. I'm only trying to say . . . I don't know what I'm trying to say. I suppose that there are things you—things that will seem like rich stories or grand adventures. But that are quite real and very sad."

"I'm ready for that." I grabbed the unfinished braid she held limply in her hand, and I undid it, combing madly through it with my fingers until my hair crackled and strands drifted across my face. "I have *seen* things that are real and sad. And I'm sorry for your loss, and maybe for all losses ever. I used to want people to fear me. I still do, sometimes. But what I really want is to be a warrior. Like in the old days. I want people to trust me to go places like the labyrinth. I want to fight their battles." The words had come so fast they were either cow drippings or my truest heart.

She looked at me with a quiet wonder. Her voice, when she spoke, was just a whisper. "I do believe you will, Thera. I believe you could."

After that, I went outside sometimes in the evening as the sun was setting. I'd tell Tamna I needed some fresh air, and she would moan and mumble and nod. I'd go to the west side of the building, near the woods, where I was least likely to be seen. I'd pick up a long stick from beneath the oak tree there and I'd practice using it as a sword. I'd slice the air, thrust at a knot in the tree's side. I'd spin and then parry an imagined blow.

Some days I felt silly. Others, I felt a promise in every movement, a grace unconnected to beauty, a certainty that went beyond hope. Some days, I felt I was learning.

One evening, just as twilight was deepening to night, just as I began to hear Bessie Holmes's frantic voice calling my name, I pivoted with my sword and was overtaken by the strange sense that I was chasing some scrap of shadow. That there was something I needed to know about this moment but couldn't grasp. The back of my neck prickled, and my heart drummed. I wandered too close to the iron fence and stepped on a tangle of vine that grew around the bars and puddled on the ground. As I kicked the vine away, I saw a hole under the fence.

A hole just big enough for a dog to squeeze through, if he was looking to go on an illicit adventure.

# CHAPTER 10

I would be remiss if I did not mention the weasel.

One fall night, just after supper, a girl screamed in the hallway upstairs. We all came running out of our rooms and clustered around a corner of the hall, where a small, gray-brown creature stood with its hair raised and its teeth showing. The teeth were so small and thin. That's what I remember—needlelike canines and long yellow incisors. Its eyes glittered in the dim light. Several girls were shrieking, and Franny Gammel yelled, "What *is* it?"

"Back away, you idiots." Bitsy put an arm out, forcing the younger girls back. I was surprised by how panicked she sounded. "It's gonna attack if it's scared."

"I used to hunt these in the western deserts," Kenna said to me. "They were the most dangerous game. The one-legged Dr. Eppler Coltrain and I used to—"

"Kenna," I snapped. "Go get someone."

Bitsy herded the girls against the wall while Kenna went to find help. The creature began to walk forward, its back end swaying side to side. It was some sort of weasel, I thought. I glanced around for Alle and saw that she was staring at the animal, her eyes blank. "It's got foam on its mouth." She spoke quietly, without looking up. The animal darted its head, and I saw she was right. Little flecks of foam dripped from its tiny jaws, and it hissed as it waddled by the line of whimpering girls.

Alle touched my shoulder. "Get the little girls away. Get 'em away." She stepped forward. The creature turned toward her. It hissed again, and its tail seemed to shiver. The foam coming from its mouth turned pink.

Bitsy and I shoved Franny and a couple of the little ones down the hall toward an open bedroom. I turned over my shoulder and saw Alle raise her right foot. The creature struck, its teeth bouncing off the bottom of her shoe, and then she brought her foot down on it hard. There was a crack, and a wet sound, and the weasel flopped on its broken back, blood smearing its chin, while the girls screamed anew.

She stepped on it again, on its head, and then it lay still.

I could only stare. At the broken animal, and then at Alle. She never took her eyes off the weasel—it was as though she expected it to return to life.

Bessie Holmes arrived a moment later. She took a look at all of us, started to speak, and then her gaze fell on the weasel. She yelped and put her hands over her mouth. Breathed hard against her palms. "What . . . *is* that?"

"Alle killed it!" Little Rina said. "It's a *Mustela nivalis*—a Least Weasel."

Bessie took her hands away, her mouth open slightly. "Allendara *killed* it?" She turned her gaze to Alle.

"It was rabid, Miss Holmes." Alle's voice was low and rough. "It would have bit somebody."

Bessie stepped forward slowly. "Listen, miss." She took Alle by the arm and pulled her down the hall. Alle stumbled but didn't resist. "We'll been taking this right to Miss Rollins."

Alle didn't respond, but fury welled in me hot enough to burn.

Bessie jerked her along. "We know what you are capable of, and we are gonna stamp that out right now."

I followed. "Let her go. Miss Holmes, let her go. She was only helping."

Bessie whirled. "You're very lucky I don't take you in too, Miss Ballard."

I backed off at the look in her eyes—a manic righteousness that seemed to have its roots in genuine fear. Whatever dastardly thing Alle was, she had the staff more cowed than I'd ever managed.

We could, I imagined, be an extraordinary team.

The next day, I was on my way to the kitchen after lessons when Denson stopped me. "Thera, would you go to the parlor, please?" There was something strange about her expression—a dreamy sort of excitement. I wanted to know what was going on, wanted to resist until I was told. Denson looked directly at me through her ridiculous glasses. "It's a good thing," she assured me.

When I entered the parlor, Alle, Bitsy, and a girl named Marcy Gates were seated in the high-backed chairs. Across from them, on the love seat, sat a young couple. The woman had close-cropped black hair and beautiful gold rose-shaped earrings. The man was dressed in a starched shirt and creased slacks. He had his arm around the woman, and the woman was smiling nervously, almost apologetically at Alle, Bitsy, and Marcy. She turned as I entered, her smile growing. "Hello. Are you Thera? You must be." Her voice started soft but seemed to firm gradually, like an apple ripening on a tree.

"Yes, ma'am." I took a seat beside Alle.

Denson and Rollins came in a moment later. Rollins's hornets' nest of hair swayed as she walked. I gripped the leg of Alle's chair between my feet and tried to imagine the hairpins as buzzing insects. I didn't know why I was so nervous. The man and the woman were not frightening, but their presence here made my chest feel tight.

"Girls," Rollins said brusquely, pulling a chair around so she could sit beside the couple. "These are the Malins. They're looking to adopt a daughter."

I hated the joy I took in that sentence, hated my own tired hope.

"Of course we'd simply take all of you if we could." Mrs. Malin smiled at me again. She seemed to be smiling at me often, and I didn't know when this had become a competition, but I wanted her to smile at me the most.

"But we only have the means for one child," Mr. Malin said.

Mrs. Malin looked at Rollins. "And we were thinking we'd . . . we'd like to get to know each of these girls individually, if that's all right?"

"Of course." Rollins smoothed her skirt. "I thought perhaps we could have each girl show you her favorite place in Rock Point. Girls, this might be your bedroom, or the supper hall, or the reading room . . . whatever you like."

My mind blanked. I could not think of a favorite place, besides Alle's bed at night, next to her. The reading room was a good place, but I wasn't sure it was my favorite. I prayed I wouldn't be chosen first, but as is mostly the case when you pray something like that, it only shines a light on you. As I led the Malins to the reading room, I began to understand just how serious a thing this was. One of us would be adopted. Given a home. And, I realized, it couldn't be me.

It was one of those things I understood in my entire being—all at once, and gloriously. I would be all right. My true dream was to be on my own and *free*. A new family would only be another sort of prison.

But Alle . . .

Alle didn't fit in here. She was too splendid, too elegant, too wise. She affected people for the better, and though she pretended she did not mind isolation, I knew it hurt her. She deserved a nice home and people who loved her above all else in the world. She was a treasure, and the Malins seemed so kind.

I knew what I had to do.

"This is the reading room," I said stiltedly, showing them in.

"This is beautiful." Mrs. Malin smiled again at me. I could tell she didn't really think it was beautiful, and I felt ashamed on behalf of Rock Point. But it seemed genuine, her willingness to see why this place might be special to me.

I shrugged and spat on the ground. "'S awright." I caught Mrs. Malin's surprised glance at her husband.

"So you like reading?" Mrs. Malin stepped forward to study the bookshelves.

"I don't like much of anything." I scratched at my arms, sniffed loudly, and when Mrs. Malin didn't look over, I began picking my nose for Mr. Malin's benefit.

They both tried to get me to answer some questions, but I only grunted or snapped at them. I was doing what I'd always done best— being repellent, undesirable. Eventually we headed back to the parlor, and I left the Malins in there with Alle and Marcy, not bothering to say good-bye.

I went up to my room and pictured the Malins falling in love with Alle. Imagined her charming them with her gentleness and intelligence. Envisioned them signing the adoption papers, telling

Alle to go upstairs and pack. Any minute now she'd burst in, grinning, and tell me she had a home. My chest ached thinking about it, but I was happy too, picturing Alle's new life. There was a flicker of envy—a tiny, secret wish that the Malins would choose me. But I doused it quickly.

Eventually Alle did come upstairs, and when I asked how it had gone, she said she didn't know.

"But you have to have some idea whether they liked you?"

"I don't know," she repeated. "I don't know if they liked me. I don't know if I liked them."

Her jaw was quivering. I would have missed it if I hadn't come to know her fairly well. "What is it?" I asked.

"Miss Holmes told them about the weasel."

"What?"

"I was leading them back to the parlor after we visited the laundry room, and Miss Holmes took them aside. I couldn't hear all she said, but she was talking about me killing the weasel."

"That awful sheep. Come here." I patted the bed. I was surprised when Alle did come over and sit beside me. I put an arm around her. "If they let that affect their decision, they're the stupidest people in Rock Hill. You were protecting us. You were brave."

She cried then, quietly. I held her, shocked and unsure what to do. I didn't experience the disgust I usually felt toward the younger children when they cried. This seemed more like comforting Franny Gammel. While I didn't want Alle to be sad, I liked having her lean against me. I liked telling her it would be okay, even though I had no idea if it would be.

A week later, Rollins told us the Malins had decided not to adopt after all. She said it as though she was apologizing to us, but deep down, I wasn't sorry. Or only a little sorry. But if the Malins couldn't love a girl who killed weasels, then I wasn't going to wait around for them to swoop to our rescue.

After that, Alle and I grew closer. More determined to protect each other, and not to need anyone else. At night, we became bolder in our kissing, and we began to fall asleep in an embrace, rather than side by side.

She was waiting for me one evening in our room when I came back from the kitchens.

"I have something you might like to see." She held out a book. It was old, its pages turning the stale yellow of a snail's shell. The cover was a faded brown fabric, and the title, in gold, was *A Conversation with the Minotaur.* I reached out, and she handed me the book.

"Where did you get this?" I rubbed what looked like a dust streak on the cover.

"The reading room. I borrowed it without officially borrowing it."

I glanced at her. "You did not."

She ducked her head slightly, but she looked pleased.

"Why?" I demanded.

"I know you like stories about the beast."

It was the first time she'd given me a gift, the first time—that I knew of—she'd broken the rules. I wanted to hug her. So I did. She tensed for a moment, then hugged me back. I sat on the edge of her bed and flipped open the cover, and she sat beside me.

The preface explained that the author had come face-to-face with the Minotaur during the beast's rampage. He had been scooped into the beast's great, clawed hand, and though he had known he was about to be devoured, he had risked speaking to her.

*"How, Beast?" I said to the She-Menace. "Look around you. Look at what you have wrought. The one who would cause such devastation must have no soul at all."*

*The Beast turned so that her blazing red eye was level with my own gaze. She smiled, and her lips rose like curtains over a platform of slathered fangs, each as long as my head. Between her teeth, I could see bits of human flesh and hair, and I knew I looked upon Death.*

*"Soul?" the Lady Heathen replied. "I do not know the word."*

"Oh, cow drippings." I rolled my eyes, flipping through the book. "He's a very dramatic writer."

Little of the text on the pages impressed me, but what did captivate me were the drawings: elaborate pen and ink renderings of the beast's reign of terror. In these illustrations, she was as tall as six men and walked upright on huge, muscled legs that ended in cloven hooves. Her arms were long and black and hairy, with hands like an ape's and claws like you'd see on a bird of prey.

On one page was a drawing of the beast holding two men, one in each hand. In a series of subsequent drawings, she clapped them together like the soles of mud-crusted shoes, and they both burst into flame. She then tied their burning bodies into a knot and hurled them into a schoolhouse.

"How many people have tried to slay her, d'you think?" I asked Alle.

She frowned. "I don't know."

"But aren't you curious? Don't you wish you could see her? The beast? And her prison?"

She didn't answer. I stopped on the next page, which showed a high-ceilinged chamber containing a mountain of treasure—a pile of gold coins with massive jewels and goblets and strings of pearls.

"What do you think the prize would be? For slaying the beast?"

She extended one foot and kicked me lightly on the back of the leg. "There's no prize for slaying anything," she said quietly. "You think there will be. But there isn't."

Not so. There was such a thing as killing for justice, and it would, I imagined, reap a grand prize indeed. "Do you think there's really a treasure?"

"Thera, I keep telling you I don't know."

"People go willingly. People dare each other into the labyrinth after a night of drinking." I jabbed at the illustration of the treasure. "How many of them actually wish to slay the beast? And how many of them simply want the treasure?"

She sighed and tipped her head back. Her curls bounced, and I smelled soap on her, and a hint of the outdoors—grass and mud. "I *don't—*"

"Quit saying you don't know. Make something up."

She crossed her arms ostentatiously, trying to hide a smile. "Don't tell me what to do."

I grinned and looked back at the drawing. "Perhaps there is something to be said for worthiness. Just like in the old tales. The greedy people fail, but the beast will be brought down by someone . . . someone . . ."

I was losing the train of thought. Someone pure of heart? There was no such person. Someone who understood the beast? I didn't put myself in this category, not yet.

We turned the page and saw a drawing of the carousel the Minotaur's mother had been working on. The animals were elaborate—the detail work on the bridles alone kept me busy for a while. There was a horse, a tiger, a giant hare, a donkey, a polar bear, and a dragon.

"That white bull must've been something else," I said. "If it was better than all this."

"These animals all look sick." She placed her chin on my shoulder and stared down at the page. I forgot all about carousels and treasure. I closed my eyes and felt the weight of her chin, the warmth of her breath. I opened my eyes suddenly, feeling a dizzying sadness.

"Maybe that's why I like them," I whispered.

She laughed softly.

"If we were that rich," I said. "We'd never have to worry about any of it. About what to do when we leave this place."

"Don't you think we'll find something to do with ourselves?"

"I personally can't see you begging in the streets. You wouldn't last a night."

"Thera. Don't be cruel."

"I don't mean to be," I insisted. "I only . . . Well, it's more than just not having parents, isn't it? Being an orphan? It means you don't have anyone in the world who cares where you end up." I was immediately ashamed of my own self-pity, and started to turn the page. But instead I went backward and admired again the drawing of the treasure.

If I had all that, people would notice me. They'd know who I was when I walked into a hat shop, or when I drove my sleek car around Rock Hill. It might not mean that anyone cared about me—but being noticed was, perhaps, the next best thing to being loved.

Her hand hovered over the page for a moment, then covered mine. I slowly looked up at her.

She closed the book, easing our hands out from the pages. Outside, the wind seemed to shove ghosts up against the glass and pummel them, and they moaned and slapped the windows.

She turned slightly away from me and unbuttoned her dress. Glanced back over her shoulder and studied me, lips parted and curving slightly upward. "Are you going to get changed?" Her body had filled out even more in the past few months; her too-small bra pushed up her breasts, creating a deep shadow between them. I was stupid and breathless and still in a world of warriors and beasts and gold.

I shucked my sweater quickly, getting tangled in the sleeves. I didn't want to stand, but she held out a hand and helped me up, and I stood before her in the dull moonlight, my breath coming too fast, my eyes, I'm sure, too wide. My chest swelled with each breath, so that my breasts nearly brushed hers, and she didn't let go of my hand.

"Can I . . .?" She stepped forward and kissed me. I felt it in my whole body. I was alive in a way that made me feel uncontainable—made my ribs seem like a corset, my skull like a cumbersome helmet. I wanted to be rid of my body and made of air. She kicked off her underwear, and I stood shivering in the chill of the room, trying not to look down. In part because I was nervous, but more because I would only have this moment once—this moment of seeing her naked for the first time. I wanted to get it right. She guided my hand to her stomach, but seemed afraid to do more than that. I moved my fingers down the slightest bit. Stopped.

"You can touch me," she whispered.

I tried. Really, I did. But my palms were damp and I was embarrassed and I wasn't sure *where* to touch her. So I leaned forward to kiss her, because that, at least, was familiar. She wound her arms around me and pulled me close. I felt the hardness of her nipples, the weight of her breasts against mine. We'd been this close many times, under the covers and through our nightgowns, but skin-to-skin was different, and I gasped as my hips slid against hers. She moved one hand up my back and into my hair. I kissed more frantically, my eyes closed.

Her other hand passed down to my lower back. Her fingers pushed under the band of my underwear, and her nails drew a light pattern on my ass. I made a humiliating sound into her mouth, a childish whimper. She tugged my underwear down, and with a little wiggling, I managed to step out of them.

The walls were thin and the windows curtainless and the staff had keys and we were not safe. She kissed me again, tugging on my hair, and I let myself move with her. She traced figure eights on my ass, the touch so light it almost tickled, and she worked her way lower as my breathing grew more rapid. Finally she slipped two fingers between my legs. I froze. So did she. Slowly I widened my stance, let her fingers spread me slightly.

"Okay," I whispered. "Okay."

She took my lip in her teeth. Met my gaze, looking fiercely determined. She used no pressure at first, but she bit gradually until I rocked against her, moaning. She ran her fingers back and forth between my legs, bringing them farther forward each time, until I was panting, matching her rhythm with the movement of my hips.

Then it was as if my entire body was swallowing convulsively. I couldn't stop the rough slide of my hips against hers, even as the motion became more reckless, became more like battering. In this welter of breath, of skin, of need, came a confusion that made me feel small and senseless. The pulse between my legs grew violent and uneven, and I gasped and collapsed against her, into her breath and sweat, her soft sounds. She caught me in her arms and held me there as the throbbing gradually subsided.

I rested my cheek against her shoulder, breathing in the scent of her hair. "It's all right," she whispered. "Isn't it? It's okay?"

I nodded. She guided me to the bed, and we crawled under the sheet. I had a sense that I was supposed to do something more, something for her, but I couldn't gather my thoughts. I was exhausted and shocked; I wanted to cling to her and I wanted to push her away. But once I steadied my breathing, the dizziness subsided, and I felt a surge of power and wonder. I kissed the side of her neck. Kept kissing down to her chest and let my hands skim her sides until I cupped her hips. I kissed the sides of her breasts, then kept going down her stomach, feeling the muscles flutter under my lips.

The cot creaked as I shifted; she let out a small whimper with each breath.

I reached the patch of hair between her legs. And paused for just a moment. Then I kept kissing.

# CHAPTER 11

Somehow, we passed over a year at Rock Point—Kenna, Bitsy, Alle, and I. We went on organized excursions into town—to the ice-cream parlor on Main Street, and to a tiny theater to see a film in which a man searched for his lost wife while a frenetic soundtrack played, and title cards showed his dialogue. We saw Rock Hill's tiny museum, which held artifacts from the Minotaur's reign. Bitsy found it all quite boring, but I studied the torn baby blanket, the bloodstained dog collar, the shattered tea set, the arrows that had failed to pierce the beast's hide, and thought about the people who had handled these objects. Wondered if I would ever meet any of those people, talk to them. The Minotaur's reign had the feel of a legend, even though there were probably many still alive who'd been present for it.

The four of us remained allies, and our dubious loyalty to one another—in addition to the Dark Tales and Denson's kindness and Tamna's odd antics—kept me from feeling too trapped. Alle's relationship with Kenna was always a bit strained, but she and Bitsy grew closer. Bitsy engaged Alle in any number of conversations that inevitably centered on Bitsy herself, and it turned out Alle enjoyed things like having her nails painted or looking at magazine drawings of elegant women in various draped fabrics, and so she and Bitsy got along well.

I found things for Alle in the kitchen, in the gardens—stones and cups and chicken bones. She stole socks for me from the laundry, and we made them into puppets and did performances with them late at night. Sometimes we invited Bitsy over to watch. Miss Ridges continued to write the Dark Tales, and sometimes we made our puppets act out these stories. Nights we curled in her bed, and we learned each other's bodies, sometimes quietly and sometimes with a desperation that made me wish I could understand every part of her and never worry she was going to drift away.

I dreamed often about a maze. About paths I knew I shouldn't take. A beast caught in tethers of vine, snorting and bellowing; men struck together like flint. Babies stolen from their cribs and dropped like morsels into a waiting set of jaws. And sometimes another current of thought seemed to join those dreams, like a stream meeting a river, creating a liquid wishbone. Someone else's dreams seemed to flow into mine, making them swell with images that were not my own.

In the months before we were all to turn eighteen, a quiet settled over us. We rarely spoke of what we intended to do after we left Rock Point. Kenna once said she'd heard people got paid to box in underground rings, and she joked that she would do that. It might not have been a joke.

One night I was in the parlor with the three of them. "What're you gonna do when you leave here, *really*?" I asked.

"Awf." Kenna shifted in her high-backed chair. "You remember I told you about my time with the sheikh in the desert? When we were lost and our camels had bumbled off and the heat woulda fried your tongue if you stuck it out of your mouth—"

"Kenna. I'm trying to be serious."

"I'm only saying I might return to the desert. I'll take a better map with me this time though."

I crossed my legs and folded my hands. "Bitsy. Any thoughts?"

She was braiding threads she'd pulled from her clothes. "Uh . . . I'd like to blow this place up."

We all stared. She glanced up at us.

"What? I'd make everyone evacuate first."

"That's kind of you," I said.

Bitsy went back to braiding. "I might leave Bessie Holmes inside. I dunno, I just want to see this place become smithereens is all."

"You know . . ." Kenna perched in the chair, drawing her knees up to her chest, wobbling slightly. "I'll probably try to get married. In title only."

"In title only?" I repeated.

"I don't want to be in love or keep house. But it would be nice to be with someone who had money."

"Being rich is overrated." I wasn't sure where my words came from, since I had once drooled over the illustration of treasure in *A Conversation with the Minotaur*.

"Then you can give all your money to me for the rest of your damn life." Kenna wobbled again. "We could always find out what the old batties here think we're suited for."

"What do you mean?" Bitsy asked.

Kenna shrugged. "They have records on all of us. They write down our skill sets and our personalities. They make note of how many times there's interest in adopting us."

"How do you know this?" I asked.

She draped her arms over the back of her chair. "I got ways."

Bitsy had looked up again, a quiet intensity in her gaze. "So where are the records?"

"In Rollins's office. I'll bet they got all kinds of stuff in there. Maybe the story of those girls who went over the cliff."

"We ought to have a look sometime." Bitsy flipped the thread braid back and forth in her fingers. "I want to know if anyone's thought about adopting me."

I wasn't sure I wanted to know. Two years ago, I'd have delighted in knowing I was too repulsive to be adoptable, too skill-less for the world outside of Rock Point. Now I wasn't so sure I wanted tangible evidence of my unpleasantness.

"You there. What are you gonna make of yourself?" Kenna asked me.

"I'd like to run away and live wherever I want." I'd make my bed in the town's schoolhouse, the library, the museum, the ice-cream parlor. Every day would be different; my scenery would be ever-changing.

Kenna raised her brows. "Well, I suppose I dare you, right after this, to go out and do that."

I thought of the hole under the fence. *I could. I could run now. Get Alle to come with me. Start a life somewhere else.* "I'd miss the Dark Tales," I said.

Kenna looked at Alle. "And you?"

"I'll get a job."

"Doing what?"

"I don't know." Alle's voice sounded strained.

"You could be an assistant!" I didn't think about the words. "To a magician or something. You're beautiful enough."

I can still remember her expression—baleful, wounded. I had meant only to compliment her, but when I look back I see my words were stones in her pockets. How it must have sunk her to be thought of as an accessory to someone else's reign. But I didn't feel entirely guilty. Part of me thought she needed to understand that if she was going to be a cache of secrets, if she was never going to let on what her true strengths were, she would have to accept being cast as an apprentice. But that day, which ought to have been a memory of friendship, has become more bitter than sweet.

It was sometime during the fall that the business with Rocky Bottom started. Alle and I had a room with a good view of the prison, and one day I found her on her knees by the open window, her arms folded on the sill, calling out, "I don't know yet!"

"Who are you talking to?" I set my lesson books on the desk and walked toward the window.

She turned to me with an exhilarated smile. "He's an inmate." She looked back out the window. "He's talking to me."

It wasn't something I would have expected her to be thrilled about, but she seemed ecstatic. I knelt beside her and gazed out the window. On the second floor of the prison, in the third window from the left, a face was visible. He was too far away for me to make out his features or expression. But he squeezed his fingers through the narrow space between the window bars and wiggled them.

"That's Rocky Bottom." She said it almost proudly. "He's in there for murdering three people and throwing their bodies in the river."

"Lovely." I waved back at Rocky Bottom. He yelled something, but I didn't catch what. "What'd he say?"

"You . . . are . . . *beautiful*!" he yelled louder.

"He thinks you're beautiful." Alle glanced at me, another smile flitting across her face. "He's not wrong."

I put a hand on the back of her head and stroked her hair. Something I'd been practicing over the last few weeks—casual contact. I still felt clumsy most times, but it gave me such a thrill to touch her.

She leaned out the window, cupped her hands around her mouth, and hollered, "I have to go now! Good-bye!"

Rocky Bottom waved his fingers between the bars again.

Alle shut the window. She walked over to her bed and flopped on it. I shifted round to look at her; a sharp bit of something on the floorboards scraped my knee through my pants. "What are you talking to prisoners for?"

She slid her hands back and forth on the cot and then gripped handfuls of sheet. "He might know somebody."

"Know who?"

She tilted her head toward me. "Somebody I'd like to know."

"How come you never tell me anything I want to know?"

"I just gotta . . . I gotta confirm some things. Then maybe I can tell you."

I grumbled, but I let it go. She seemed more relaxed than I'd seen her in ages, and I took the opportunity to climb onto the cot with her and run my hands over her body until I saw goose bumps on her arm. She smiled at me. Got up before I could say anything and left the room.

In the days that followed, I sometimes found her kneeling by the window, staring out at the prison. Or I'd come into our room to find it empty, the window open, a draft rolling in.

I grew some dark chin hairs. I tried to pretend I didn't mind them, but they did make me self-conscious. I feared it was my punishment for making fun of Van Narr's mustache for the last year.

Denson worried about wrinkles, though she wouldn't admit it. I enjoyed watching people check out their own reflections, and noting where their eyes were drawn first. Denson spent a fair amount of time investigating the lines between her eyes and around her mouth. And there was one day I'd caught her outside the reading room, trying to gather her hair into a bun, little wisps escaping. She'd muttered in frustration and said, "It's getting so *fine.*"

One afternoon we were supposed to go to town for ice-cream sundaes. Bessie Holmes was busy fixing up the prettier girls, instructing them how to act around boys. Some listened eagerly, and some rolled their eyes.

Everyone was in a mood. Bitsy was playing chess with Rina and griping about the cold. "Who gets ice cream in this weather? Let's get cocoa, you lumpy boxes."

Kenna came into the parlor wearing an honest-to-God *skirt*—black with a bit of ruffle at the bottom. It was paired with a yellow blouse that made me want to warn her not to get too near the kitchens or Tamna would mistake her for corn. But a glance at her face stopped me from joking. She had black makeup smudged unevenly under each eye, and her lips were rouged slightly. Her hair, which was longer than it had been in some time, was pinned up.

Bitsy looked up and her mouth fell open. "Oh. Heavens."

"I know, I know." Kenna waved us off. "Laugh all you want. But when I was on the Gordon-Wargar islands . . . Oh, shit, I can't do this." She started to take her hair down.

"No, no." I grabbed her wrist. "Leave it."

She actually looked better without makeup. But she'd made the effort, and I wanted her to go out feeling confident.

"I know I look like a tart." She glanced miserably at me. "But seeing as I do want to get married in title only . . ."

"I understand. Only, it'd be a real piece of rotting rind who likes you just because you've got makeup on. You know? But you look nice."

"I don't. I look like I'm trying to be everyone else."

Bitsy suddenly slammed a rook onto the table. Everyone in the parlor jumped. Bitsy lolled in her chair, sliding it back from the table. "Ohhhh, God." She rolled her eyes and blew her bangs out of her face. "I am so *tired* of thinking about where we're going and what we're supposed to be. Can I just play a game without listening to everyone in the damn world feeling sorry for herself?" She turned to us. "I'm starting to think the murderers in the prison next door would be better company than all of you. They may be going to hell, but they've had some fun along the way, huh?"

Alle stood. I watched her hurry from the parlor, and I waited a moment before exiting and heading upstairs to find her.

She wasn't in our room. I stood there, staring into the small mirror in our closet, when someone rapped on the door. "Thera?" Denson's voice. "May I come in?"

I sighed. "Yes."

She pushed the door open and stepped inside. I faced her. "Are you all right? I saw you run up here. I know you're supposed to be heading to town soon."

"I'm not going."

"Any reason?"

I took a couple of deep breaths. "Since you are the only person here who's ever really been honest with me, maybe . . . Could you tell me something?"

She waited.

"I'd like to know about Allendara. The reason you and the other staff act afraid of her." I didn't want to learn about Alle this way. I wanted her to trust me, wanted her to tell me her secrets. But if she was going to be so closed off, and if Denson liked doing me favors, then why not ask?

Denson's mouth tightened. She pulled out a handkerchief and coughed into it. I wouldn't dare tell Alle's secrets. Wouldn't tell about her talk with Rocky Bottom. But I wanted Denson to understand I *knew* something was up.

Finally Denson folded the handkerchief and tucked it away again. "I am not at liberty to disclose other girls' histories."

"I'd like you to make an exception." I sounded as adult as I could manage.

"Would you like knowing I was gossiping to other girls about you?"

"I wouldn't care."

"I see."

I tried another tack. I furrowed my brow with all the sadness I could manage. "I only want to understand her better. To be a better friend." I collapsed on the edge of the bed and slumped my shoulders.

Sure enough, after a moment, Denson was by my side. "Thera." She spoke with a near-conspiratorial urgency. I leaned slightly closer to her. "Perhaps it is time you worked on understanding what *you* want. For yourself."

This surprised me, but I said nothing.

"I know Dr. DuMorg has probably talked to you about your future, but it wouldn't hurt to think, *really* think, about the best path for Thera Ballard." Her voice was rough, as though she was holding back tears.

"That's a hard thing to know," I said tentatively.

"Tell me what you want." She sounded so sincere, and her eyes were so gentle, that I became inexplicably angry. How was I to know what I wanted—and if I knew, why would I tell her? She who had the power to disappear, to disperse my secrets, to side with my enemies. She was a prison guard and I a prisoner, and she could walk away.

I considered telling her the truth—that I wanted freedom, a life spent wandering wherever I chose, bound to no one. I wanted to watch her try to deal with how improper a dream it was—how different from what the other girls wanted.

But I suspected it was a dream Denson might admire, and I saw a better game to play. A game that would take my mind off how much her question frightened me. With effort, I softened my own expression. Glanced at the floor, then up at her. "All I want is a home." I let my voice tremble. Oh, I did a whole lost-little-girl circus. "A family. I want to feel like I belong somewhere."

Denson's shoulders went slack. She rolled her eyes upward, and I thought for a second she hadn't bought it. But then she put a hand on my hair. "I know," she murmured. "I know, dear." The word sounded all wrong coming from her. She was not sentimental enough to pull off dears or sweethearts.

Still, I let her stroke my hair, and I ignored the guilt that drifted like scum on my surface. If she wanted to see me as someone in need of comfort and rescue, I would let her. And if she loved me in a way she oughtn't, I would offer her just enough to keep her shut up in dreams. When her fingertips brushed my ear, when I felt her breath near my cheek, I didn't protest. I leaned closer. Her lips met my cheek in a quick shiver of a kiss.

# CHAPTER 12

The first time it snowed that year, we were all up early, our faces pressed to the large, dirty window of the parlor. You could look down the line of girls and see the muted wonder in their eyes, in parted lips that didn't dare smile. We were skilled at tempering excitement with wariness—all except for Kenna, who whooped and banged on the glass to make an icicle fall from the molding. She was the first out the front door, racing across the perfectly white yard and leaving a trail of dark footprints behind her. We all followed, and we continued to trek coatless through the drifts and to throw snow at one another, even when Bessie Holmes yelled at us to come back inside.

I pulled Alle down into a drift and was surprised when she retaliated, pinning me and stuffing snow down my shirt, laughing as I shrieked. She grinned, her hair brushing my cheeks. I'm sure I was a sight—my nose running, my eyes watering from laughter and cold.

"Awf!" Kenna shouted at us. "You two BDs, quit your wickedness."

I sat up immediately, shocked. No one had ever accused Alle and me of anything untoward, but I suppose it was always something I feared, even if I tried to pretend I didn't. But when I looked at Kenna, she merely threw a snowball in my face and went off to harass the other girls.

Later, Alle and I went for a walk around the grounds, the snow soaking our thin, patchy shoes.

"Hey," I said quietly, long after my toes had gone numb and I'd grown tired of walking. We were completing our umpteenth circle of the grounds. I felt her gaze on me, and I forced myself to continue. "Do you think you *will* stay on here?"

"I don't know what I'll do."

The white world around us was so lovely—the branches heaped with little walls of snow, drops of ice clinging to the broken end of twigs. "I'm going to try to go somewhere and live as I please." I paused, trying not to think too hard about my next words. "You could come with me, if you wanted. We could help each other." I didn't dare look at her. But she stopped walking, and I was forced to stop too.

When I finally glanced her way, she wasn't smiling. But she didn't look disgusted either. She stared at me with a caution that made me feel, for a moment, dangerous. "Do you mean it?" she asked.

"Of course." I was puzzled.

"I need you to really mean it. I don't have anywhere to go, and I'm not skilled at getting things for myself. So I'll go with you, if you promise we're going together. Otherwise I'd just as soon work here, in the nursery."

I could've burst into a reckless dance that would have obliterated the peace of the snowy world. "We *will* be together! I promise. We'll figure out how to live, and we won't need husbands or parents or anyone telling us what to do."

She grinned, shyly at first, then more boldly as I took her hand. "All right, then."

"We've got a plan."

"Well, it's not much of a plan." She knocked me lightly with her shoulder.

I pulled her against me and kissed the side of her neck, not caring if anyone saw us. "It is a plan. Our plan is to be together, and you're not going to be sorry, because I'm going to take care of you."

She stiffened slightly, and I wasn't sure what part of my speech I was supposed to be ashamed of. So I was, for a second, ashamed of all of it.

She turned to me. "Together," she repeated, her dark eyes seeming once again to hide the most important things from me. She could mix laughter and sorrow in a way I could not. But we had all the time in the world stretching before us, time enough to learn each other's secrets. The sun under its veil of cloud had tinted the snowdrifts a gentle blue, and I felt valiant. My dreams that night were not of the beast or the maze, but of the wide world, and the million homes I might make in it with Alle.

I wanted to give Alle a symbol of my promise. During craft hour each day, I braided yarn into a circle and stuck little charms in it—coins and knickknacks I'd found or taken from other girls long ago. I set the yarn circle on my head to test it out. Looked at my reflection in the window. Alle sure as hell wasn't going to look like a princess in this, but perhaps that was all right.

You can, I have noticed, find the whole idea of princesses fairly stupid, and yet think of no better way to tell someone she is perfect than by giving her a crown.

But really what I wanted was to show her that I was kinder now. That my desire to be feared had given way to a desire to be more admirable, at least in her eyes. I'd spent a fair portion of my life taking, but I could now see the appeal of doing the opposite. Could imagine that it was its own sort of power, to do murder on somebody's heart with a gift.

I completed my ridiculous crown, and I kept it stored in the closet inside the left shoe of a pair I'd outgrown but refused to give away. I was unsure whether to wait until Christmas to present it to Alle. Then one day, as I hurried from lessons, ready to change and prepare for work in the kitchen, I passed a group of younger girls. They were whispering and glancing at me, and one called Etta Bowen smirked as I approached. I'd have liked to stop and demand to know who she thought she was. But I kept going.

Then Etta said, loudly: "Yes, when she came here, she was a hophead. Snowed out of her mind."

I was used to girls being too frightened of me to be cruel—even the younger girls, who knew me by reputation only. But now I felt lost. I didn't want to lash back, but I couldn't let this girl get away with speaking to me like that.

"Reckon she'll end up like the cook here," Etta went on. "No man wants a junkie for a wife. 'Specially not an ugly one."

I managed to squeeze past Etta, bumping her too hard with my hip, and I ran upstairs to my room. I took out the gnarled crown I meant to give Alle and twisted it, breaking off the charms until eventually the yarn braid came apart. I sat there for a long time, and was late to the kitchens—though Tamna acted as though she hadn't noticed my absence. She handed me glass jars of corn, the bright kernels floating in cloudy brine, and I whacked the lids on the counter's edge until they popped off.

I remember Christmas that year. Officer Grenwat and Denson put up a small tree in the reading room, and a present for each girl appeared underneath it. Bitsy and Kenna and I drove Denson crazy but made her laugh with our raucous renditions of Christmas carols. Even Alle joined us once for an "O Come All Ye Faithful."

Walter raced around the orphanage, and nobody seemed to mind. It was decided a group of us would go into town to hear Bessie Holmes sing in her divorced women's choir, but the night of the concert was deemed too snowy, and so Bessie went to Rock Hill and sang alone. At the time, I didn't mind missing the concert; I was having great fun throwing snowballs at Kenna out in the yard. But now I wish I had heard Bessie sing.

On Christmas Day, after a corn-drenched meal I had helped Tamna prepare, Denson gave me a little hand mirror. I wanted both to keep the mirror because it was from her and to smash it, because she clearly didn't know me at all. I had no desire to look at myself; I was not some silly girl who would gaze obsessively at her own reflection. Then I saw the image on the back: a woman with purple skirts and dark hair whirling around her, holding a curved sword high above her head.

I don't know that Denson gave gifts to any of the other girls. She put her hand on my shoulder as I gazed at my mirror. "I thought of you," she said softly.

I wished then that I had a mother. That Denson was my mother. That all the love in the world was mine for the taking. I think our wishes often get as muddled as dreams. In our wishes, people are their better selves and walls lose their permanence, and no matter how heavily we populate our fantasies with friends, with family, with lovers—we are ultimately in them alone.

Later that night, Alle and Bitsy and Kenna and I headed downstairs to meet Miss Ridges for a Dark Tale, but I stopped to listen to a ruckus in the dining room. I peered in through the open door and saw Van Narr and Officer Grenwat polishing off a bottle of wine. Van Narr was slumped in a chair, and Grenwat perched on a table.

"A house!" Grenwat exclaimed. "How can she afford one?"

"She's been saving for years." Van Narr took a swig from the bottle. "Got herself a little cottage in the heart of Rock Hill. Don't know how much longer she'll stick around here."

"Ah well. Never could tell w—" Van Narr belched. Silence, then they both laughed. "What went on in that head of hers."

*Say a name*, I urged them. Up ahead, Kenna had turned to look back at me. She mouthed a question, and I waved her on.

"A cottage." Grenwat shook her head. "She's going soft in her old age."

"She's an odd one. Always h'ssss loved that scrappy beast, T. Ballard."

Grenwat raised her glass. Van Narr raised hers, and they clinked. "To Riley Denson," Grenwat said.

"Riley Denson," Van Narr agreed.

They drank.

Alle and I were sitting on Rock Point's side lawn, watching the prison. It was nearly spring, and I was stripping the petals from an early-blooming flower. "My sister and I used to pretend we were detectives, solving murder cases." I showed her the flower. "The key to every case was always a flower. Pinned to the victim's lapel as a calling card, or trod upon by the killer's boot."

It wasn't true; Rachel and I had seldom played games like that. But now that I thought about it, I wished we had, or I wished Alle and I would.

Alle's fingers brushed mine as she took the flower. "I didn't know you had a sister." She rolled the stem between her fingers.

I nodded. I hadn't thought about Rachel or Auntie Bletch in a very long time, but I was surprised by how clearly and quickly they came back to me. "I ruined her wedding."

Alle cocked her head. "You're not going to tell me any more than that?"

The story of the wedding was one I'd never told anyone, not even Denson. And I was damned glad I hadn't told Denson, at whom I was still—unfairly but bitterly—furious. A cottage in Rock Hill? And when did she plan to tell me she was leaving? "Do you really want to know?"

"Yes." Alle looked at me and twisted her mouth to one side. "Please."

And so I began.

My sister had an outdoor wedding. She had no money beyond what Auntie Bletch could spare, and Marc's family wasn't much for frivolity, so the decorations were simple: Gold lights, wound around the rail of the back porch of Marc's family farm. A long wooden table covered in a clean white cloth. On it, a roast turkey, a huge bowl of salad, a plate of rolls, and three different casseroles. And a cake—not tiered and decorated, but a single layer vanilla cake with *Happy Journey, Marc and Rachel* in pink letters.

I wasn't jealous, exactly—I had no desire to be married, especially to someone as bland as Marc. But I was, perhaps, thrown by the attention Rachel was receiving. I didn't see what the big accomplishment was in hitching yourself to someone and borrowing his future for your own. I was fourteen; I had no strong opinions on love, but Rachel and Marc's utilitarian partnership seemed sad to me—barren and ill-fated.

There were only a handful of people in the wedding party. Three pairs of bridesmaids and groomsmen would walk down a makeshift aisle in the backyard and stand by the well that would serve as an altar. The guests sat in mismatched chairs chattering and eating. Auntie Bletch, by this time quite frail and reliant on a daily cocktail of pills to function, sat by herself in a wooden chair that tilted precariously on a grassy incline. My sister's friend Marie tried to prop up a sagging petal on one of the lilies in her bouquet.

I was standing at the food table, wrapping appetizers in a napkin for later and eyeing the turkey, when Marc came up to me. "Pretty dress."

I turned, startled. He was staring at the neckline of my pink gown. My breasts had recently gotten quite large, and I was uncomfortable with the way they swelled against the bodice. His stare annoyed me, but I wasn't afraid.

"I don't normally wear dresses."

"You should. You look nice. *These* look nice." He tapped the top of my right breast with one finger, as though pointing out an important clause in a document. Then he cupped his whole hand around it.

I stared for a moment at his hand. Then I shouted. Everyone turned. Marc jumped and yanked his arm away. I scanned my audience. "He touched me! My . . . He touched me where he oughtn't."

A few murmurs, and one woman laughed. I heard Auntie Bletch say, "Thera!" Rachel looked horrified. She turned from me and strode toward the house. After a moment, everyone else went back to what they'd been doing.

Marc grinned at me and gave my backside a swat. "Naughty girl. Telling on me."

I hit him. I felt the bones of his nose cave under the heel of my hand. Damp flecks on my face. He shouted and put his hands up to his nose. Blood poured between his fingers, running in mangled ribbons over his lips and down his chin. Everyone turned. Most of the focus was on him—people were yelping and murmuring and rushing to offer handkerchiefs. But some had started to look at me.

"Heavens, Thera!" Auntie Bletch stood, nearly falling over. "What have you done?"

Marc pinched his nose, but it wouldn't stop bleeding, and when he took his hands away, his nose was off center. Rachel ran over to us, dirt flying from under her white slippers, graying the hem of her dress. "Oh, oh no," she said, taking Marc's face in her hands. It surprised me, that she was willing to get his blood on her dress. But she held him as though nobody in the world existed but her injured boor of a future husband.

At the reception she ripped her veil off and went to cry behind some trees. And when I found her, white gown puddled around her hips, face streaked with cried-away makeup, she said savagely, "You couldn't have just kept your mouth shut?"

I don't know why it works this way—that we blame the one who shatters the illusion, rather than the illusion itself, or ourselves for buying into it. What ruined that day for Rachel wasn't that her lying sister told tales and grabbed the spotlight. It was that she believed those tales. She knew her husband was an ugly man inside and out, and she still hoped for a decent future with him.

I returned to the yard, furious and hurt. One of the groomsmen was getting ready to carve the turkey. I walked up to the table and shoved bird and platter onto the ground.

It should not have brought me so much joy, but once you've stood in front of a crowd with power rolling over you—*through* you—with secrets and meanness junked up in your passages like a virus, your mind concussed and your heart out of the picture, it might be easier to understand.

I kicked the turkey like a wet, fleshy football. The crisped skin split and the meat spilled out. I kicked it again. People got out of the way and rust-colored bones sprang from the flesh. Rachel arrived and shrieked when she saw what I was doing. It was rude and cruel, but it was one of my most satisfying moments, to kick the shit out of my sister's turkey and watch her cry. I had no desire to hurt her; I only wanted to answer her ignorance, to repay her compassionless moment with one of my own.

Auntie slapped me later. She made me stand still for it too; it wasn't spontaneous and skillful like slapping in stories. She had to take aim. Her arm was trembling, and she was clumsy and clubbed half my ear. I let her do it because I felt a rough batch of guilt rising inside me. I wouldn't apologize to Rachel, though.

I still haven't. I didn't tell Alle that last part. About the joy I took in hurting my sister, about my refusal to apologize. I lost the words I needed to make her understand the way fear becomes pain, becomes the need to cause pain. But knowing what I know now, I doubt she needed me to explain this.

She stared at me after I finished my story, her dark eyes tracking mine. "I'm sorry for you." She shook her head with a worldly sorrow I envied. "That shouldn't have happened."

I wasn't sure if she meant Marc touching me or me behaving as I had.

"It took a long time." Her childlike voice was strange against a backdrop of guarded ferocity. "But now I'm not afraid of anything."

I didn't believe her, and I wanted to know what she had been afraid of before. I looked at her and wished we were under a blanket together. I wanted to be her worthy hero and worthy opponent and I wanted to her to think that I had grown and hardened since my turkey-kicking days. I was suddenly very ashamed that I'd told her about Marc's hand on my breast.

"Neither am I," I told Alle.

I lay back in the grass, unable to look at her anymore. Shame is perhaps both a form of self-pity and a form of loneliness. In the heat of embarrassment, it's possible to believe you are the only one who has ever felt such guilt, such a profound understanding of what an impossibly evil thing the self is. It feels good to be martyred on your own terms. It is a bit like being sick and wanting someone to bring you soup. If you're guilty enough, someone may have mercy on your kicked-cur soul. Someone might ease you from the worst of your darkness.

Alle settled next to me, her hair brushing my temple. There was a jitteriness, almost a buzzing in my chest. I had always wanted her to like me. But part of me wished to be adored like a painting—admired for my inscrutability, loved only as a very carefully decided-upon version of myself. And part of me wanted to be loved for what I truly was—afraid and unsure and in awe of a girl who made me feel less alone.

Alle took my hand. A gesture familiar to both of us, but it made my throat tight. I ran my thumb over her knuckle and stared at the sky. I thought about that time Auntie Bletch and I had held hands on Main Street. The whirling of the lights and people and the jingle of the bells on the shop doors and the whistle of the train. The sense that if I let go, I might get lost in all of it.

"Rachel's pregnant now. Auntie Bletch wrote me." Auntie Bletch hadn't written me, and probably never would. The scabby bat was probably dead. Though Rachel might well have been pregnant. I rarely knew exactly why I lied, except that it felt good sometimes to see how easy the truth was to pull aside, how easy it was to hang something else in its place.

"Oh."

I turned toward her suddenly. "Do you ever think about having children? Someday?"

Her mouth curved up slightly on one side. "Depends on what happens."

She was always saying things like that. *I don't know. Depends. I don't know.* I watched a barely there puff of cloud in the sky. "I always feel bad for mothers. I'd hate to stand around with some squally thing hanging off my tit."

"Well they're not hanging off your tit forever."

"Yeah, I know that." The buzz moved into my throat, forced it tighter. I turned away, but there was no escaping—I was crying in front of her, and I could feel her watching. "I don't hate children. I don't know much—" I just barely stopped a sob "—about them, and I don't know'f I've got the patience for them. But I don't h-hate them."

She squeezed my hand. "That's like a lotta people, then."

She didn't understand. "I can't *be* a mother. Look at me. I'm gonna leave here with no money, and I can't . . ."

"Thera. You don't have to worry yet. Denson, Rollins—they'll help you find a job."

I opened my mouth to denounce Denson as a traitor, to tell how she planned to abandon us to go live in a cottage in Rock Hill. Stopped myself.

*Maybe I do want a child. A daughter. Maybe I want to take care of her when she's sick, and tell her stories—the Dark Tales—and I want her to love the wickedness of them. And if they give her bad dreams, she can climb in bed with me.*

If I had a daughter, I wouldn't ever leave her. And I wouldn't tell her to keep her mouth shut if something hurt her.

I took a deep breath. Saw the darker swirls in the gray space above me—sometimes the clouds seemed to grow on the sky like ivy. "What if I'd be a decent mother? But I won't ever know."

"I think you would be." She kissed my cheek.

There are perilous cracks in what we know. And a deceptive smoothness to all that we don't. I didn't call it love then, what I felt for Alle. But it swept beyond friendship, beyond sisterhood, and it felt like the kind of adventure I craved.

"I feel sick when Rocky Bottom talks to you," I muttered. "I really do."

Her lips looked full and soft, and I wanted to lean over and kiss them. I didn't want to be shy or delicate. I wanted to know what it was like to ravage a body with a misguided admiration for it. To know that skin got in the way of the truth of the person, and yet that truth, that soul, was untouchable, and so you had to settle for skin. "He's only lonely."

"Well, I wish he'd go bother someone else with being lonely."

"You want to fight with me, Thera?" Her voice was quiet, but there was a firmness to it that stilled me. Her long neck was elegantly arched, and the curve of one breast was visible under the thin fabric of her dress. She crossed one arm over her body and brushed my temple with her fingers. I could see every pore, the slight lines that formed when she gave me a closed-lipped smile. The folds of skin where her neck twisted, the sway of each black curl that hovered around her face. "Don't you think you do enough fighting?"

"Not nearly," I whispered. If I had any sense, I'd fight *this*. This joy, this hope that made a warren of my mind, that flashed through me quicker than I could follow. If I had any sense, I wouldn't need her.

# CHAPTER 13

I went to chapel on Sunday with Alle. The staff had organized trips to town on Sundays for girls who wanted to go to church. Alle went most weeks, but I'd never been. I wore my black trousers and Kenna's yellow blouse, and I felt like a banana going bad at the bottom, but I liked that my shirt almost matched her shawl. She seemed distant that day—chilly and distracted.

I hadn't realized the coming Tuesday marked the anniversary of the end of the Minotaur's reign. The preacher was a black woman with white hair and liver spots all up and down her like the world had rained blood on her. She said Darwull, the architect who'd built the labyrinth, had spent nearly three years designing it. He had put it on the promontory, both to keep it away from the town and in the hope that the beast wouldn't see it and destroy it before it was done.

I tried to imagine Darwull and his crew slowly building a palace, stone by stone. I wondered how they had decided on the twists and turns. How they imagined they might baffle a monster. How Darwull had managed to put aside his love for his daughter and do what was best for the town.

I pictured the Minotaur's mother carving the white bull. She must have been smart, must have known the slopes of an animal's body, the regality and power of the creature she carved. She knew which art was worth keeping close to her chest. And her daughter, she knew what people feared, so that when she began her horrific slaughter, she succeeded grandly.

I had always pictured that decade as one of relentless destruction. But as the preacher told the story of those years, I realized the

Minotaur had come to Rock Hill to wreak havoc only once in a while. Many of the people who were killed had sought her where she slept in her lair by the sea. She woke, killed them, and then came into town to demand a price for having her slumber disturbed.

People can be very stupid. If there is a monster, they must slay it; if there is a secret, they must know it. If the whole world were to go up in flames, there'd be someone wandering around with flesh hanging in burnt strips from a charred skeleton, looking for a reason.

During a hymn, she crept into my mind—the beast. I didn't panic, and I didn't put her out. I let her snuffle through my visions of her prison. A large, dark, lumbering shape; she grinned at some of the things I imagined. Shook her great horned head at others.

Alle stood in the doorway to our room and held up a massive ball of ratty thread in all colors. It was as big as her head. "Do you see what he gave me?" She was nearly breathless, smiling. "Do you see?"

"*Who*? What the hell are you talking about?"

"Rocky Bottom. I stood in our yard and he stood in his and he threw it to me. He's been collecting it." She stepped closer to me and held it out as if I might want to see it better. "For years, he's been collecting the thread he gets to use for craft projects and tying it together."

"Why would they give prisoners thread?" I asked. "Suppose they tried to strangle a guard with it?"

"He gave it to me. He gave it to me and asked if I want to marry him."

For a second I couldn't speak. Was this why she was so excited? "But . . . you can't mean . . ."

"I told him no, of course. But I said if he really loved me, he'd get me the information I need." She placed the thread on our desk.

"You can't keep doing this." I tried not to sound as angry as I felt. "Either tell me who you're trying to get information on, or stop talking about it."

"Thera." She turned back to me, and her expression grew serious. "I will tell you one day. I'll tell you all about it. But for now, I just . . . I need to figure this out. Please?"

I glared at her.

She tilted her head. "Maybe I will say yes to him." For the first time, I imagined I heard a note of genuine cruelty in her voice.

"Shut up."

She laughed. "Thera, come on. You can't really be jealous. You can't really think I would?"

"Just knock it off, okay? I'm not in the mood to hear about it."

Our plan. The two of us, together, helping each other survive. How could I guarantee she'd stay with me once we had our freedom? That she wouldn't get married in title only—or worse, marry for love—and leave me on my own?

When you fall in love with someone, you fall in love not only with her face and eyes and heart, but with her vision of the world. Love leaves no room to stand back and pity another's delusions. You share them. You join hands lying down and draw an arc across the sky and tell a story about what a cloud looks like, a story that becomes your shared truth.

But what of the pieces of her you don't understand? The notes in her voice you cannot hit with your own? The words she uses, but that you cannot remember the meaning of? I wasn't sure what I wanted in that moment—to share everything with her, or to take back my secrets and begin again in a version of our story where I was aloof and intriguing. Where she begged to know me, but I gave her nothing but cool stares and cryptic promises.

# CHAPTER 14

There came a two-week period where Miss Ridges had laryngitis. Denson tried to take over reading the Dark Tales for a couple of nights, but she couldn't do the voices. She was a terrible reader, and we knew it, and she knew it, so for several nights there were no stories, and we were all bored.

It was Bitsy's idea to sneak into town.

We used the hole Walter had dug under the fence. The gap wasn't very big, and we had to do some of our own digging. Our hands and clothes were dark with mud when we arrived on the other side. I looked down at my sweater and couldn't even see the gold threads anymore. It was just Kenna and Bitsy and me. I hadn't asked Alle—I'd assumed she would disapprove. Bitsy was thrilled with that decision. "It's about time you acted like anyone else exists, Thera."

Our actions and their potential consequences were not real to me that night. The whole time we were digging, I found myself glancing over my shoulder at Rock Point, imagining lights snapping on, shadows hurtling toward us. Officer Grenwat shoving me to the ground and dragging me to Rollins's office. I imagined Denson's disappointment. But everything I imagined only bent back some magnificent, supple wickedness in me and let it fly, made me waver with pleasure. I was never going to be what anyone expected. Was never going to live under anyone's thumb.

Bitsy led the way to town. In the dark everything looked strange, and I realized I'd never seen the world outside of Rock Point by night. It was a soft blue dream, layers of mist and the dark curves of mountains like the bellies of sleeping giants. As we passed the prison, I thought about the men sleeping there on hard cots, perhaps lonely.

The road down to the village was steep and rocky, and I watched my feet in their ragged black shoes; for some reason I was more afraid of falling than of being caught. Kenna kept shaking dirt from her hair. Bitsy's blond ponytail bobbed, and she walked with purpose, not at all like a scared girl doing a forbidden thing.

Main Street still had plenty of lights on. The pub was open and leaking laughter and music. People were dining outside at a couple of restaurants, despite the chill in the air. I stared at the patio railings with their flower boxes and gold lights, watched couples leaning across the table toward each other. Heard the clink of silverware and the soft glug of wine being poured.

I expected people to look at us. I thought maybe they would know we weren't supposed to be here. But a band of three ragged girls seemed to make no impression. An old man with a gummy beard and a filthy brown coat grinned at us around his cigarette as we passed. I moved slightly closer to Kenna, and then was ashamed of myself for doing so.

We walked into the pub—a squat wooden building with a lit-up sign. Bitsy tried to order a gin and tonic and was told to "Go on home, little girl." We were spat back out onto the street.

"Awf, what'll we do now?" Kenna asked.

"Hey, look there." I pointed across the field behind the pub at an old shed sitting in a cluster of weeds.

"That looks like a ghost's paradise. What are you thinking, Ballard?"

"Nothing. Maybe that's where I ought to live someday."

"I'm going to get us a bottle of wine." Bitsy crossed the road and led us to a garishly lit convenience market that had a neon sign and a crack in the glass door. I stared inside, wondering how exactly she planned to convince anyone she was old enough to buy a bottle, if she'd just been called a little girl at the pub.

I was about to suggest we send Kenna in, since nobody was likely to question Kenna in full bully mode, when Bitsy said, "Be back in a jiff," and disappeared inside.

She was gone awhile, and we could see through the window when she brought the wine up to the counter. Saw the clerk's lips moving, then Bitsy's. Saw the man shake his head.

I shifted, agitated. "He's not gonna let her."

Kenna was already heading into the shop.

"Kenna!"

I had no choice but to follow Kenna in. Bitsy was arguing with the clerk. "*Just* one bottle. Who will it hurt?" She spotted us. "There. These two. They'll vouch for me that I'm old enough."

I opened my mouth, unsure what to say, but Kenna boomed, "Oh, yes. She's certainly old enough. By far."

"If she can't prove it, I don't sell," the clerk said.

I grabbed Kenna's arm before she could start forward. "Bitsy, just put it back. We'll get it somewhere else."

Kenna muttered and pulled away from me. I walked toward Bitsy and took the wine from her hand. I could see how badly she wanted to keep arguing. I gripped her wrist and led her away. "Where's Kenna?" I demanded as we exited. Kenna came out a moment later, and then I rounded on Bitsy. "Why would you argue with him? We're not supposed to be out here. We can't draw attention."

"He was talking to me like I'm an *infant*," she said scornfully.

"Well, maybe—"

"Hey!" Kenna interrupted, holding up two foil-wrapped rectangles. "Look what I nicked."

Two chocolate bars. We split them up and ate them.

And that was what started the game.

We went into town twice more that week and stole small things—candy bars, sodas, a manicure set. We were not so much interested in the items—at least, I wasn't—as we were in knowing we could get away with it. Knowing that, in an emergency, any one of us could go into any store and emerge with food or drink—it seemed to me a valuable skill to carry with us into our uncertain future. We came back to Rock Point giggling and hid our inedible treasures in Bitsy's room. Alle was always asleep or pretending to be when I got back, and I wished she would awaken, ask me where I'd been. I didn't know what I'd tell her. But I wanted her to ask.

We didn't go out every night, but I'd say at least five times during the two weeks Miss Ridges was sick, we were in town, practicing discretion, patience, and thievery. I have nothing to say in my own defense. I have grown, and I have regretted, and I have softened, but it is indeed a world where the dogs chew the bones of their own kind. I grew annoyed, though, at Alle's increasing distance. I had noticed, over the past two weeks, a change in her behavior toward me. She was tense when she kissed me. We touched each other less. On the nights I was out, I climbed into my own bed when I came back, not hers. I didn't know whether it had to do with me or with whatever she'd learned from Rocky Bottom, but it occurred to me that maybe I couldn't spend an entire lifetime with someone so closed off.

"Would you like to go out?" I asked her one evening.

"Out where?"

I tried to sound casual. "Into town. Bitsy and Kenna and I have been going there at night, since Miss Ridges isn't well enough to read. *Don't* tell anybody."

She looked up from her book, lips parted. "What do you do there?"

"Just walk around, mostly." I didn't tell her about the game of taking small things from shops. "There's a hole beneath the fence. We're always back before morning. You should come with us." I suppose I was giving her a test. Trying to discover whether she could be trained in the art of wildness, whether she could ever want the mayhem I wanted.

She was silent a long moment, and I began to wonder if she'd actually say yes. "I don't want to risk it," she said finally.

"No, Miss Prim." I tried to sound teasing and failed. "I didn't imagine you would." I knew my anger was irrational, but I wanted to know if she could be dared.

"I haven't asked where you've been going." She glared at me. "But you're damn lucky no one's come in here looking. If we both go . . ."

"You mean you're afraid." I pulled on a black sweater over a flower print blouse that looked like a damn curtain. I yanked it into place.

"What are you gonna do if you get caught?"

"I won't get caught."

"You might."

"I won't."

She shut her book. "I don't like how you've been acting. Since you started sneaking off."

I turned, my hair crackling from my sweater. "Oh *really*? Well I don't act the way I do to make you happy."

"I'm not prim. It's stupid that you think that. You have no idea."

I thought of Rocky Bottom, of her excitement over a ball of thread, and my fury grew. "So prove it. Come with me."

A long silence. I grabbed my shoes, intending to storm out.

"Okay."

I almost didn't hear her. "What?"

"I said I'll go."

I sat on the bed to put on my shoes. "If you go, you can't wear a dress."

"Why not?"

"In case we have to run. And you can't get scared and mess everything up."

"I won't."

"Okay, then."

She lunged off the bed and went to the closet. She searched through our things, coming up with a pair of slacks, and she yanked them on then shucked the dress she was wearing. I forced myself to look away as she found herself one of my sweaters. The blue one with the waves.

"There," she said when she'd put it on. "Now can we get going?"

The walk into town was mostly silent. Kenna kept glancing at Alle, and I stayed tense, silently daring Kenna to say something. Bitsy kept up a steady stream of chatter—about which lessons she hated or which of the recent baby shoppers had looked the strangest. Alle didn't speak to any of us. I knew the other two were angry with me for inviting her, and as we got closer to town I became increasingly unnerved. Kenna and Bitsy would want to lift a couple of items from a shop, as always. And how was I supposed to explain that to Alle? What if Alle argued, or tried to rat on us?

We ended up in the pub. Alle had looked horrified when Bitsy suggested it, but she'd followed us in without a word. We didn't try to order booze this time, just some soda. We sat at the bar like we belonged there, and no one questioned us.

There was an older couple next to me, maybe in their fifties, and when I could no longer stand the stilted conversation with Kenna and Bitsy, or Alle's sullenness, I turned to them. "Hello there."

The man nodded. "Good evening. What brings you here?"

"I'm just unwinding after a day of research."

The man rubbed his lips together and held his empty glass up as the bartender walked by. "Research?"

"I'm writing a book." I tried to sound as serious as Kenna did when she told her stories. "About the Minotaur."

"Thera?" Bitsy whispered from a couple of stools down. I ignored her.

"Oh-ho-ho." The man nodded. "Another one of those."

The woman leaned across him to speak to me. "Honey, I don't think there's room in the world for another book about the monster."

"Well, I don't know much about her," I said. "So it'll be a learning experience for me."

They both look me over. The man squinted. "You couldn't have been alive when all that was going on."

"Were you?"

They exchanged a glance. "We were children," he said.

I bent toward him, excited. "And were you afraid? I've heard those were the darkest of times."

"Well." The man passed a hand over his mouth. "Certainly it's better now that the beast is'n prison. But we still gotta send her tributes. She still holds sway. Doesn't she, Em?" He nudged the woman.

"She does. She does." Em's head bobbed up and down.

"What would happen if we stopped sending tributes?" I asked.

"Dunno, missy. I wouldn't want to find out."

I leaned closer still. "Do you believe she can escape?"

"Don't know, don't know."

One of Em's curls came unpinned and bounced against her cheek. "All we know is, if she escaped, it would be the end of Rock Hill."

"No bullet can kill her," the man said. "No steel, no . . ."

"Arrow," Em supplied.

"No arrow. No rope."

"No poison."

I feared that unless I stopped them they would go on indefinitely, naming things that couldn't kill the beast. "And did you ever see her?" I asked.

"See her?" The man's brows shot up. "I was there for the *sacrifice*."

I cast a quick look at Kenna, who was talking to Bitsy. Then I looked back at the couple. "What's the sacrifice?"

"Mmm." Em smiled a bit dreamily. "There was a mother— How's it go, William?"

"A mother," William continued. "And the beast had snatched up her little one. Was about to devour the child. The mother begged. She lay down in the street, and she begged for the beast to take her instead."

"The beast put the little girl down," Em said. "Killed the mother, but let the child go."

I took a shaky breath, my mind snagging on the image of the sacrifice. "Was it the only time she let someone go once she'd caught them?"

"That we know of."

Alle tapped my shoulder. "Thera. We need to leave."

I ignored her. "Did anyone know the beast when she was human? Anyone know her as a child?"

Em nodded. "My grandmother. A troubled girl, she said. With a witch's eyes."

"Thera." Bitsy was beside me, tugging my arm. "Time to go."

"But it's always easier," William said as I was pulled to my feet. "Always easier to say someone looks like trouble once they've proven they are." He held up a hand in a strange salute.

I reluctantly followed the others out the door. It had rained, and the empty street was a slick blue-black. "Why'd you do that?" I demanded. "I was having a conversation."

"You can't go having conversations," Bitsy said. "We don't want people remembering us."

"'Sides," Kenna said, "we've got to get back soon, and Bitsy wants to stop at the convenience mart."

"Can't we skip that tonight?" I tried to sound offhand.

Kenna glanced at Alle, then grinned slyly at me. "Awf, you haven't told the nice Miss B. that you're a thieving tough, have you?"

"There's no one out!" I insisted. "They'll notice you more, because there's no one else around."

"What's going on?" Alle glanced at each of us.

"Come on, babe, don't worry about it." Bitsy led the way down the street toward the store.

"Bitsy's just gonna run in and get something here," I told Alle as we arrived at the store. "I'll wait here with you."

"Naw, naw. Come in." Kenna motioned to us. "You might see something you want."

"Leave them be." Bitsy shot us a quick look and stuck her hands in her coat pockets. "I'll go alone. We don't want to attract attention."

She went in. I stared at the ground and waited, holding my breath. I could sense Kenna staring at me, and I could feel how rigid Alle was. Why I'd ever thought bringing her was a good idea, I didn't know.

Bitsy emerged at last, hands still in her pockets. "I got us chocolate," she said. "A whole bunch of it. And lipstick." I turned gratefully, ready to start for Rock Point, when suddenly the shop doors opened again. Two men walked out, one taller and one rounder. Both in uniform. Cops.

I motioned Bitsy toward us, just as the taller cop said, "Hold it there, honey."

Bitsy stopped and faced them.

"Bitsy!" I called. "Let's go."

"What were you doing in there?" the rounder cop asked.

"What business is it of yours?" Bitsy asked.

*No. No, no, no.*

"It's my business what's in your pockets, sweetheart."

Taller stepped closer to Bitsy. "Hey, blondie. What'd you need from that store, hmm? New eyelash curler?"

"She probably uses it on her front doormat." Rounder grinned. "Keeps it nice and springy for the boys. Or are you bald down there, baby?"

"Wanna show us?"

Bitsy's hands clenched at her sides, then released. She walked toward them.

Kenna tensed as though intending to go after her. "Bitsy, you lug, *no!*"

"What did you say to me?" Bitsy demanded.

The cops were still smirking.

"No, really. What did you just say to me?"

I stood frozen. Some sick part of me wanted to see what would unfold. But I knew this was dangerous, knew we had to get Bitsy back to us and return to Rock Point.

Bitsy stopped a few feet from the cops. "My cunt hair is none of your business, you clogged chutes." I had never seen her so angry. At Rock Point her temper was amusing, or annoying, but it never really frightened me until now. Kenna and I moved closer. "And everything in my pockets was mine to begin with."

Rounder glanced at Taller, then looked back at Bitsy. "That's, ehhh . . . disrespecting a police officer."

"And just where are you from, honey?" Taller asked. "What're you doing out so late at night?"

"I'm sorry," Bitsy said snidely. "Do I have a curfew, daddy?"

"Bitsy, let's just get on home," I said again, hating my own cowardice. But I was afraid, and I wanted to be back in my room, sleeping next to Alle. There were so many ways this could go wrong— if the officers knew she'd robbed the convenience mart, if they found out we were from Rock Point . . . I'd have taken the girls' home over prison; any of us would have.

Taller smiled. "Ought to listen to your friends, blondie. Unless you want a ride to the station."

"Maybe she's armed, Toby," Rounder said. "You ought to search her."

"Not a bad idea." Taller reached forward. At the same time, Bitsy lunged, bashing his jaw with her fist. The man staggered back in surprise, and Rounder grabbed Bitsy, laughing. Taller blinked and moved his jaw in circles, pressing his fingers to the spot she'd hit.

"Bitsy!" Kenna shouted.

Bitsy elbowed Rounder in the throat, and he let her go, but Taller caught her. I raced toward them, hearing Kenna and Alle behind me. The officers were genuinely struggling to contain Bitsy, who wasn't screaming, but was fighting as hard as she could.

"Let her go!" I yelled.

Bitsy sank her teeth into Taller's hand. He shouted, then raised his other fist and punched Bitsy in the side of the head. Bitsy's knees buckled, and she dropped to the ground.

Kenna, Alle, and I stopped running. The cops stared down in shock. There was a moment of complete silence while we all looked at Bitsy's motionless form.

Then I started to scream.

"Holy shit," Taller said. "Holy shit."

Rounder had bent down and shook Bitsy, feeling for a pulse. He glanced up at Taller, and though he didn't speak, I knew what he was saying.

I tried to run to them, but Kenna held me back. "Murderer!" I shouted at them. "You *murderer*."

"Bitch *bit* me." Taller suddenly glanced at his partner with mingled panic and despair. "She came at me."

"You're the bitch. You're the bitch, you pansy cowshit! You toad, you trash!" I pounded at Kenna's arm, trying to get her to release me.

The officers fled. I broke free of Kenna and ran to Bitsy. Knelt beside her, searching for a pulse. I knew she was dead. Her eyes were frozen, wide and blank. I clutched her hand. I don't know how long I stayed there, snarling and weeping, before Kenna dragged me away.

# CHAPTER 15

**B**ack at the fence of Rock Point, Kenna shook me. "Pull it together." She hissed the words fiercely and yet somehow managed to sound like a little girl. I was vaguely aware of Alle standing silently to one side, her arms crossed. She'd done nothing. She'd stood there, silent, while the police officer had killed Bitsy. I wanted to shout at her for it. Kenna kept shaking me and said, "Shut the fuck up. You understand? We're in major *goddamn* trouble."

I bared my teeth at her. "She's dead. She's dead." I chanted it like I was casting a spell, and I shook my head so my hair swept my neck, and I shoved Kenna away.

"You fucking idiot!" Kenna grabbed my shoulder. Her touch was rough. I wanted nothing so much as to have Bitsy with us, snickering and going on about how stupid the men were in the pub. Slapping the dirt from her arms and dragging the tangle of vine back over the hole. "We need to walk in there and get in our beds. And tomorrow, we need to act like nothing. Fucking. Happened."

"She's dead," I repeated. "They'll know she's dead."

"They won't know anything. They won't know a damn-fuck thing until her body turns up. And even then—"

"They'll *know*."

"They'll think she ran away."

"Something did happen. Something *did* happen."

Kenna slapped me. Harder than Auntie Bletch had ever managed. I didn't even put a hand up to my cheek; I just stood there and let it sting. "Shut up." She glanced at Alle and then looked back at me. "Go inside and get in bed. If you can act normal until they find her body, then we'll be fine. Once they tell us she's dead, bring on the hysterics."

She turned without another word and slid open the basement window we'd been using. I followed her through the darkness of the laundry room. When we got up to the kitchen, Kenna pushed me ahead of her. Everything we did seemed loud—the shuffle of our feet, our breathing, Kenna's whispered commands.

Kenna walked Alle and me to our room. She gave me a pat on the shoulder that was half shove. "Not a word." When I looked at her, the damp sheen in her eyes caught the moonlight. She was trying not to cry.

*Dead.* The word tunneled through my brain, writhing like a worm in the meal of an apple, and chewed its way through feeling and memory. When it got in deep, that word—when it touched on the memory of Bitsy falling—my heart whirred like a wound clock and then ticked on.

It was hard to talk to Alle. She nodded when I said things that could be nodded at. But she didn't really reply. She kept her head down. Sometimes at night, if there was enough moonlight coming through the window, I could see her huddled form on the cot, shaking. But I never heard her cry.

*Don't you care?* I wanted to scream at her.

Kenna kept reminding us to "keep quiet" and "hold it together." She even promised we'd go back and find those officers and kill them ourselves. But she didn't mean it. She was, in her way, as lost as I was. Most people I have met seem skewed toward the idea that death, real death, will shake the dreamers lose from their trees. You can't shut the book on real death. You can't break at a chapter's end then pick up three months or a year later to when things are easier for the characters. You can't unleash an act of good to tame the tragedy.

Losing my parents felt more like a dream—blurrier, less permanent—than storybook deaths. I used to tremble with empathy for lost heroes in stories, for friendships cracked apart, for those who were fictionally lonely. The girls who felt unworthy and scabrous and consulted with false stars to negotiate better fortune. I cringed at descriptions of death, while the real thing only left me woozy and confused, like I'd wandered unknowingly onto a playing field and been whacked by a ball.

But Bitsy's death ached me where it ought to. I was as much a wreck as I had been the day I'd arrived at Rock Point, and yet Kenna was right—nobody seemed to notice. Miss Tophitt lectured me on my posture and Bessie Holmes hustled us all through our morning routines and Miss Ridges asked in a still-croaky voice if I was ready to resume the Dark Tales. The whispers among the staff were the only sign that anything was wrong. They were looking for Bitsy in the house and on the grounds. They'd sent a search party to the cliffs.

This drove me nearly mad. Someone in town ought to have figured out by now that a girl of Bitsy's age with no identification on her could have come from Rock Point. Had something happened to her body? Had some glop-faced drunk from the pub dragged her off to give himself a few good tugs over her lifeless form? Had someone thrown her in the river, in a ditch, burned her, buried her?

One day I was in a history lesson, trying not to look at Alle or Kenna, trying to focus on a religious crusade, when a cry came from the hall.

Immediately several girls stood, despite Miss Tophitt's orders to stay put. Kenna moved for the door, and I followed her out of the room.

Liz, Bitsy's roommate, was on her knees in the corridor, her white tights torn, her black shoes scuffed. She was sobbing—blubbering—and pounding the tile with her fists. Bessie Holmes was bent over her, large breasts swinging. I could see right down the front of her sweater to her grayish-white bra.

"I know, dear, I know." Bessie's tone was different from her usual faux-mama nonsense. She sounded genuinely sympathetic. "You must miss her so much. But the police'll be finding her. They will."

*No. Not the police. Not the fucking police.*

"She's not coming back." Liz's voice arced from a whisper to a wail. A chill went up my whole body. "She's—she's—she's—"

"Sweetheart." Bessie tried to draw Liz to her feet. When that failed, Bessie knelt slowly beside her. "If you been known anything about what might have happened . . ."

"She used to sneak out!" Liz said between gulps. I froze. Behind me, I could feel Kenna ready to lunge. "At night, she'd sneak off sometimes."

Bessie gave a dramatic gasp. "Lord, Liz. Where did she go?"

I actually heard Kenna growl. At that exact moment, Liz looked up at the small crowd that had gathered. She spotted Kenna and me, and her face went slack. "I—I don't know," she stammered. "I don't know if she went with anyone. She might have . . . I think—I think she said she sometimes met a boy in town."

*You liar!* I wanted to shout. But it was a lie that we needed, Kenna and Alle and I. A lie that made Bitsy into a silly, love-struck girl rather than a criminal. Which seemed still another level of injustice.

Liz looked away from Kenna and sobbed, a hand over her face.

Bessie moved her mouth in a sort of fish-gape. "Sweetheart," she said finally. "I'm taking you to your room. I'll been needing you to tell me everything." She led Liz away, and I couldn't protest, could only watch them leave.

I couldn't sleep that night. Kenna and I had attempted to find Lizzie after dinner and figure out what she'd told Bessie, but Liz hadn't come to the dining room and the door to her bedroom was shut. She didn't answer my knock.

The only one who noticed the change in me was Denson, and she cornered me one day in the parlor and said, among other things, "I know you must be worried about her."

I gazed at Denson with perfect calm. "If she's run off, she's run off. I've thought about doing it plenty."

Denson's expression barely changed, but she tilted her head slightly. "Did she say anything about running away?"

I studied her glasses. God, but they looked thick enough to make bullets bounce like raisins. "No." I looked away.

"She took nothing with her."

I felt a slight vibration just under the surface of my left temple, as though a small fly were trapped between layers of skin. "Then maybe she hasn't run off." I turned to Denson again. "We're not happy here, you know. We all want homes, families." I was pleased to see Denson flinch a little. "You send us out of here with nothing but slave skills," I went on. "Can you blame Bitsy if she took off? If she went looking for something outside this place, even if it was just for one night, and—"

"*Do* you know where she is?" Denson's voice was as close to severe as I'd ever heard it, and it bashed everything out of place for a moment. The walls were crooked and Denson's body looked like it was stacked wrong.

I began to cry. It started like glass cracking—the smallest, barely audible *cricht*. A web of faults reached out from that center point, long tendrils of weakness lengthening and branching. I had to find a way to go back to that night. To keep Bitsy safe and Alle happy. To keep Denson on my side. Or I had to find a way to push a lie forward, to doctor this broken tale. "I don't know. I don't *know*. But I th-think Lizzie's right. She used to sneak out to meet a boy."

Denson coughed. And coughed and coughed, leaving blood in the crook of her elbow. I'd encountered enough tragic coughers in stories to know it was not dust in the air that did this to Denson, and the thought that she was ill made me feel even more hopeless.

Denson looked up, wiping her mouth. "Please don't lie to me."

"I don't know!" I stepped backward. "Why won't you find her? Why won't anyone *find* her? Look near the pub! She always came back smelling like booze."

Denson stared at me, and it looked too much like Rachel's stare when I'd yelled that Marc had touched me where he oughtn't. Like Auntie Bletch's dismayed contempt when she'd realized why her pills were disappearing. "Go away!" I shouted. "Go *away*!"

Denson did, and I hated her for it. But I would have hated her more if she'd stayed, if she'd pushed, if she'd discovered what I really was. If she'd loved me anyway and told me I could still be saved.

I knew the day they found Bitsy. I saw Denson and Miss Ridges go into the reading room together. I was supposed to be on my way to grammar, but I'd forgotten my book and had doubled back. Now, instead of going upstairs, I went to the half-open door of the reading room, and I listened.

"—all three of them," Denson was saying.

"In town?"

"Yes. And he claims to have seen them that night."

"But no one saw who killed her?"

I clenched my hands so hard my bitten nails put a blunt, unsatisfying pressure on my palms. They knew. They knew Bitsy was dead, and they knew Kenna and Alle and I had been in town with her. Or . . . No. *Three* of them, Denson had said. But there had been four of us that night.

I heard a series of small gasps. I didn't understand at first, and then I peered through the door and saw Miss Ridges's heaving shoulders. She wiped her face sloppily with her arm. "I read them those stories. Do you think they . . . that's where they got the idea to—"

"No." Denson sounded firm. "I don't."

"If I'd known what it would cause them to do, I'd never have shared those tales."

"Your stories didn't cause it," Denson assured her. "If anything, you gave them further inclination to make their own decisions. If they have made the wrong choices, that is on them, and not on your tales."

Silence for a moment. "Do you think Allendara might know anything about it?"

"Perhaps. It's worth asking. I know Thera is hiding something. But I don't know if . . ."

I had to step back then or risk being sick. I fled to my room and shut the door. It would all fall apart now. They knew about Kenna and me, and they'd want to know why we were in town and who killed Bitsy. And if we told on the police officers, the officers would have us arrested for stealing.

I went to the bathroom and was sick for the better part of an hour.

Then I washed my face and went to find Kenna.

## Death Notification
## Report By: Dr. Brenda LiPordo

*B Lacombe's body was found in Rock Hill Cemetery yesterday. Coroner believes cause of death to be trauma to the head. This loss is a shock to Rock Point, and Dr. DuMorg and I are discussing how to break the news to the girls. Police are looking for the killer. Though the head wound could be accidental, there is evidence her body was dragged into the cemetery postmortem.*

## Security Staff Report: Officer Molly Grenwat

*I for one would like to know HOW she got out. Van Narr and me keep a good eye on things.*

**DuMorg's Note:** *Really? Because Darla Ling always said you two played cards most of the night.*

**Bessie Holmes's Note:** *if you don't mind my saying, there has been certain ways a lady can behave that brings such trouble on her.*

**Rollins's Note:** *I do mind you saying.*

"They know," I told Alle. "They know Bitsy's dead. They know we were all in town that night. Well, maybe they don't know you were there." *"Three of them,"* Denson had said.

Alle was staring at her lesson book, but she didn't have a pencil or paper, and I knew she wasn't doing homework. Anytime I was in the room with her, she had to be looking at a book, or folding clothes, or pretending to write a letter. I grabbed my own lesson book from under my bed. Took it to the desk and dropped it beside her. The spine cracked. She started.

"Look at me," I demanded.

She whipped her head up, anger and fear in her expression. "What?"

"I want to tell."

No response.

"I want to tell them what happened. Denson. We could tell Denson."

She shook her head. "Kenna said we ought to keep—"

"And now I'm saying we need to tell. They already know."

"You said maybe they don't know about me."

Rage flared in me. "So you want us to leave you out of it?"

"If you hadn't made me come with you . . ." She trailed off, shaking her head more rapidly. "Why the hell'd you have to go into town, huh? Why couldn't you just be *normal*?"

"I'd rather be anything but a coward!" And yet I slipped into cowardice so naturally. I used friends and I bullied strangers and I searched for enemies.

She stood. "Enough. Thera, enough. I mean it. We can't. They can't know I was involved."

"Why not?"

"They just *can't*. If you only trust me on one thing, let it be this."

"Alle," I whispered, suddenly exhausted. I started to lean my forehead against hers, and I placed my hand on her shoulder.

She pulled away. "We can't do that anymore."

I stepped back. "What?"

"We— I can't. I'm sorry."

"Don't you . . .?" What the hell was I going to ask her? If she loved me? My God, we were sick, the two of us, twisted in words and dreams. And if she didn't need me anymore, then I sure as hell didn't need her. But then who did I have? If Denson thought me a liar, and Alle didn't want me anymore? Who, then? Kenna?

"Forget it." I let my hand fall. "Forget every fucking thing."

I left the room and went downstairs. Then outside into the night, where I pressed myself against the iron fence of Rock Point and waited to feel something grand and be a better girl. But the wind whipped through my hair and all else was silent.

So I steadied myself and looked up at the few stars that weren't obscured by gray mist. God and all those liar's tales, all the false things we go down on all fours like a dog for . . . I didn't need or want anything except to find those two officers and make them pay. Terrible things happened in the world, but we could put them right if only we were fearless. If only we were not hampered by a weakness like love. I vowed I would never love anybody. That as a warrior I would concern myself only with justice and heroics—and never, ever with pretty girls who had scared souls and fools' secrets.

# CHAPTER 16

Two more weeks passed, and nobody on staff approached me to talk about Bitsy's death. DuMorg had a brief session with each girl at Rock Point after the news was announced. I mumbled through my session, assuring DuMorg that I was all right to continue with my lessons and my chores. The girls' home had a moment of silence in the dining room each night for a week in Bitsy's honor.

Kenna said we ought to have a memorial service for Bitsy, on our own. I didn't care in the least, but thought perhaps I should keep my newfound coldness private for the time being. So I agreed.

We discovered, Kenna and I, as we attempted to write speeches, that we knew very little about Bitsy. Where she had come from, when she had arrived, what her middle name was.

"We ought to look at her file." Kenna glanced up at me, that spinning, wobbling energy making me uncomfortable. I stared at her for a moment, not sure what she meant. "We could find out everything about her."

"Don't be stupid. We can use the things we already know."

"And we could look at the report on her death." Kenna's tone grew more desperate. "See if they suspect we were there for it."

"That's what you want? To see if they suspect us?"

"It's gonna matter, isn't it?" She crumpled the paper on which she'd been trying to write a eulogy. "When we leave here? We'll need letters of reference. Don't you want to know what they've been saying about us all these years? Hell, didn't Bitsy say she wanted to know if anyone ever thought of adopting her?"

"I don't care what she wanted," I said. "I don't care if I am a suspect. I don't give a shit about who wanted to adopt Bitsy."

Kenna's desperation vanished, replaced by what looked like pity. "Awf. You sad old thing. You remind me of a drunken barman I once knew who'd whistle through a hole a bullet had left in his leg. His name was . . ."

In the end, I went along with it because I didn't know what else to do.

Kenna claimed only Rollins and Dr. DuMorg had the keys to the file cabinet, but I had learned to pick Auntie Bletch's medicine cupboard, and I felt sure I could manage this.

We slipped away during dinner, and I followed Kenna into Rollins's office. It was tidy—a wooden desk, a chair, a file cabinet, and little else. Kenna walked past the desk to the cabinet and immediately began inspecting the lock. I was almost there when I saw a folder on its surface, pages sticking out. I don't know what made me open the folder and look.

Adoption papers. Signed by Rollins, some legal so-and-so . . . and Denson. Under Denson's signature was a blank line for me to sign on, my name printed under it.

Riley Denson intended to become my legal guardian.

I stared and tried to breathe. Kenna was rattling the cabinet. "C'mere, Thera. I need your help."

I couldn't move.

I would have hit anyone and anything, gladly. I would have broken a nose; I would have bruised an eye, split a lip, hurt someone until they cried.

*That traitor bitch.*

She hadn't asked me.

She hadn't fucking asked.

She'd had these papers drawn up, and—what? She'd just assumed I would sign them? That I'd throw my arms around her and cry, *I have a mommy at last!* Where did she expect me to live? In *this* place? The cottage, I realized. The cottage in Rock Hill. She'd bought it, perhaps knowing she was going to ask me to live there with her.

I gazed at that blank line. At the way the tail of Riley Denson's Y came down to touch it. I didn't deserve a mother. Denson had no idea what I was. And did she want to be my mother, really? Or was it just that she couldn't quit thinking her devil's thoughts about me?

"Come *on*, shit-weed," Kenna whispered. "We've got to find those records."

I closed the folder, blinking against the sting in my eyes.

*Almost two years. Is that how long it took you to decide I might be worth it? Or to feel sorry enough for me that you'd have those papers drawn up?*

I went over to the filing cabinet. Picked the lock numbly with a hairpin, ignoring Kenna's *hurry ups*. At last the cabinet sprang open, and we rooted through the files. Kenna pulled Bitsy's out and opened it. "Jane. Elizabeth Jane Lacombe." She looked up. "Doesn't she sound like the heir to something? A minor throne, or perhaps a stellar racehorse?" Kenna returned to reading. "She came here three years ago. Father died in a factory accident. Mother was institutionalized. Awf, look here. Someone tried to adopt her a few months after she got here, but decided not to go through with it because Bitsy was sick. They thought she was dying."

I listened without feeling much of anything.

"Thera, c'mon. You read our files while I look at this. See if they think we're criminals."

I searched the folders until I found my name. Pulled the folder free and opened it up. The words all jumbled together, but I was fairly sure there was nothing surprising here. Notes on my violent behavior. My dead parents. My bullying. My medications. No mention of anyone trying to adopt me. Nothing about me sneaking into town, or hiding facts about Bitsy's death.

"There's nothing," I murmured. "They don't think we're hiding anything."

"Well, that's good, huh? Oh." Kenna let out a breath. "Oh, this is sad."

I turned toward her, my vision swimming. "Hmm?"

"Just, it says here Bitsy really likes horses. She told DuMorg in all her early sessions that when she grew up, she was going to ride professionally." She flipped the folder shut. "I don't know. It's sad, isn't it? That she never got to ride that fine bangtail she was to inherit?"

I nodded.

"Ballard? You aren't listening to me at all."

I was staring into the file cabinet again. I'd spotted a folder labeled "Beadurinc."

Kenna put Bitsy's file back and took out her own. Spent a few minutes reading it and snorting, then replaced it without telling me any of what it said. "That sounds about right," she muttered when she'd finished. "Come *on*, Thera. Put your folder back and let's go."

I put the folder back. And when Kenna wasn't looking, I grabbed Alle's and stuffed it under my sweater.

I sneaked down to the reading room that night, opened Alle's folder, and read a story.

I read about a girl of twelve who'd hidden in a woodshed with her parents when two men had come to the farm to collect on her father's gambling debts. I read how her parents had seen the men approaching their hiding place and had ordered her to go out the back—she was small enough that she could crawl through the shed's window and into the tall grass. Her father would distract the men by going out to meet them face-to-face.

The girl hadn't wanted to leave, but her mother shoved her away, told her to go quickly and not to look back. But the girl had, of course, looked back, and had seen one of the two men cut her father's throat. Heard her mother scream and saw her run from the shed with a shovel and attack the man. She'd knocked him unconscious, but the second man had stabbed her and left the blade in her chest while she died on the ground.

And so the little girl had doubled back. She'd pulled the blade from her mother's chest. She'd sneaked up on the second man while he crouched alongside his unconscious friend, and she'd plunged the knife into his neck.

A strange case, the police report said. Not precisely self-defense, but an understandable desire for revenge and self-preservation. Alle had not been prosecuted, but she'd been passed from one foster home to another. She'd been counseled by a church and then finally sent to Rock Point. The man she'd stabbed had died, but the other man, Aaron McInroe, had awoken. He'd been charged with murder in the first degree. Sentenced to twenty years in prison. There was a picture of him in a newspaper clipping attached to the report. He looked like a man who hadn't slept in a long time.

The story sounded so clinical, written as it was—just the facts and none of the feelings. But I could imagine that little girl peering through cracks in the shed, could imagine her clinging to her mother and being forced away. I felt her terror, and I wondered what to do now. Could I tell Alle I knew?

I looked through the rest of her file. Saw DuMorg's notes from an early session.

*Nothing I have seen leads me to believe A Beadurinc is a danger to the other girls here. However, a therapist she talked to soon after the incident claims A spoke of finding Aaron McInroe and killing him.*

Aaron McInroe. He must be the reason Alle spoke to Rocky Bottom. To find out if McInroe was still in prison. And if he was, what did she intend to do?

I sat shivering in the parlor, half hoping a monitor would walk by, that I would have the distraction of being in trouble. I could not be any of the things I wished. I couldn't be Denson's daughter, and I couldn't be Alle's protector. I was no warrior; I was a girl who played with sticks. All this time, I had been sleeping beside someone who truly knew what violence was, who had chosen action over bitter dreaming.

Some girls at Rock Point begged to know what happened next if Miss Ridges left off at the end of a suspenseful chapter. I would happily leave characters dangling from a cliff's ledge or trapped in a basement with a lunatic. I left them to suffer alone in the dark. I saved their fears for later. I wished it were possible to do this with myself—wished I didn't have to know what happened next. Perhaps it would be a mercy if nothing happened—if I could eat and sleep and grow old and forget myself, forget my own story, and die untroubled in my sleep.

I swiped the thought away angrily. No self-pity. No regret.

Just make it right. Make it right.

I look back now, and I do pity the girl I was that night. It's not that revenge has no place in the world. But we so often clamp our jaws around the things we think we want, while the real prizes escape between our teeth, slide down our necks in rivers and are lost in our skin.

# CHAPTER 17

I was in the parlor plucking my chin hairs. It was just after dawn, and I was using the gray light and my hand mirror, which I'd had to wedge between the table and the wall to keep it upright. I needed both hands for plucking, one to hold the tweezers and one to pull my skin taut.

Denson entered the parlor. She didn't reprimand me for being out of bed. She just said, "You're up early." Her voice was hoarse, and she tried unsuccessfully to stifle a bout of coughing.

All at once, I was breathtakingly grateful to her for her kindness toward me when I'd first come here. It hit me like big news, that Riley Denson had probably saved my life. And just as quickly, I was furious.

Not just about the adoption papers—though that still made me feel sick and uncertain—but because she knew. She knew we'd been out that night with Bitsy, and yet she'd said nothing.

"I'm doing my chin." I could see her in the mirror, watching me. I forced a smile. "If you're worried about your hair going thin, I could lend you some of my fucking beard." Denson let me say *fuck*. It was a privilege I tried not to abuse, but that I did like to make use of.

She smiled, and sadly.

I always thought loneliness must be a quiet thing. Up all night with frog sounds, wandering an empty room by day, resenting the sun squares on the floor. Guilt too seemed like it ought to be a silent kind of suffering. But what was going on inside me was a filthy and violent underground. Jeers and wagers and the sound of creature versus creature.

"You don't need to worry about your chin," she said softly. "You're beautiful, Thera."

Something in me broke apart then. I set my tweezers down. "I don't think you know me at all."

"I do know you. And there's something I'd like to talk to you about."

I turned. "The adoption?"

She opened her mouth but didn't speak right away. "Yes. I . . . Did Rollins tell you?"

"No. I found out, though." I stepped toward her. "And I have to tell you, it's not a good idea." I kept my voice very calm.

Her brow furrowed. "Thera? Are you ill? You don't look well."

I nodded solemnly. I was close enough to touch her now, to feel her breath on my face. I reminded myself that love was a weakness. That this woman kept secrets—mine and her own. That she'd had two years to rescue me from this place, to take me to a cottage in Rock Hill, and she'd waited until it was too late. I let all the anger from the past two weeks, all my pathetic hope from the past two years, collide in me.

I grabbed her. Spun her so she faced away from me, and wrapped an arm around her neck. She didn't resist; her body was as easy to move as a pillow—light and yielding. She gave a small gasp, but other than that, she was silent.

"You don't know how dangerous I am," I murmured in her ear. "I'll make you hurt. Oh God, I'll make you hurt." I said it like the idea was appealing to me. I closed my eyes and twisted any goodness that remained in me into the bliss of imagined pain. Her pain, and mine. She writhed gently, not like she was trying to get away, but like she was trying to get more comfortable. She finally let out a frustrated breath and went still.

"Please," she whispered.

I opened my eyes. "What do you want from me? Should I tell them what you want from me? Rollins? Grenwat? Should I tell?"

She twisted her neck in an apparent effort to see me. Said, in a shaky voice, "I don't want anything from you, Thera, but happiness."

I tightened my grip. "You think I don't know how your appetites run? At this late stage, what would an adoption be but your attempt to wed me the only way you can?"

"Thera, stop!" She sounded genuinely shocked.

"It's all right," I whispered, pushing my arm against her throat. "I'm unnatural too. Perhaps I was made so by spending so much time with you."

"Please," she said again between gasps. She coughed, and I felt the vibrations through my skin. "Please."

I let her go. She stepped away, breathing hard like she'd been chased and looking at me like I was something she hoped never to see again. "Stay away," I warned. "And don't tell."

I left her there and went to my room.

I remember being driven to Rock Point Girls' Home in my Auntie Bletch's wheezy, rusting car. Auntie was talking to me about the squirrels that kept getting in her bird feeder. She seemed guilty, each squirrel-grumble a peace offering. She could barely drive—her hands shook on the wheel and the car shook and twice she pressed the gas when she meant the brakes.

I thought it cruel I was being sent away. But I slouched in the seat, too blanched of feeling to dwell much. I had slipped a bottle of phenacetin into my coat pocket, out of revenge and necessity.

"Goodness, Thera," Auntie said, glancing over. "Sit up straight. Don't you want to make a fine impression?"

I laughed then, hysterically. I don't know what all I was on, but my head seemed to be floating away from my body. I imagined it was a balloon on a string, and the string was tied to a skeleton hidden in an ill-fitting dress. I watched the gray sky as though a future might resolve from it like a vision in the mists of a crystal ball.

I thought she would stop and force me out of the car, and then I would be alone in the middle of the road with the world spreading in all directions and no one to tell me ever again that I was wicked or strange or unwanted.

But Auntie Bletch kept driving, her jaw tight, and my panic turned to a delirium. My underarms sweated and tears dripped from my jaw. I shivered and jerked, and Auntie Bletch reached over and dug her pointy purple nails into my knee like claws. I screeched and pushed my face against the window, sobbing. *"I don't want to go. I don't want to go."*

And soon I had no capacity for words, only a terror worse than nightmares. I don't remember reaching Rock Point. I don't remember saying good-bye to the Bletch, if that even happened. I remember the shock of cold water and rearing up like something freed from an enchanted lamp, swinging my fists and screaming.

The next thing I remember is waking in the solitary room, morning pouring in through the window. I stared out beyond the gates at the freedom I felt sure I'd never have again. I checked my pocket for the bottle of painkillers, but I didn't even have a coat anymore. I was in a drab gray jumpsuit.

And then Riley Denson came in.

## Security Staff Report: Officer Molly Grenwat

*T Ballard, #11305094, has been missing since early this morning. We suspect she has RUN AWAY. Van Narr and me are searching the grounds now. ANY information anyone has is appreciated.*

**Rollins's Note:** *Denson claims not to have seen her at all this morning. Bessie, the night monitor, saw Thera in her bed last night at lights out.*

## Rec Report: Glenna Formas

*Rec not the same today without #11305094. Between losing her and the blond girl, the non-wiener contingent is fast dissolving. I will help look for this girl if it means a soccer game where somebody actually scores a damn goal.*

**Bessie Holmes's Note:** *Yes, T Ballard was in bed last night. i was been unclear how she escaped, as i am always watching that hall.*

**Van Narr's Note:** *Except when you fall asleep.*

**Officer Grenwat's Note:** *Except when most kids here are SMARTER than you, Bessie. Wouldn't be surprised if these children are running off just to get away from YOU. Also, no one has mentioned the single clue: A purple unicorn was left outside of L Beecham's room.*

**Van Narr's Note:** *It was pink.*

**Bessie Holmes's Note:** *i know what you think of me. Stupid ugly woman & i'm not good with the kids & i'm in a pathetic choir. But i'd like to tell you something. i used to have a little girl. i know this will surprise you, but i was been a good mother & i loved her very much.*

*i had considerible mental difficulties in this time & my husband thought i wasn't fit to be a mother, but my baby was my joy i told him. Over & over i told him.*

*i hadn't gone out of the house in months. i was been home every day with the baby. i wanted to go to the cinema & asked my husband if he could stay with the baby for 2 hours but he said no. So i took my little girl with me.*

*She slept in my arms for the first ten minutes of a spectacular film—Crudzie's Ovation. You might remember it. it had splendid dancing and the font on the title cards was exessivly lovely. My daughter began to be fussing quietly. i rocked her but she cried louder. People was starting to look over but still i rocked her. i hadn't been out in so long & i was enjoying the film so very much.*

*Someone finally said get that baby out of there because people are trying to enjoy the film. i said she'll stop fussing in a minute just be patient. But then more people started telling me to leave. i didn't leave. i wanted to see how the movie ended. i just shushed my little girl & held her close & prayed she would sleep again.*

*i could barely enjoy it anymore because of what people said. They were been making more noise than my baby! Someone yelled you stupid cow, that babys unhappy in here. Go away. i was so embarrassed i started crying.*

*i got up & ran out of the theater & called my husband to pick me up. My skin was hot as fever. As soon as we was out in the lobby, my baby stopped crying.*

*i don't know why i stayed in a cinema when she was crying. I don't know why i was having been so stupid sometimes but after that my* ~~psy~~ *mental debilitations was such that my husband left & he took the baby. A judge said that was only right since i was unwell. if you think i don't regret that, your wrong. if you think i don't care for the girls here, your wrong. i am being haunted each day & i only want the best for people. You all make fun of my dog & my hobbies but nightly i pray for happiness for all of you.*

**Officer Grenwat's Note:** *Somebody call DuMorg in.*

**Van Narr's Note:** *DuMorg is a youth specialist. I don't know what she could do about a case of the Old 'N' Batties.*

**Rollins's Note:** *Bessie, we are very grateful for the work you do here. I do not doubt your compassion or your good intentions. I hope you'll join me in my office after three today. I have some new tea my uncle sent. Anyone else is welcome too if you are not on duty at that time.*

# BOOK TWO

# THE LABYRINTH

# CHAPTER 18

It was a month before I was found. In that time, I lived fairly comfortably on a thief's salary, stealing what I needed from the shops in town. I slept in the shed across the field from the pub. It was a mess of broken glass and rotting wood and spiders, but nobody bothered me there. I still sometimes felt a wonderful quiet, a sense that my rage was a surface disease that crawled on my skin, rather than a consuming, permanent thing. But mostly I was lonely and tremendously bored.

I turned eighteen. I found myself increasingly able to deal with Bitsy's death, though I didn't lose my desire for revenge. I walked Main Street many times, looking for those two officers. I staked out the police department, hoping for a glimpse of them. But I never saw them.

It was Alle who occupied my mind, and to stave off thoughts of her I concentrated on opening my mind to the beast. My dreams became darker and darker still. I was ready to know her. I was ready to *be* her. I became convinced that the labyrinth was my destiny, the beast my mirror, and that once I was inside the maze everything would make sense.

I awoke one night to a tapping on the shed's broken window. I got up, grabbing a steak knife I'd snatched from the pub's kitchen weeks ago. I went outside and called, "Who's there?"

"Awf, you loon." Kenna crushed me in a hug so hard I dropped the knife. "You stupid thing. Why'd you run off? Denson's ready to call in the military for a search."

My stomach clenched at the mention of Denson. I backed up. "What the hell are you doing here?"

"Looking for you. We've left the dungeon, both of us."

"Both of . . .?"

Alle stepped forward. We stared at each other for a moment, saying nothing. She appeared distant, almost blank. Something in me twisted when I looked at her.

"Can we come in?" Kenna pushed past me into the shed. "God, Thera, you don't know what a ruckus you caused."

I followed her in and listened to Alle's footsteps behind me. "I was ready to get out. I just went a few weeks early."

"Well, happy eighteenth, anyway." Kenna glanced around my lair. "My, you're a slob."

"I just had to get out of there. After Bitsy . . . and Denson was on my case . . ." I still felt sick every time I thought of Denson. I'd hoped that would fade, the same way the edges of Bitsy's death had dulled over the weeks. But my guilt over what I'd done to Denson didn't lose its sharpness.

Kenna pulled me aside suddenly into the shadows. She jerked her head toward Alle. "I told Miss B. what a shitty thing she did to you. Claiming to be your friend, but then bailing when the going got tough. I mean, I could see it, after Bitsy. She barely spoke to you, and I know she thinks we're crooks and all. But when I told her I was gonna look for you, she wanted to come." Kenna rocked back on her heels and shrugged. "I thought you should know she's been worried about you."

And I'd thought about her every day since I'd left Rock Point. But it didn't matter. "I really don't care. Right now, I'm concerned about one thing. Which is getting enough money to live off."

"Got any grand plans?"

"As a matter of fact, one." My heartbeat felt soft and erratic, like the flickering of a candle.

"Awright. What, then?"

"We steal the treasure from the labyrinth."

Kenna's mouth opened for a moment, then lifted in a grin. "You're getting as bad as I am, the way you lay out your horse patties with a straight face."

"I'm not joking. I mean to go into the labyrinth. And come out with the treasure."

"Okay," Kenna said slowly. "And you do know there's a beast in there with the head of a bull who eats people?"

I smiled. "I've heard something to that effect." *She will not eat me. She knows I am coming. She knows I'm meant to be there.* "Are you in or not?"

Kenna looked at me and said, very solemnly, "Back when I was fighting in a global war—7th Cavalry Division, basic soldier, first class—I had a commanding officer who told me something."

"Kenna. Please. You never fought—"

"Shh." She put a finger to my lips and stared at me. "He said, 'Private Murphy. If you don't take these risks, someone else will. And that someone will chow forever on glory that should have been yours.'"

"Beautiful."

"I'm in." She kicked a piece of glass across the floor and into a corner. "But what if the beast wakes and finds us thieving?"

"Then we kill her." I said it decisively, and my heartbeat became stronger, more even. In truth I couldn't imagine killing her, didn't know whether she was my enemy.

"Right, right. The two of us against a beast. Or is it three?" Kenna looked over her shoulder. "Miss B.? Thera has a proposal."

Alle came toward us cautiously. I tried not to look at her, tried to turn her into a shadow. I told her the plan, sure the news would send her scurrying back to Rock Point. But she nodded. "I'll go with you."

I lifted my head and gazed at her, unable to help myself. She seemed older than Kenna and me. Even holed up in this broken place, in her stained yellow shawl and secondhand clothes, her hair full of twigs—she looked worthy of a crown.

I shared some of my tinned food with Kenna and Alle, and Kenna offered a stream of tales from Rock Point, most of which I knew were horse patties.

After dinner, Kenna went outside to "answer nature's call," leaving Alle and me alone and silent.

"You'll really go with us?" I asked her.

She nodded.

I noticed she held something in her lap. Rocky Bottom's ball of thread. She saw me staring at it and drew back, a hand hovering almost protectively over the ball. "Because of Aaron McInroe?" I asked.

She glanced up in surprise.

"I've read your history."

She stiffened. "How?"

"Kenna and I looked at our files, and Bitsy's. I read yours too."

"So what?" Her voice was cold. "Now you know I'm a murderess."

"I know you were brave."

Another bout of silence so long it set my teeth on edge. How could she feel like such a stranger to me? At last she spoke, her voice less harsh. "Rocky Bottom says he thinks Aaron McInroe went to the labyrinth several weeks ago."

"So that's it. Why you talk to him?" All around us, night creatures whirred, and out the window of the shack, tall weeds rustled. "But isn't that a good thing? He's beast food now."

"I want to do it myself."

I stared at her. *There's no prize for slaying,* she'd told me. "But if she's already done it . . ."

"She hasn't."

"How do you know?"

She hesitated. "He's in my dreams. All the time, he's there. I know he's alive. I don't care if you think I'm crazy."

"No." McInroe was in her dreams, same as the beast was in mine. I understood, and I wanted her to do what she was meant to do.

"If we're going to the labyrinth for different reasons, we might . . ." I didn't know how to say it. We'd be separated. Her quest might compromise mine, and vice versa.

"We're not."

"What do you mean?"

She held my gaze. "I know you're not going for the treasure. You're going because you want to kill the beast."

I sat there in the dark and listened to Kenna humming outside. Was it true? I had no idea anymore. What did she imagine would happen? That we'd enter the maze, go our separate ways, then meet up again once she'd killed McInroe and I'd slain the Minotaur and Kenna had grabbed us a sack of gold?

The whole idea seemed doomed, and yet I didn't care. Did it matter why each of us went? Together, we stood a chance of facing whatever waited for us in the labyrinth. Of not becoming lost forever in the maze. I curled my toes, then stretched them, feeling the grit of the floor.

"You know what they told me?" Alle asked quietly. "That I had one chance at Rock Point. And if I did anything to hurt anybody, they'd send me to jail."

"Who said that?"

"Bessie Holmes. DuMorg. Shit, Thera, I started to like it there. I started to think I could have a life, that I didn't need revenge at all. Like more killing wasn't gonna do a damn thing. But then I . . . when I started talking to Rocky Bottom, I remembered."

I was silent.

"There's something I'm *supposed* to do." She shook her head. "Only reason I don't want to kill him is I'm afraid once won't be enough."

Kenna came inside then. I couldn't tear my gaze away from Alle. I didn't know what to think, what to say. I finally turned from her and said loudly, "We'll leave tomorrow at dawn for Rock Point."

"Rock Point?" Kenna's face looked slack, dull in the shadows and moonlight.

"It would take hours to walk to the promontory. It's a gamble to ask for a lift in town—most people won't go anywhere near the labyrinth, and some might turn us in if we've been reported missing. If we go to Rock Point, we can hide on the grounds and stow away in the back of the prison truck when it comes."

Kenna clapped. "You are a madness."

"It won't work," Alle said. "We'd be caught."

"Listen, you weasel-stomping baby doll." Kenna walked over to us. "This is Miss Ballard's waltz. If she says we're going in the prison truck, we're going in the prison truck."

I glanced at Alle, daring her to protest. She was silent.

"Well, then." I made a mock bow. "Friends. I say we pay a visit to the beast."

I would have liked us to march on the labyrinth's gates, throw open the doors, and step inside as though I were coming home. As it was, we returned to the outskirts of Rock Points Girls' Home with our limited food. We stayed in the woods and kept an eye on the prison. Kenna and I took turns sneaking inside and pilfering from the kitchen as needed. More often than not I volunteered to go, as it was hard for me to be around Alle without Kenna there. Finally one evening the truck showed up to the prison to collect tributes. We saw it coming up the gravel road and hurried toward the fence, grateful for the lack of moon.

We went under the fence and sneaked toward the prison.

The truck stopped in front of the prison's gate, and one of the men got out to open it. We stayed crouched in the shadows. My heart was pounding, but more with excitement than fear. The truck drove through and stopped, and before the second man could close the gate, Kenna threw a rock. It hit one of the truck's wooden slats with a crack, and the man near the gate whipped his head around.

The driver leaned out the window. "The hell was that?"

While both men were distracted, Kenna, Alle, and I slipped through the gate and huddled along the fence.

It was more frightening now—the prison yard was wide open, and we could see a light in the guard hut. We pressed against the chain-link, and I was certain one of the men would spot us. But the driver pulled his head back through the window, and the passenger closed the gate and got back in the truck without so much as a glance in our direction. They drove up to the front of the prison.

We were familiar enough with the routine from watching the prisoner loading and unloading over the years. Both men jumped out. One opened the back of the truck to get cuffs and chains out. The men were armed with long rifles, and the passenger had what looked like a silver charm around his neck that flashed briefly in the glare of the truck's lights. They went inside to collect the prisoners.

While they were gone, we went to the back of the truck and climbed in. There were sheets of burlap covering bales of straw. A rubbery tarp on the floor and loose straw that pricked our feet through our flimsy shoes. Kenna and Alle crouched behind a straw bale in the far corner and I threw some burlap over them. Then I climbed in beside them.

"D'you think the guard saw?" Kenna whispered.

"Shut up. If he did, he'd be here."

"I just want you to know . . ." Kenna poked me. "That I've never done anything exciting. I was never lost in a desert."

"I know."

"I never killed a zebra."

"I know. Would you can it?"

"This will be my first time doing anything noteworthy. So thank you."

I held Kenna's hand, and wished I were holding Alle's. Eventually we heard voices. The clank of chains. The shuffle of feet on gravel. The truck rocked slightly as the prisoners were loaded. Their chains banged against the floor. One man was protesting, and I realized I knew the voice.

Rocky Bottom.

"You can't do this to me, man," he said. "I don't wanna go there. Man, you can just kill me here. You getting me? You can kill me here."

"Shut up," the driver muttered. The prisoners took a seat on two of the straw bales in the middle of the truck. I could see a pair of legs through a gap in the burlap.

"I mean it, man!" A chain dragged against the tarp, and I heard a gun cocked.

"Get back!" the driver warned. "Or I'll make it slower than the beast would."

The chain *slinked* as Rocky Bottom sat again. The door slammed. It was completely dark.

The driver and the passenger climbed in up front, and the truck started. I could feel Kenna and Alle lying tense beside me. The truck made a circle, heading for the gates again.

I have no idea how long we drove. The night had been chilly, but crammed under the canvas with Kenna and Alle, listening to Rocky Bottom's protests, I began to sweat. There was straw digging into my back, but I was afraid to move. I tried to hang on to the idea of myself as a warrior, vengeful and brave. I was as scared as I'd ever been. As scared as when I'd been told my mother and father were gone. As scared as when I'd been dragged into Rock Point.

We hadn't thought about how we'd get out of the truck once we arrived on the promontory, but we lucked out. After they were ushered out of the truck, the prisoners made a break for it. We could hear the shouts and the swinging chains. By the time the driver and the assistant had tackled the prisoners, Kenna and Alle and I were out of the truck and hiding in the hedges that lined the path to a towering stone building.

We could just make out the shapes of the prisoners as they were led to the entrance. There was a soft sheen of silver light cast over the pathway. We saw the armed men herd the prisoners to a huge wooden door. The driver of the truck grabbed a heavy-looking iron ring and pulled the door open.

"No!" Rocky Bottom shouted. "No, please!"

Both prisoners were shoved roughly inside, and the door fell shut behind them. The men got back in the truck and drove away.

Slowly, Kenna and Alle and I stood.

The outside of the labyrinth did not look as much like a castle as illustrations had led me to expect. Castles had an ancient and staggered elegance. This was a long building, dirty stone and greasy windows, the whole thing so perfectly rectangular it was hard to imagine anyone getting lost inside. At the front entrance stood spindly, pocked columns that looked like gnawed bones. I couldn't tell whether the high ceiling was glass, like in the pictures, but there was indeed a massive clock tower such as one might see on an old railway station.

The only numbers on the clock's luminous face were nine through twelve, and they were a deep, rich red. In the clock's center was a brutally detailed rendering of a human heart. There was no minute hand, but when the hour struck, a thick blue vein snaked out from the heart and latched on to the number 9.

"What in the hell?" I whispered.

We watched for several minutes as "blood" flowed from the number into the heart, turning the vein red and very gradually sucking color from the symbol.

"So after an hour, the nine will be gone?" Kenna asked. "Like the numbers before it?"

I was enthralled. I thought my soul dark enough to take pleasure in the famed palace's ugliness, in its promise of death. If I went inside, I imagined, I would feel no fear. My kinship with wickedness would protect me.

Alle's tension was evident—she seemed trapped and restless in her own body. And Kenna, well—she was playing tough, but her bravery was like satin draped over a wire frame. Walk by and pinch it, and it would all collapse to the floor with a *fffwwwsss*.

"What'll you do when you're rich?" Kenna didn't look at me as we walked to the wooden door. "I'd buy a place nicer than this. I'd have servants."

"I don't know." I thought about what Alle had said—that I wasn't here for the treasure at all.

The men who'd brought the prisoners had simply opened the door. That seemed too easy, and yet when I pulled on the giant iron ring, the door creaked open. Inside, there was darkness, broken by red-gold blurs of candlelight.

"Well," Kenna whispered.

"Go on," I urged. She and Alle entered while I held the door. I cast one last look over my shoulder at the misty cliffs.

Fearless and foolish, I stepped into the labyrinth.

# CHAPTER 19

T he entryway was inelegant—a hollow chiseled in the rock, lit by a limp candle in a brass dish. The walls were scuffed, the stones uneven. The floors were sleek black tile, and in front of us a hallway stretched into darkness. There were no decorations, nothing beautiful at all. The door fell softly shut behind us. We walked across the tile, and Kenna giggled as though we were breaking curfew at Rock Point, rather than looking to steal from the most formidable beast in all of legend. I searched for any sign of the prisoners, but the tiles were dusty, as though no one had passed through in some time.

"Where d'you think they are?" Kenna asked.

I watched a gob of wax slide down the candle. "I don't know."

"Do you think they've tried to hide? And how long does it take the beast to find them, I wonder? I'll bet she knows all the good hiding places."

Alle stopped suddenly. I paused too. "What is it?" I asked.

She glanced at Kenna. I stepped closer to her. "Are you all right?"

Several yards ahead, Kenna turned and looked back at both of us. "Have you got cold feet?" she called.

Alle shook her head, but then looked at me pleadingly. "I don't . . . I don't want to do this."

"What about Aaron McInroe?" I whispered.

She shook her head again. Her breath came in faint gasps. She stared ahead at the dark hall that lay before us. She was clutching Rocky Bottom's ball of thread in one hand. "I'm going to die here. I know I am." The words were spoken quietly, and they chilled me all the more for that. Her eyes were vacant, her body trembling. "It's a trap. My dreams . . ."

"Shh-shh." I glanced over my shoulder and was puzzled to find that while the anteroom was much as it had been, I could no longer see a door. I blinked several times, and the door was there again, but I was shaken by its momentary absence.

Kenna strode over. "What the hell?"

"Kenna, get stuffed." I turned as though to shield Alle.

Alle pushed past me and faced Kenna. "No treasure is worth our lives."

Where was the girl who'd told me killing Aaron McInroe once wouldn't be enough? What had happened to convince her we were in certain danger? And why didn't I feel it? The labyrinth was eerie, but I didn't feel afraid.

Kenna clapped a hand on her shoulder. "Grow some tits. We're in the most amazing place ever. We're gonna become rich, and you're being a child about it."

"Someone needs to stay here," I said suddenly.

They both turned to me.

The idea had only just dawned on me, but I was pleased with it. "We'll lose our way in the labyrinth—we could easily become like those people who are said to be lost here forever, so deep in the maze that even the beast can't find them. But if Alle stands here at the entrance and holds the ball of thread, and if I tie the end of the thread around my wrist, we'll have a way back."

Kenna did not look impressed. But Alle let me take the ball from her and wind the thread around my wrist. She helped me tie it.

It was a foolish plan, but I felt a desperate certainty that it would work. "I do want to find him," Alle whispered as she finished tying the knot. She glanced up at me. "But I have a bad feeling about this. I wish you wouldn't go."

My heart beat faster. *If I thought you loved me. That you'd stay with me and help me survive, I wouldn't need a fucking treasure. I wouldn't even need to be a warrior. I'd just be yours.*

I turned away. "We'll be back as soon as we've got the treasure."

"I'll be here," she said softly behind me.

We both must have known there could be no leaving this place the way we'd entered. If that were the case, wouldn't every unwilling tribute turn and walk back out the door as soon as they were in? I felt the beginnings of dread then.

Kenna and I started forward.

"Wait," Alle called.

I spun.

"If you see him . . ." She hesitated. "If you see him, I don't want to know."

I felt a flash of my old irritation toward her. I *liked* vengeful Alle. I wanted her to never rest in her pursuit of Aaron McInroe. How could she do it—be above her anger, push aside that injustice? I burned so often over things I couldn't even put words to. My abandonment. My preferable sister. My own stupidity and cruelty, my fear that I'd never be able to make things right with Denson. And yet she could feed her anger to her fear and have it vanish.

I nodded, then faced forward and continued on.

The thread unwound gradually as we went.

"Awf, she's a sap, isn't she?" Kenna muttered as we ventured down the corridor.

"She's smarter than both of us put together."

Kenna glanced sideways at me. "Oh *Lord*."

"What?"

Kenna shook her head. "Nothinnn.'"

The hall was tall and narrow—black stone lit by red, thin, snakelike flames in brass candleholders.

"This," Kenna said, "is *wild*."

It was. I began to lose myself in old dreams, take pleasure in the strangeness of the place. We found ourselves on a square patch of grass within the stone hall. The grass looked odd in the orange-gold light from the torches. The wall to our right no longer went up to the ceiling—it was about six feet high, and over it, all I could see was blackness.

"Oh!" Kenna elbowed me and pointed.

From the end of the hall a man was coming toward us, gray-haired and stooped. Walking several paces in front of him was a black-and-white sheepdog with one yellow eye. Before I could think about running, the man gave a sharp command, and the dog dropped into a crouch, its yellow eye trained on us.

"What. The. Hell?" Kenna whispered.

The man whistled, and the dog started toward us—silent and swift, its hackles up.

"Shit!" Kenna shouted as the dog picked up its pace.

"Kenna, up here!" I gripped the uneven stones of the wall to our right and started to climb.

I slipped, heard Kenna scream, and then the dog's jaws closed around my leg. It wasn't a painful bite, but the animal shook me a little as it pulled me from the wall. I landed hard on the grass and struggled, finally nailing the dog in the jaw with my foot. It yelped and retreated.

I clambered to my feet. The man whistled, and the dog circled away from me. I leaped and tried once more to scale the wall, calling for Kenna. This time I made it to the top, the thread pulling taut. I balanced on the narrow edge with my arm out, not wanting to break the thread. I turned to see what was going on. The dog had Kenna against the wall. It was growling low in its throat, but didn't look like it intended to attack. The man hurried toward it, muttering something.

"Come on, then," I heard him say when he reached Kenna. "Come on, come on."

"Get away!" Kenna shouted, holding her hands up in front of her. "Get the fuck away. Who the hell are you?"

"Come on," the man repeated, whistling again. The dog began to herd Kenna down the hall, snapping at her heels so that she jolted and cowered, but moved where the dog wanted her to.

"Kenna! Run!"

But she continued down the hall, whimpering at each nip from the dog, the old man following both of them, whistling an odd tune.

"Hey, you!" I called to the man. "Hey!" But he didn't turn. I crawled along the wall on all fours, but I couldn't move fast enough to catch them. There was more slack to the thread as I went, though. Alle must be unraveling the ball. "No!" I shouted, crawling faster. A stone crumbled under my hand, and I slipped to the right. I plummeted over the wall and into pitch black.

I got to my feet, shaking more with anger than with fear. I tried to climb the wall again in the dark, to get back to Kenna and the hallway with the grass, but the stones had become slick and wet. Even when I managed to get to where the top of the wall should have been, there were more stones. I slid to the ground.

I could hear my breathing echo in the lightless space. I gathered the slack in the thread, looping it in my hand. I gave it a series of tugs. A moment later, I felt Alle tug back. That brought me some comfort. I began to walk, feeling my way along the wall, letting out the thread as I went. Every now and then I heard a sharp bark, and a girl's shriek, but they sounded farther and farther away, and eventually I heard nothing.

I reached a room with red carpet and high, dark wood ceilings supported by carved beams. In little alcoves stood candelabras so clumped with wax they looked like snow-covered branches. There was nothing in the room but an old wooden trunk I could not open and a door in the opposite wall. Beyond the room stretched another dark hall, but I was tired of dark halls. I went to the door and tried it. It opened easily, and I stepped through.

I was outdoors, standing on a rock ledge. The wind immediately tore back my hair, and I looked down about ten feet to a brown beach covered in shallow, murky puddles. All around the cliff was a dark-gray sea, roaring and foaming. Sticking up from the water were great mounds of black rock. Joy and terror burst in me with each crash of a wave against the rocks. The endlessness, the sight of something that existed so far beyond *me*, that mattered so much more, was splendid.

Waves hit the beach and burst, ropes of white water flinging themselves forward, clawing at the shore and leaving veins in the sand. I am ashamed now to say I forgot about Kenna in that moment. I pulled twice on the thread and felt Alle's answering tugs, and then I began to walk along the rock ledge.

A wave crashed at the base of the cliff and I swelled with excitement. I began to run along. The waves seemed to chase me, smashing against the rocks, their spray hitting my feet, soaking my shoes. I stopped and stared down at the water. I can't explain the power I felt in that moment. I took several deep breaths, and then I raised my arms as though I hoped to lift the sky.

The largest wave yet rose from the sea. A plume that was level with my face, spitting froth and awaiting my command. I swung my arms apart and downward, and the column sprayed in all directions and plummeted back into the ocean. I laughed, half-amazed and half-terrified. But that seemed perfectly all right. Life had given me a moment of wonder and set fear beneath it like a flame.

I raised my arms again and brought them down. Repeated this several times, watching the waves obey. I spun on the ledge and watched one of the spouts become a swirling funnel. I thrust my arm forward like I was pitching a baseball, and the spout arched away from me, serpentining through the air before it collapsed. I was breathless, but I wasn't finished. I looked at the clouds and beckoned them toward me. They came in a jumbled stampede. I tilted my head back and raised my palms, and lightning shot down in white thorny branches, striking the sea and electrifying the spray. Gold light marbled the gray water and I watched, enchanted, as flames burst from the foam, then died.

I clambered down the cliff's wall, completely unafraid of falling. When my feet touched the wet sand, I felt a jolt. I stared out at the gray water, which had grown calm in the absence of my commands. I began to run along the beach, and the sea's current mimicked my direction. The thread dragged behind me, its myriad pieces knotted together. All it would take was one undone knot, one too-hard tug, and I would be separated from Alle. Yet in this moment, I didn't care. I wanted to be alone and in command of this world. The clouds had opened and were pouring rain; the drops pelted so hard they stung my skin and left pocks in the sand.

I stopped when I saw something several yards ahead.

It was a shark, as long as I was tall, gray bodied and black eyed. It lay on its side and whacked its tail against the beach, sending wet sand flying. From its gills spewed pink mush, streaked through with red. Lightning webbed the sky as the shark's rows of needle teeth met. It fell still suddenly, its tail giving two more convulsive jerks.

I began to shiver. I almost wanted to touch the creature. The shark arched again, its head tilting upward, its black eye rolling back to reveal a white membrane. Thunder sounded, knocking me into the sand. Each time I tried to rise, another rumble shook the land and goaded the sea, and I lost my footing. I didn't like it anymore, this illusion of power. The clouds had formed an odd shape—a towering, hulking form. Lightning flashed, outlining the figure of a bull, and the sea careened in all directions, waves knocking into each other, white foam whipping into vortexes in the dark waters.

I fled then, hearing the sea roar after me, the waves once again giving chase, though it no longer felt like a game. I followed the thread back to the cliff, the sand beneath my feet now covered in water. I started to climb but I was not fast enough, and the water rose beneath me. I gasped as salt stung the backs of my legs. I had never held any power here; the power was all hers. I had borrowed it, tried it on, and now I would suffer for it.

A wave lashed upward. I had just enough time to see it over my shoulder before it was pushing me up, up . . .

It deposited me on the cliff's ledge, in front of the door I'd come through, then plummeted back into the ocean. The rain stopped. The clouds became gray and uneventful. The sea crashed against the rocks, sending spray up to me, but there were no massive waves or whirlpools.

Panting, I got to my feet and stepped into quiet darkness, shutting the door behind me.

# CHAPTER 20

The labyrinth seemed at first to be a series of corridors, but eventually I found myself in an open space that had grass and trees and hedges, and a very high ceiling in which I could see a reflection of my movement. The sky was visible through the vast pane—first white-gray, then eventually midnight blue as I wandered, uncertain, across the prickly grass. I felt less claustrophobic here but more exposed. I felt watched, hunted, and I tried to keep close to the trees. I saw a shipwreck half-buried in hedges—a moss-covered hull, broken masts, an unreadable name—and was almost tempted to explore it.

Eventually I came across a man in a sickly garden. He was bleeding from a dozen stripes on his back, his lips peeling from dehydration, his breath rattling through his body. All around him, brown vines curled and flowers looked fuzzed and ugly, like baby birds. He panted and held out an empty glass jug to me. Patted at his throat with one hand and mimed drinking with the other. I didn't understand why he was so thirsty—there was a stone fountain a few feet away, clear water burbling from the mouths of three carved fish.

The vines on the fountain were fat and brown and slimy. They seemed to pulse as I approached.

"Fill it," I snarled. "You ass. There's a fountain right there."

The man's thin white beard reminded me of cobwebs. He shook his head, and I winced again as his wounds snapped their scabs and began to bleed afresh. He staggered to the fountain and dipped the jug in. I watched him pull it from the water, full and dripping. A moment later, the water faded and was gone. He turned to me, shaking the jug as if to say *See? See?* Then he set it aside and dipped his hands in the fountain. Once again, they emerged dripping. But when he went to splash his face, his hands slapped dryly against his cheeks.

He stuck his whole head in the fountain, then pulled it out, sucking at the water's surface. A second later, his hair and beard were dry, and he was rubbing his throat. The water was disappearing from the basin before he could swallow it.

He looked at me. "Please," he rasped. "Please."

I went to the fountain and dipped my hands in. The water was cool and clear and stayed in my cupped palms. I held my hands up to him, and he leaned down and drank. He looked up at me gratefully, his beard dripping. I got him another scoop, and he drank it too.

"More?" I asked.

All at once, there was a crack, as though from an invisible whip, and the skin over the man's shoulder split open, dropping a gush of blood so suddenly I gasped and stepped back. Flecks of warm liquid hit my skin through the holes in my shoes. The man moaned in agony, his body convulsing. The invisible whip cracked again, and he went to his knees, blood fanning down his back like gory wings.

He looked up as the ground began to tremble. I looked up too. There was nothing above us but dark sky and our blurred reflections in the glass. Then all at once, a wide, luminous stone pillar descended toward us. The clock tower. It crashed against the ceiling, shaking the whole labyrinth, sending bits of stone into the fountain. But the glass didn't so much as crack. The clock's massive face stared down at us, bright white as a moon except for the heart at the center. The vein snaked out and began to pull color from the number twelve, turning from blue to red. The heart seemed to pulse against the glass.

I looked at the man, who was standing with his head tilted and his mouth slightly open. "It's fallen!" I said. "The clock tower's fallen." I had no idea what that meant—if the labyrinth was coming down around us, if the beast was trying to escape.

The man nodded, raising his gaze, and I looked up and saw the tower moving upward again, slowly disappearing from sight.

"Why did it do that?" I demanded. But he had his fingers in the fountain and was flicking the water halfheartedly. He looked less substantial somehow—his brown skin thinner, the veins beneath it more visible. I scooped more water into my hands—there was much less in the fountain now, even though I'd taken no more than a few handfuls. I offered it to him. "Tell me where I'll find the beast. Tell me where they might have taken my friend."

He drank with a gentle slurping sound. Droplets of water rolled down his forehead, spreading over his eyelids and lashes. The droplets seemed to take bits of his skin with them, leaving raw pink trails in their wake. He raised an arm and pointed down a narrow hall to my right. As I looked, a series of chandeliers came to life in the hall—small, simple, but nonetheless welcome, as I had no wish to go farther in the dark. The man was dissolving into droplets, his skull visible in one patch of his forehead, skin sliding in strips from his arms. A few soggy wisps of his beard caught between my fingers like cotton, then blew away.

He collapsed onto his side, and the grass drank him slowly, skin-first.

I turned and ran toward the hall, shaken. There was no reason to trust the man, but I didn't know where else to go, and at least this hallway had light. The walls here were not stone; the bottom halves were wood paneled, and the upper portions papered in faded pink. Several times I had to slow and wait for Alle to unravel more thread. There were doors to my right, but I had no idea which one to open.

Finally I saw a door narrower than all the others, with a brass knob shaped like a cat's head. It was holding what looked like a real mouse by the tail. I placed my hand on the knob, breathing hard, and yanked it. The mouse in the cat's jaws began to struggle, and I gasped and jerked my hand away. The brass cat's mouth opened, and the mouse fell at my feet and darted down the hall. I stood there for several seconds, my heart pounding.

I walked into a room that was mostly in shadow, except for a few yellow splotches of light coming from long-necked lamps on the shelves. Oh, the shelves. They covered three walls, all the way up to the ceiling. And on each one were toys. Mostly dolls, lying limp or else propped with their legs dangling. They were wooden or plastic. One looked expensive and pale—china, I supposed.

I left footprints in the dust. I turned in a circle, trying to see all the toys. There was a wooden train engine. Marbles in a glass jar. A plastic clown in blue and green polka dots bending close to a little plastic dog, a hand cupped over his ear as if the dog were telling him a secret.

I heard a sound like water dripping steadily from a faucet. I looked around, but I couldn't tell where it was coming from. Then a skittering in one corner. I walked forward and my foot slipped. Looking down, I saw the weak lamplight was catching the edge of a puddle. A rustling came from one of the shelves. I turned, intending to run from the room.

But then I saw her.

The doll had a heart-shaped face and black, shoulder-length hair. She was stuffed into a frilly, peach-colored dress with a lacy collar. Her eyes darted back and forth in the shadow, and she had a tight, tiny, bow-shaped smile painted on. Her lips, though—her lips underneath the paint were sewn shut with spider-leg stitches, and she was *moving* them, trying to get them open. Each time she did, the stitches strained, and she whimpered.

Her arms had a slight sheen, like plastic, but they looked . . . warm. They looked alive. I gazed at the doll's face again, irked by her strange familiarity. I reached out and tipped one of the lamps toward her.

Kenna. The doll was Kenna.

Kenna, with her lips sewn shut, that awful, painted smile on her face. She sniffed, and a drop of clear liquid fell from her nose into the small puddle.

"Kenna!" I reached out to touch her, but she wobbled and fell. I caught her and tried to right her. She pulled away from me, stood on her small, hinged legs, and leaped from the shelf. She collapsed to her knees upon landing, but immediately scrambled up and ran behind one set of shelves, her nose still dripping.

"Kenna, come back! I'll help you," I promised desperately. But she had vanished. I shined the light on some of the other toys, and noticed new horrors. Some of the dolls still had human skin—moles and downy hair and the shadows of veins. Some moved. Others were inanimate except for their blinking eyes. The wooden train engine was actually made of a tiny, folded leg, a pink shoe forming the smoke stack. The marbles in the jar held miniature body parts. One was a pair of lips encased in glass. Two were eyes, the glass distorting them, making the blood vessels swell and the irises blur. I saw fingertips, locks of hair, yellowed teeth with bits of gum clinging to their roots. My stomach churned, and I had to turn away for a moment until the nausea passed.

A movement in the corner caught my eye. Kenna, looking shy and so small—she only came up to my knee. I dropped the lamp and raced to her. She froze, as though I might not spot her if she didn't move. Her nose was dripping faster, and as I approached, a tear slid down her cheek, and she began to gush water from both nostrils, like a faucet. She let out a cry through her stitched lips and started to run, splashing through the trail she left.

Calling her name, I chased her from the room and out into the hall, where the chandeliers flickered out one by one until I was in darkness, listening to Kenna's fading whimpers echoing off the stone.

I don't know how long I walked, feeling my way along one papered wall, my breath coming in shallower and shallower gasps. I stopped several times to listen for Kenna, but I heard nothing. Every once in a while I slipped on a wet stone, or imagined I heard water dripping. I kept going, determined that Kenna could be found, could be fixed. That I would not be responsible for the loss of another friend.

I paused once, thinking I heard someone else breathing. But each time I stopped, I was met with a silence that seemed to have weight, temperature—a thick, cold haze. At last, I saw a faint light at the end of the corridor. I ran toward it, and I burst out of the shadows and into another wide space beneath the ceiling of glass. This time I was in an artificial jungle. Enormous leaves arched up around me and vines unspooled from crevices in the walls as I ran. I collided with a solid figure, and gasped and staggered back, my body throbbing with pain.

A woman stood before me, hunched and staring. She was middle-aged, with long black hair in careless curls down her back, wide eyes caught in nets of wrinkles, and thick, fanning black lashes. Her lips were rough and chewed looking, her face slightly lighter in complexion than mine. She held up her hands as if to ward me off. Her nails were almost perfectly square. She wore rags.

I'd seen women artfully, tastefully clothed in rags in illustrations. But this woman . . . Her filthy right breast was exposed, the shreds of a once-white linen dress were streaked with dirt and hanging from her. It was hard to tell which marks on her face might be bruises and which were dirt. And still there was something lovely about her, a beauty that bruises couldn't touch.

"Go away!" I shouted at her. "Go away, right now!"

Her head bobbed forward as she walked, like a bird's. "Shh, shh. What are you crying about? Shh, now, no. Shh, no, don't. Do you want the beast to hear you? Hmm. Do you want it wide-awake? Do you have a plan for when it comes; are you in here all alone?" She extended an arm toward me. "Shh, don't cry, my baby, don't shake."

I tried to calm my gulping breaths, thoroughly ashamed to find that I was very nearly crying. "I'm not afraid! Only I—I'm lost."

She took my arm and pulled me closer. I resisted, but she was surprisingly strong, sweeping me into the curve of her arm. "Well, you're going to get killed; you're going to get us seen. This place is full of madness and wonder and the worst kind of dreams." Her voice was singsong, her words seeming to tangle and collide in strange rhymes.

"Who are you?" I pulled away from her, my mind filled with visions of dolls and of men who couldn't drink. Of the clock tower falling and that great heart throbbing against the glass. I needed a weapon. That was what I needed—something in this damned place that I could use to defend myself. "Don't come any closer."

She tipped her filthy chin up disdainfully.

"I mean it," I snapped.

"Oh, dear, dear." The leaves rustled as she walked around me, her stride steady and graceful, her head still bobbing slightly. She had grime-smeared welts on her calves. I had a sudden memory of rubbing mud into my sister's hair while she winced and asked if I was sure this would make it grow longer.

"Don't!" I turned with the woman, glowering, ready to attack.

"How long have you been here? Pretty little girl; pity, little thing . . ." She lunged at me suddenly, and I shoved her away. Her body felt heavy; her dirty rags swung out, then fell against her skin.

"I have no business with you."

"No business, no business . . ." She chanted as she circled me. I refused to let her out of my sight.

"Have you seen a doll?" I demanded. "A doll that looks like a little girl with short black hair?"

"No, dear. No doll. Have you lost your dolly?"

"Get out of my way if you haven't!" I shouted.

She stopped moving and lowered her voice to a harsh whisper. "Be silent! You'll bring the beast right to you." She stepped forward again. "What are you? A prisoner? A debtor? An *unwanted* girl?"

"No," I said, surprised by the sting of the lie. "I am here of my own will."

The woman put a hand to her throat. "Not a tribute, then?" Her eyes were a murky riverbed brown. The pupils contracted and dilated to a rhythm like a heartbeat. Her lips parted, and a soft light seemed to slide from her temples down her cheeks. "Are you . . . here to fight?"

I couldn't tell if she was mocking me, but never in my life had I so wished to be a warrior. Why should warriors be a thing of the past? Why couldn't I be one now? One who was always ready to fight, who looked on death and remained unshaken. Who had mastered both stillness and violence and whose life was comprised of quests with clear beginnings and ends. I thought of the horrors I had seen so far, and I found myself saying, without really meaning to: "I'm here to kill the beast."

A silent moment. Her mouth twitched up every few seconds. A small choking sound came from deep in her throat. Her eyes lost their hardness, and she gripped my hand. "Oh. Tell me it's true. Tell me it's *true*."

"Who *are* you?" I repeated. "Tell me now."

"My name is Asteria." She shuddered, as though her own name was repugnant to her. "I don't know how long I've been inside the labyrinth. I serve the beast." She glanced over her shoulder.

"What?" I jerked back.

"No! I do not serve her willingly."

"Explain yourself."

She glanced around again, then smiled, two tears leaking from her left eye and leaving pale tracks on her dirty cheek. "I was captured soon after I entered the maze. I thought the beast meant to kill me, but—"

"You've seen her?"

She crossed her arms over her chest. "She said I might be u-useful."

"Useful how?"

"I'm supposed to be a spy. I tell her who enters the labyrinth. I tell her where I saw them last—the boys, the girls, the heroes, the men, the mice. And then she hunts them."

For just a moment, fear pulled me into a too-tight embrace. A fern brushed my leg, and I shivered. "Does she know about me?"

Asteria clasped my hand tighter. Her palm was rough, callused. "That is the beautiful thing. She knows that tributes were brought here. Two men. But you . . . she has said nothing of you. But . . ." She let out a soft, slow breath. "Are there others with you?"

"Only one. My friend Kenna." Something stopped me from saying anything about Alle. Alle, to whom I thought I'd given the least dangerous role, and whom I had intended to protect. I should have known better. Putting a queen behind a line of pawns only makes her look more of a prize. "I found her in a room back there." I gestured down the hall. "It was full of—of toys—but they were—she was—"

"Yes." Asteria nodded frantically. "Yes, yes. I know the place."

"Does the beast know, then? Did *she* turn Kenna into a doll?"

Her throat worked as though she were trying to swallow. "There is a chance she does not know. For all her magic, she has grown old. She is not as perceptive as she once was. And there are enchantments here that would make a victim of anyone. Most likely your Kenna did not encounter the beast directly, but simply wandered into the spell."

Asteria kept looking at me with such hope—yet all I wanted now was to find Kenna, follow the thread back to Alle, and leave this place. "There was a man," I said suddenly. "When we first entered. He knows we're here. He had a dog, and he separated Kenna and me."

"He is not real." She tugged me closer. "The beast creates phantoms. Sometimes out of tributes' bodies, sometimes from her own mind."

I thought of the man who could not drink, who had dissolved when I'd helped him. "Then how do I know *you* are real?" I asked.

She surprised me by placing my hand on her chest and splaying it over the rips in her garment. The tip of my first finger nestled in the hollow at the base of her throat, where I felt a slow, steady pulse. She looked at me, all anger and slyness and grubby beauty. "Do you believe I'm a phantom?" Her breast swelled just beneath the heel of my hand and her heart seemed like a trapped bird, beating its wings beneath her skin.

"No," I replied honestly.

"Good." Her whisper made me shudder. "I can take you to her. I can tell you when she is weakest. Tell me what you need from me, and I will aid you however I can."

I did not know what I needed. "How long will it take to get to her?"

She studied me with a thoroughness that made me uncomfortable. "Two days, perhaps."

"And what about finding Kenna?"

"If you can slay the beast, Kenna will be freed from her spell. The tributes who remain alive—the ones who are so lost even the beast cannot find them—they will be free too."

"How do you know this?"

Her expression softened. "I know only what she has told me. She is afraid of death, and has often confided what she fears will happen when she dies."

"It's a gamble, then." I struggled to keep my voice steady. "If I don't go after Kenna now, she may be lost. And even if the beast is slain, Kenna may remain trapped in that spell forever, if the beast has lied to you."

"But if you find her now, what will you do? The spell must be reversed by destroying its source."

I didn't know whether to believe her, but I felt I had little choice. And had I not come here with a mission that was secret from everyone but Alle?

"All right, then," I said. "Take me to her."

# CHAPTER 21

**A**steria led me across the jungle and into a black marble corridor. We passed through many halls—some wood, some stone. Through a cold blue cave where gems gleamed, half buried in the rock like glittering parasites. Through a narrow corridor with cracked walls and a floor that slanted. There were tables along the walls, small round tables of varying heights, some with vases of wilted flowers.

"Did she make all this?" I asked. "I've heard she did her own decorating."

Asteria walked with such a long stride that it was hard to keep up. "It was a maze. But she has made it a hell."

"And is there truly a treasure?"

She paused—the slightest break in her easy rhythm. "Indeed, there is a treasure. And many gluttons, many thieves have come looking for it. All dead now." Her bare feet shuffled over the stones. "You may come here to play hero, you may come to be a slave, but you may not come to take what isn't yours." I couldn't tell if she was warning me or if she meant *you* in a wider sense.

"She lives in the very center," Asteria went on. "All routes lead, eventually, to her chamber, no matter where you might stop on the way."

"I saw the ocean. Through one door, I saw the sea."

"An illusion."

But I'd felt the sand and the spray. The water had lifted me. Those moments I had commanded the waves and sky had seemed more real than any in my life. "If I'd tried to swim it?"

She glanced at me. "I imagine you'd have drowned, little girl. Little pretty, hoping thing."

"I'm not a little girl."

She stopped walking suddenly. I nearly ran into her. "What's that on your wrist?"

I started, tucking my arm close to my body. She stared at the thread, and I offered my arm hesitantly to her. "I've tied the other end in the entryway. So I'll be able to find my way back."

She touched my wrist. "This is clever." She tugged lightly on the string.

"Don't."

"But easily broken." She met my gaze and said nothing else.

We arrived in open space again, the clear ceiling partly obscured by the branches of two massive gray leafless trees that we passed between. The ground beneath us was uneven—troughs of dark earth and small pools of mud. Rocks staggering up like broken teeth.

"I used to think I was like the beast." I hopped from one flat stone to another to avoid a pool of mud. I was more confident now—excited, even, about our adventure.

Asteria was a couple of steps ahead of me, and I saw her shoulders rise slightly. "Why?"

"I don't have any magic—at least, I don't think so. But certainly enough people have called me a monster." I hopped onto another stone. I felt tension in the thread, and stopped to pull it carefully over the rocks, then raced to catch up to Asteria.

"I was immensely unpopular." I halted beside her. She was staring at something beyond the trees. "I went to a very fine school, but I was considered unteachable. My problems arose from my family situation. My mother murdered my father with an ax."

She walked on. "Oh my. Things are bad, aren't they? Sometimes, in the world?"

"My mother said it might be best for everyone if I was shut up somewhere."

Asteria didn't answer. I wanted more from her. Wanted to know everything she knew about the beast.

"Can't she leave?" I asked. "If she's so powerful?"

No response.

"I mean, she terrorized a town. No one could kill her. And now she's stuck here? Isn't she magic? Isn't this ceiling made of glass?"

"I don't know why." Asteria's voice took on that singsong quality again. "Magic is brittle; minds have their own bars. Silence, now—we are coming to dangerous places."

I got a thrill at that. With Asteria by my side, even if she was strange and cracked and untrustworthy, I grew braver. The ground became very dry. Broken stones and brown grass, shrubs that would have snapped at a touch. A sludgy brook that slunk past us like a snake. "Perhaps it's all about mothers. Do you think? If mine had lived. If the beast's had been—"

"Get down!" Asteria pulled me to my knees behind a dry brown hedge. I heard skittering nearby, and then a small, plaintive wail.

"What if it's Kenna?" I started to stand. "What if she's looking for me?"

"Hush!" Asteria whispered.

Over the stones came a steady *clop, clop, clop*.

Hooves.

I shrank closer to Asteria. I saw a shadow on the far wall—hulking, horned. It was there for a second, then gone. My heart pounded. I felt suddenly very small, like I would be useless against that shadow. *The danger you can't see is always more frightening than the danger you can*, I reminded myself. *When you confront her, no matter how fearsome and horrible she is, it will be easier, because you can see her.*

But I wasn't so sure of that anymore. I might have chosen more hours in dark halls, listening to whimpers and footsteps over the images that now haunted me—Kenna's stitched lips and the bloody back of the man at the fountain.

I could hear the beast's harsh breath moving closer. A snuffle, almost a sigh.

Asteria suddenly flicked her wrist. From the marshy area we'd just crossed came a tremendous crack. I peered around the hedge and saw a branch plummet from one of the huge trees, hit the ground, and splinter. A silence followed.

I held my breath as the *clop, clop, clop* moved slowly in the direction of the disturbance. I heard the suction of mud as the creature retreated the way we'd come, through the muck and between the trees. Then an enormous snort, then a bellow that rattled the walls and made me clap my hands over my ears. I was trembling when it ended, and I looked at Asteria, lowering my hands. "You have magic."

Asteria closed her eyes briefly. "It's why she wanted me. She thinks I might help free her."

"Can't you use it to fight her, then?" My voice rose with excitement.

"Shhh," she whispered. "She knows someone is close by. But she's frustrated, tired." She stood. "I must get back. She'll be returning to her chamber soon and will want my news."

"Wait . . ." I struggled to my feet. It had not occurred to me I would have to be alone in the labyrinth again. "You're just going to leave me?"

She studied me. "I want you to keep going through this hall." She motioned at a corridor to our right. "It is a long stretch, and there are few forks. The signs." She nodded at the wall, where a purple neon sign read: *French's Fish Sticks*. "If you come to a divide, follow the signs. Eventually you will reach a cottage. Wait for me there."

Something jolted in me at the mention of a cottage, but I pushed it aside. "But you're going to her chamber. And isn't that precisely where I need to be?"

"I have ways of getting there faster than you ever could. I must go to her now so she sees nothing is amiss." Asteria leaned close to me. "If she finds out about you—that I am helping you—I will be tortured to *death*. It is very important that you listen to me."

I nodded, enlivened by the promise of such high stakes.

"The journey should take you several hours. I will find you at midnight."

She gave me a quick kiss on the forehead and vanished down a small, hedge-lined path I had not even noticed until that point.

I was alone in the labyrinth once more.

For what seemed like miles, I followed the signs. They were spaced every few yards or so:

*Dr. Arnet Lauer, DDS.*
*Fizzy Pop.*

*Stage Door.*
*Skodal Studios.*
*Hotel.*

Some of the signs had arrows, but I never saw anything but the black hall.

I worried sometimes about the thread—that I would run out, that I would be forced to sever my one connection to Alle and venture deeper into the maze with no hope of getting back to my starting point. That Asteria would abandon me, or betray me to the beast, and I would have nothing, no one.

I started to wish I had simply given Asteria a head start and then followed her down the hedge-lined path to the beast's chamber. If I had done so, perhaps everything would be over now—I would either be dead or triumphant. I closed my eyes and searched for the beast in my thoughts, but even there I found silence. I felt alone in a way I had not since my earliest days at Rock Point. Loneliness is like having a wound sewn shut with barbed thread. We close off the parts of ourselves that are open to others and pretend to embrace the privacy of our bodies—and yet we do the closing with something that will hurt every time we move. That will remind us of the secrets we've tried to stow away.

I thought of Alle often. The faint smell of sweat on her skin and the whiff of soap in her hair and the weight of her breast in my hand. The promise I'd made that day in the snow. The thoughts became so consuming sometimes that I'd find myself tugging the thread too hard and too often. Each time, she tugged back, and I imagined that she understood. That she had a wealth of compassion, a panoramic wisdom that caused her to look upon me with a warm, amused pity and whisper that I would be all right.

I came upon a hallway lit with gold, glass-walled lamps. The hall was narrow, with blue tiled walls and a high ceiling webbed with stucco. Music filled the corridor—a symphony that alternated between languid and triumphant. There were five dark doorways, two on either wall and one at the corridor's end, and as I walked by, I peered into each one.

In the first room was some sort of banquet—high tables, silver platters, the clink of glasses. Laughter and happy chatter. And then as

I watched, a shadow leaped onto the table—wolf-shaped, long-nosed. It began to devour a woman, pulling her from her chair headfirst. She screamed until there was a crisp crunch, like biting into an apple, and then the screaming stopped. Others were shouting; I heard thumps and crashes. The wolf's bristling tail flung plates to the floor, and the snap of bones seemed deafening.

I hurried on, my heart striking slow, sharp blows to my ribs. *Phantoms. They are phantoms.*

In the next room was a symphony—rows upon rows of instruments playing softly and sadly and out of tune. But there were no players. Just instruments and empty chairs. A saxophone dipped slowly. The valves of a trumpet moved up and down. I walked on.

The third room was dark. The fourth door was closed.

In the fifth room, a man sat slumped in a chair, his head on a desk. Pale as a fish's belly. A single weak bulb in a wire cage cast a whitish light throughout the wooden room. There was something familiar about the man. As I stepped inside, he opened his eyes, and I knew.

His eyes were Denson's eyes.

I was frozen for a moment, looking into them. His mouth was open, and there was a dark pool of liquid under his chin. When I ran to him, when I asked if he was hurt, if he could move, he moaned and tried to lift his head. The dark pool grew.

A single steel bolt passed through his tongue and chin and into the wood of the desk. He stared at me, eyes wide, body trembling. I hovered with my hand near his mouth. "Oh God," I whispered.

Asteria. Asteria and her magic. Perhaps she could fix this.

"Hold on," I told him. "I'll go for help. There's someone who can . . ."

He closed his eyes, his breath shallow. Then it slowed and was finally silent.

He vanished slowly. First his legs, then his body, then his arms and his head, then his blood. All that was left in the table was the steel bolt.

Then the light went out, and I ran.

# CHAPTER 22

steria was waiting by a small cottage in a little square of woods. I ran to her, nearly in tears. "There's someone—someone being tortured." I could barely get the words out between gasps. "Bolted to the table. There are—I don't know if anything's real! I need your help."

"Oh," she murmured. "Pretty little doll, you have not obeyed. Where did you go?"

She wrapped her long, dirt-streaked arms around me, and my head went under her chin. Her hair smelled like earth. Her body was soft, and yet I was certain she could lift me, pin me, do whatever she wished. She guided me down onto the gritty floor, and she held me. I could feel the tension in her at first, as though she wasn't used to doing this. When I looked up at her, I saw wonder in her gaze. It made me think of Denson, and then everything hurt. She tightened her embrace. I shook, though my eyes remained dry.

The clock tower fell against the glass, setting the palace trembling. I watched the vein latch onto the number twelve. I clutched Asteria harder.

"Does it always do that?" I murmured.

"Every midnight." She stared up at it. "I used to dream it would break the glass, and that I'd climb up there and fly away."

The tower lifted off the glass and righted itself. Asteria stroked up and down my back, and for a moment I pressed my forehead to her shoulder. "I should never have come here," I murmured.

"But you did." I suspected she took some satisfaction in the words. It was only the ghost of smugness—could easily have been my own paranoia. But I feared, for a moment, that she wanted me to suffer. That I always would. Kenna and Denson's brother and Alle and Asteria—all of us tortured endlessly until the beast saw fit to end it.

"I said I was ready to come to this place. I thought— I thought I didn't care if I lived or died, but I do."

Asteria kissed my forehead. I imagined a mountain of treasure, the slide of gold coins and silver cups down the sides. I pictured the cottage behind us as Denson's home in Rock Hill. I wished that on the night of Bitsy's death, we had all stayed in and Miss Ridges had read us a story.

But what I had right now was Asteria. And she was, under the layers of grime, beautiful. Whatever I wanted to believe about the unimportance of beauty, it couldn't change the fact that she *burned* with it—her black hair and wide eyes, her firm jaw. I loved the faint vertical lines between her brows and the way her hair clung to the sweat on her neck. I could have wrapped my body around hers and pulled her into me; I could have fucked her until our cries twined and drowned out the music of suffering.

I thought of Alle, and a savage pain cut me at the middle. "Alle," I whispered, tugging the thread and getting no response. "Alle." Louder. "What if something happened to her?"

Asteria writhed for a moment, as though my pain hurt her too. Then she went still. "Alle?"

I held up my wrist with the thread on it.

Sometimes it would happen, in a Dark Tale, that a character would do something quite stupid—spill a secret to the wrong person or wander off when she ought to stay with her group. I always loved these girls best when they were doing the stupid things. They weren't witless; they made good choices along with the bad. It was just that sometimes they fucked up in a single, irreversible instant.

I knew I shouldn't tell Asteria about Alle. I have nothing to say in my defense, except that you should have seen her—Asteria. Ragged and sure and mysterious. This woman could have sung with no regard for tune, and you'd still have heard a song. I told her the story of my friendship with Alle; it seemed to come out of me unbidden. I admitted I had not gone to a fine school, that my mother had not killed my father with an ax. I told how I had failed Alle, lost her affection. How Alle now held the thread at the labyrinth's entrance.

When I was done, my breathing had calmed. The image of Denson's brother bolted to the table seemed like a bad dream. Asteria was rocking me, and I felt light, almost as if I were floating. "It's strange," I said. "I know she doesn't want me anymore. But I'd still do almost anything to protect her."

"Anything?" Asteria repeated. She had seemed to go into something like a trance when I told her about Alle and the thread.

"Well, *almost*. I feel I've already let her down in so many ways. But I still want to— I want to do good things for her."

"I may know the feeling." Asteria was silent for a moment. "My parents put me here."

"Your parents gave you up as a tribute?" I gazed up at her, stunned.

She sighed, her breath ruffling my hair. "And yet I still sometimes think, if they wanted me back, I'd go. I suppose that's simply the way love works."

"I don't know if I've ever really loved anybody," I admitted.

"Of course you have." Her voice was so sharp I nearly pulled away. "You have loved. And you know that love is a miracle."

"I don't know that," I said harshly. "It only seems to get in the way."

"No. No, no, no. It is a brave someone who would fall in love. And a fool who would let it go once she had it."

Did she mean that as an accusation?

"Have you ever been in love?" I demanded.

"I think perhaps I have."

I plucked the thread.

"She's safe enough, if she stays there," Asteria said finally.

"What?"

"The beast cannot find the labyrinth's entrance. No matter how hard she tries."

"Can you find it?" I asked.

She shook her head slowly.

I stared once more at the thread. "Do you want me to take you to it? We could both leave, quickly—"

"It would not work the way we want it to."

I shrugged out of her embrace. "How do you know?"

"The beast will still be here. The town will still send tributes. Your Kenna would still be trapped. This is my prison, and it is yours now too. And will be as long as she lives."

We stopped talking then. Asteria went into the cottage and came out with food—tins of meat and canned vegetables. She opened the containers with a casual spell, and we ate in silence. When we were done, we positioned ourselves among some shrubs at the side of the cottage and lay down.

It was cold. And though she held me close to her, I did not grow warmer. I felt restless and helpless, and she seemed as fitful as I. We fell asleep, both of us in our broken prison, rattling like coins in a box.

In the morning, she was no longer holding me. In the instant before I spotted her standing by the cottage, I feared she had been an illusion too, and for some reason this made me furious. "These phantoms," I snapped at her. "Are they—are they *true*? What I see, is that really what happened to these people?"

"I don't know." She seemed a bit wary of me. The cottage stood behind us like a stage set, empty and pathetic in the gray light coming through the ceiling. The air, though, smelled fresh, earthy.

"What have you seen? Did you see her kill Denson's brother? Did you see her kill that man in the garden?"

"I do not watch her kill. I only tell her where she might look for tributes."

"You are sick," I snapped at her. "And you're a coward. Why don't you use your magic to defeat her?"

"There are powers far greater than mine. And aren't you the one who wanted to run last night?"

I turned away.

"Perhaps I am a coward," she said, as loudly as I'd heard her dare speak till then. "I am *afraid*!"

"If she has done the things I've seen—tortured people . . . She is truly a beast, then! She is as bad as they come."

"Good and bad have no place here. There is only survival."

"And that is how you justify it? Doing her bidding. Leading her to her prey?"

Asteria's glance tossed shadows like a candle flame. She headed for the cottage. "I need no justification. I do what I must to survive.

I am her slave, and I will indeed be free one day, but serving her has bought me my life. Why should I be displeased that she has taken a liking to me?"

I shrugged. "I would not want to be the sort of person a monster takes a liking to." I thought guiltily of my dreams, the ones the beast had seemed to infiltrate. How I'd felt strangely honored—*chosen*.

Asteria stopped suddenly and bent over with an arm across her stomach, as though she were ill. "I miss freedom," she whispered. Tears fell from her closed eyes, and her lips curved up in a bitter smile. "God, I miss it."

"There's no time to feel sorry for yourself. You get your freedom by *acting*."

She opened her eyes and gave me a cold stare. "By being like you? Bumbling into the labyrinth for a chance at the treasure, with no idea what you're up against?"

So she'd guessed, then. Guessed I was not a warrior, but a greedy fool.

"I thought it was about the treasure, at first." I met her gaze, not sure why I wanted so *badly* for her to understand. "But I want to fight. I want to stop her."

I realized, with a gradual, slinking terror, that this confrontation would be nothing like I imagined. I was a new soldier in a long-standing war, dreaming of the day I'd arrive for battle. Preparing for the front lines by imagining over and over that I would be brave when it counted. That I would defend my brothers and sisters and slay my enemies. Only to find myself, when the charge began, divested of my shield, separated from my fellows, and hacked apart by enemies.

Asteria got a strange expression on her face, like she was watching the end of something rather than the beginning. She smiled, though, a slight but luminous thing. "Pretty thing," she said, "you may yet win."

She looked sad, bitterly sad. And it dawned on me that perhaps the reason Asteria was alive—and the reason she had never tried to kill the beast—had to do with love.

"Are you lonely here?" I asked her softly.

She gave a laugh that seemed unsustainably light, a stone pitched through the air. "I used to think no one could ever be lonely, as long as she had eyes. I used to think the world was full of strange and wonderful places, and that I would find a home in one of them." She said no more than that.

I had never, in all my memory, felt safe or wanted. Fear kept me sharp, kept me alive. But the more breaths I took alongside Asteria, the more I looked into eyes the color of earth, the more I wanted to believe that I would win and she would protect me. That I would learn to avoid pain, that I'd never again see Kenna with her lips sewn shut or Bitsy falling to the ground or Alle's face as she stood holding the thread, watching me disappear.

"What do I have to do?" I whispered.

Her expression was kind, almost pitying. "We'll make you an armor. I can do that much for you. And when you finally meet the beast, you'll be protected."

We spent the next few hours hunting through the cottage, picking up any metal objects we found along the way. Bolts and silverware, discarded food tins. Jewelry. An old brass carousel pole we found lying across the floor of an otherwise empty room. Asteria knelt beside the pile of metal.

I didn't see how she did it. I only saw the carousel pole begin to melt, slowly. And then it swallowed bolts, and a fork's tines dripped away. She rose with sheets of molten metal tossed over her shoulders like garments. She walked to me and began to touch me. Softly, her head tilted back, her lips parted, her hair falling between her shoulders, getting caught in the liquid gold. She ran her fingers between my breasts and tugged down my shirt. Lowered her head and licked down my chest, her fingers gliding along the sides of my jaw.

I gasped. Felt the heat of the metal, sweat falling down my forehead, catching in my eyelashes. The fluid gold swirled away from her body and circled mine. I cried out at the pain, but soon I was in love with it. I moved like a snake, sliding against that source of pleasure until it wound around everything inside me—my stomach, my heart, my shoulder blades. It swept up into my throat until I could have screamed fire.

I was pulling hard on the thread. I could feel Alle pulling back, a series of frantic tugs as though to ask what was wrong. I knew a panic bound in a wicked ecstasy as the thread started to slip from my wrist.

I'd tightened it three times this morning, and still it seemed to want to be free of me.

The metal began to harden around me, forming plates. Asteria pushed her palms against my back and front, and she breathed into the plates until they grew hot once more against my skin. And then she herself seemed to liquefy, to flicker and then melt into gold, and she became part of the armor. I looked around for her, to make sure she hadn't simply stepped out of my line of vision. But she was gone, and I smiled softly at the space where she'd been and put my palms to the metal. The plates cooled gradually, and the gold turned to burnished copper. I believed I could see her shadow swimming in it like an eel. Then she appeared again before me, fragile, colorless, but smiling. Her middle had become a sheet of dark glass, and I gazed at myself.

I saw all that I could be, and I was grand. Not beautiful. But powerful. I would no longer have to settle for being transformed—I would do the transforming. I would draw Alle and her mysteries like a magnet; I would be needed and admired and confided in.

As I stared at my reflection, it began to move and change. From the slough of what I had been rose some crystal version of myself, glinting in brilliant patches like ice mounded on a road. Not a street tough but a warrior, holding a sword. My jaw was set, my brow heavy, my eyes dark and burning. I looked ready to slay the beast. I'd come this far, and I was going to free the labyrinth's prisoners—free the town from this creature—and then go back to Alle. We were going to make a life together like the one we'd dreamed: endless freedoms to be tried on and then cast aside, each of us the other's only certainty.

"What do you think?" Asteria whispered. She sounded strained. Blood vessels netted themselves across the glass, and then fat and muscle and skin grew over it until the mirror was swallowed. A hint of fragrance—vanilla and fruit—seemed to cover something that lurked beneath the surface of the fresh air and forest smell. Not rot, but age. An undusted room. An underground place.

"I want to be that," I said honestly, ignoring my moment of mistrust.

"I cannot make you anything that will last." Her voice was soft with a regret that sounded a little too smooth, too practiced. "I can take things from the labyrinth, I can patch them together, but the armor will fade. I cannot give you a sword, but I can tell you where one lies. Do you know how to fight?"

"Not really," I admitted. "I practiced with sticks at my—back home."

"A blade hangs in her chamber. Just above the fire. If you can get hold of it, you'll know what to do." She leaned forward and kissed me. Her lips seemed to have sharp edges—I started to draw back. But then she softened, and the kiss became as pure and deep a thing as I have known.

The thread pulled tight, and a soft cry vibrated through my body. She pushed me back against the wall, and I yielded to her, all boldness and despair and a rhythm that had become familiar to me. The thread fell from my wrist. And when we pulled away and started once more into the dark reaches of the maze, I left it behind.

# CHAPTER 23

To pass the time as we walked, I told Asteria my favorite Dark Tales. Another midnight went by. The armor disappeared, but I felt as if I still wore it, as if it were under my skin. I learned to recognize trees that bore fruit, and to search the labyrinth's rooms for secret feasts. I resented it when she left for hours at a time to visit the beast. In her absence I grew bored and was spooked by shadows. I often imagined that I still had the thread, that I was tugging in patterns, sending Alle messages. I was aware that I should be more upset to have lost that connection, lost my way. But I was freer somehow without it.

I grew harder, too, in the hours I spent on my own. I was easily spooked but not afraid. Once I found a rushing stream that cut through the floor of a wide corridor and seeped under matching doors on either side of the hall. There were wide flat stones in the stream, and the crossing was easy. But I stopped on the middle stone when I noticed a dark shape beneath the water.

I peered down, and the current seemed to slow so that I could see. Rocky Bottom lay on the shallow riverbed, his cheeks bloated, his eyes wide. I experienced a moment's sickness, but then I remembered: Phantoms. Illusions.

Rocky Bottom reached up with one arm. I started, nearly slipping from my stone. He banged on the underside of the river's surface, with a sound like he was knocking on glass. His eyes bulged and a jet of bubbles came out his nose. I crouched and tried to reach into the stream but found that beneath a few inches of burbling water, the surface was hard and smooth. Water sloshed into my shoes, soaking the cuffs of my pants. I went to my knees and pounded, coaxed, tried to dip my hand in the water as I had done at the fountain. Then I stopped.

*He is a murderer, and not worthy of your pity. What, will you pity the beast when you stand before her? Will you lower your sword?*

I stood. Rocky Bottom continued to knock. I stepped onto the water. Felt it rush around my feet. Looked down at Rocky Bottom's wide eyes and frantically moving mouth. And then I walked on.

"I don't think you have been honest with me," I said with a practiced coolness.

Asteria had just returned from her latest visit to the Minotaur. We were in a room that looked a bit like Rock Point's parlor, except crumbling and dusty. As usual, she had been reticent when I asked what she and the beast had talked about, what the monster had required of her. "I think perhaps you have some love for the beast."

She did not answer. So perhaps it was true. I didn't know whether I was disgusted or pleased. Or envious.

We made our way through a creaking door and found ourselves in a ballroom. Huge white pillars supported a mezzanine, and a mahogany piano stood on one corner. Above us was a night sky with far more stars than I'd seen before in my life and smoky white clouds drifting across the darkness.

"Is she not wholly a monster, then?" I asked. "Did she really kill a mother who sacrificed herself for her child?"

Asteria turned to me, and in that moment I felt more frightened than I had been so far in the maze. "I have no love for her," Asteria said calmly, her gaze blank. "My only wish is to stay alive."

"What about the people before me who have tried to slay the beast? Why didn't you help them as you're helping me?"

One side of her mouth curved up slightly, and her eyes moved slowly back and forth. "I have seen many fools try to do what you are doing. They are doomed and were not worth the risk to my own life to aid them."

"So why am I different?"

"Because you *think*." She crossed the ballroom, leaving dirty footprints on the blond wood floor. I followed. "The brave are not the ones who merely answer the call. Any fool can embark on a quest. The brave are the ones who do their duty and come away, not with a monster's head on a pike, but with some new *knowledge*."

Miss Ridges had said once that reading meant nothing unless you could articulate what a story had given you. But I'd always disagreed— though I'd never found the words to argue. You didn't have to be able to analyze to appreciate a story. You had only to be able to feel, deep in a place that didn't deal in words, how that story was yours and everyone else's too.

"But the monster's head on a pike doesn't hurt," I said.

She smiled. "No. But it is not the most important thing." She paused before the piano. I waited for it to start to play by itself, but it was silent. "So tell me. What will you learn here?"

"I want to be unbreakable."

I didn't think it was true, even then. Invincibility wasn't learnable. But I look back now and can't think what I would have said in its place.

Still, it gave me some satisfaction to tell Asteria I wanted to be unbreakable. And to be unable to see, in her eyes, in the slow nod of her head, whether she thought I was a fool like the rest of them.

I cannot say who began the kiss, only that the clock tower could have made its midnight collapse and I wouldn't have noticed. A dampness formed over my skin; my shoulders went slack. She touched my breast, slid her thumb around my nipple, and I gasped against her lips. When we parted, I retreated, panting, and stumbled to the floor.

She was violently hungry. She crawled on all fours toward me, her back end swaying, clots of thread hanging from her ragged clothes. Her exposed breast swung as she crawled. Her black hair was like a lion's mane, bending and shivering with a life all its own. Her smile dared me, jolted me. I wanted to be on my back, my spine jerking and arching like some broken piece of a puppet. I wanted her to sew my mouth shut like one of the beast's dolls and let this confusion bleed from me, tumble in bad rivers from between my legs.

I knew a moment's repulsion, an accusation that never made it out of my mouth—*How can you be a slave, when you are so clearly wicked? How can I pity your tattered clothes, your sharp ribs, when you were born to consume?* And then I was guilty, thinking of Alle, who didn't love me and wouldn't love me, but whom I still wanted, with a childlike desperation, to impress.

And then I stopped thinking, because she swept over me like flames, and all that is best about living—the small wonders, the darknesses that get folded inside, the thrill of *taking* from a world that wants you to wait politely with your hands out—seemed to hiss across her skin in terrible currents.

Oh, I was alive then. And I was far from unbreakable.

We were interrupted by a *plink* high above us.

The stars dropped out of the sky one by one and shattered against the ceiling. They were the size and shape of Christmas ornaments—not balls of gas at all. They burst, and their points skittered across the glass, frosting it like ice. Finally one hit so hard that a cracked web appeared in the ceiling and the star fell through. It plummeted and then fractured at our feet.

Asteria pulled me close. "Watch out!" She sheltered me with her body as the stars continued to fall.

Finally the whole night came down, the black sky fluttering like a banner and draping itself over the ceiling. Stars' points lodged in it, glinting down at us like teeth. Through the spaces where the fabric of the sky didn't quite cover the glass, I could see only blankness, an endless white, and it frightened me.

"Nothing is real here," I whispered, watching the bits of star on the ground fading. I gripped Asteria tightly, digging my fingers into her shoulders. "Fuck. Damn this whole shit-slimed world. I thought this place . . . It's all just spells; it's all nothing."

"Not nothing," she whispered back, burying her face in my hair. "I promise you, there is something real here."

I wanted to believe her. To trust that I had found the real thing, that every moment before entering the labyrinth, I had been a prisoner, and that this was freedom. But I only felt alone.

The next day, we passed two men pulling cartloads of fish across a wide, empty clearing where grass grew between stones and an odd carnivalesque tune climbed the walls until we could no longer hear it. A lizard scuttled near my feet, and I stopped and watched it for so long that Asteria was nearly out of sight when at last I bolted forward to catch her.

I told her, that day, about the storm and the ocean. About playing on the beach, making the waves rise. She smiled, and I felt the warmth of that smile—not deep inside me but on my surface, fleetingly. It was a ribbon that caught in my hair and between my fingers before blowing away. "You must have a tremendous power, Thera. Very few can command anything in the labyrinth."

"But why would I have power? I mean, I've never done anything magic that I know about, not in my whole life. And there are plenty of times it would have helped, to be sure." I was babbling excitedly, spurred by this new idea of power, wondering what I might do with it.

"Perhaps you were meant to come here." She said it very softly, and I looked at her, puzzled. I had a flash of memory—on the floor of my childhood bedroom, playing with little animal figurines. Looking up suddenly to find my mother in the doorway, watching me. I remembered staring at her red lips and the lines around her eyes and trying to figure out if she was smiling or not, because her mouth curved upward slightly, but she did not seem happy.

"I have thought that too, at times," I said.

Asteria touched my shoulder. Her hand was scuffed—abraded knuckles and streaks of dirt. I followed her.

We came upon a large iron gate in a dark plot of land that looked like a cemetery without graves. In front of the gate, a bird was choking on a worm. I couldn't tell if the creature was trying to swallow the worm or spit it out, but eventually the worm spilled from the tiny yellow beak, growing longer and longer. I watched Asteria go up to the bird, lift it in her hand, and twist its neck until it broke with a twiglike snap. She tossed it to the ground and pulled the seemingly never-ending worm from its mouth. She hauled open the iron gate, which creaked, and used the worm to tie the gate open.

"I dislike having gates shut behind me," she said, ushering me through.

The ease with which she'd killed the bird called to mind Alle and the weasel. It surprised me, how easily I sometimes forgot to be wary around Asteria.

"The beast," I said, watching her carefully. "Was she ordinary, do you think? Until she became a monster? Or was she always damaged?"

"She must always have been troubled, I suppose."

"But she was human, once. How did she justify killing so many people?"

Asteria walked ahead of me. I noticed then, that part of the bird's wing was stuck to the bottom of her foot—a bruise-colored mat of feathers. "Is it so hard to see?" She put a hand on my shoulder, urged me to walk beside her. "Violence starts as a discovery—of power, of ambition. Of a force that rests with its head against your heart. It is always there—a shadow, featureless. Until you turn a certain way, and the silhouette resolves itself. You see the nose, the lips, the curve of the shoulder. You see what you are capable of. You feel both the danger and the ordinariness of it. Because in the end, the blood comes out of each of us the same way. And one dead human, weighed against the world and the galaxy and everything beyond, means very little." She paused. "Every act of violence is a disappointment before it even begins."

I thought about fights I'd started over the years. The satisfaction of striking out was indeed short-lived. But connect enough of those brief moments of power, and couldn't you braid something out of it? A fearsome legacy? An enviable façade? I wasn't sure whether I hated the beast or hated that she and I dreamed together.

She guided me in a strange dance that took us through trees and over odd bulges in the grass, until we were walking along a low stone wall covered in vines. Time seemed to fall away, and I wondered if there was such a thing as spirits, as a web of life as old as the world, and if we had known each other, Asteria and I, when the earth's greatest battles were between fire and earth, mountain and ocean. When there were no bodies like ours, no words, and no grief.

I realized we had stopped. She was looking at me with that strange almost-smile that suddenly unnerved me. "You'll reach the center tonight."

It was as if my heart became liquid for an instant, and spilled through my ribs. "I will?"

"I will meet you outside her chamber. I will create whatever diversion you need. The ivy that grows along this wall? Follow it. Do not stray. You'll be where you need to be in a few hours' time—a room of stone with paintings on the walls. If you follow the ivy, it will lead you directly there."

I gazed at her. *You would not betray me?*

A fool's question. She would. Anyone would.

*There is no good or bad. Only survival.*

My armor seemed to tighten around my bones. Why did I obey her? Why was it always, *Follow the silver lamps* or *follow the ivy* or *I must return to her now, but don't be afraid; she does not know you're here.*

The beast knew I was here. She had given me that storm by the ocean. She had taken Kenna from me. She had breathed with me in the dark halls. We're taught that a predator is an obvious thing, stalking and fanged and hungry. But the best are the riddlers and illusionists, the ones that hide their teeth.

I broke our stare, turning toward the ivy wall. "All right," I said. "I will see you there."

# CHAPTER 24

I did not obey. I followed the ivy-covered wall until doors began to appear, and then I walked through the first one that drew me. I found myself in sunlight, standing on warm, prickly grass. The sun shone over a green plain. The sky was almost comically blue, and no matter how I looked, I couldn't see glass above me. I thought for a moment that I had escaped. That I was no longer in the maze at all.

I saw figures—silhouettes at first, resolving themselves into people. Lounging in the grass, picking flowers or watching birds through binoculars. I would have thought it all false, some painted idea of happiness. Except I felt the warmth of this place immediately. I knew Asteria had told me to find the room with the fireplace and paintings on the walls. I vaguely remembered her telling me how to reach it. But all I could do was walk across this plain toward the figures, who looked up as I approached.

I knew by now not to trust anything in the labyrinth. Knew I ought to be more afraid of this idyllic scene than I had been of the room with the toy shelves. But the warning was all in my head and not at all in my gut. The warmth here was unlike anything I'd known before. Different from being pressed against Alle on a narrow cot, different from the ferocious heat of Asteria's body. I continued toward a shady tree, where a woman was lying. She had red hair that fanned and shone on the grass. She opened her eyes as I drew near, and she smiled.

I am not sure whether she spoke. It was like a dream where you know you are welcome or know you are in danger without anyone having to say a word. I understood her, and when she rose and walked toward a long, low wooden building with rows of windows, I followed. Without any verbal instruction, I began to work with the other people.

Our only job, it seemed, was to sort through maps and place them where they could be seen. We plastered them to tabletops and tacked them to trees. We papered walls with them. We stepped into gardens and used rolled maps to stake tomato plants.

The maps were not of any world I knew. Continents spread over blue backgrounds. There were deserts and rivers I'd never heard of, mountain ranges and bridges the names of which I had no desire to memorize. I was happy. At night, I curled up in that low wooden building, in the nearest available bed, with whomever happened to be in it.

Every now and then I would be out in the field, taping pieces of map to the backs of leaves or creating a map tent to shelter stones, and I would spot a shadow in a window of the wooden building. I would frown, trying very hard to remember whom I had left behind and where I had once lived. And then I would feel the worry leave me like released air, and I would go back to work.

In truth, I am not sure how long I spent in that paradise. But I passed that time in a glorious haze. I frequently stood still and daydreamed. I was in no more of a rush than the sun. But I was troubled occasionally by shadows in the windows. I began to feel there were eyes in the trees, watching me, and I carried out my work with a wariness that made it less joyful. If the others noticed, they said nothing. I began to spend all my nights outside, rather than in a bed. I watched the stars draw into themselves until they were nothing but freckles, then watched them expand again.

One morning, a baby was crying somewhere in the garden. I mostly ignored it, or loathed it. But sometimes I wandered through rows of vegetables and sunflowers, looking for the source of the sound. I encountered the red-haired woman and asked her about the baby. She frowned, a slight furrow appearing between her eyes.

Nobody else I spoke to heard the crying either.

It became more difficult to do my work. My maps rolled back up whenever I tried to spread them out, and I couldn't find any uncovered trees or rocks or walls. I wasn't sure if I imagined it, but the sky seemed darker too.

I wandered around the wooden bunkhouse. The crying sounded closer when I was there. But no matter where I looked, I couldn't find the child. And every time I thought I'd gotten closer to it, a moment later, the sound was far away again.

I began to sob. I, who hated crying, walked across meadows and around map-covered trees, weeping for an invisible child. The others tried briefly to comfort me, but they soon went back to work, and eventually their diligence was an inspiration. I returned to my duties too, but I was a quieter, colder worker. I tuned out the infant's crying and manufactured a silence that shrouded me well.

Until the day I woke beside a woman with dusty hair, and the sun was shining, and I realized that we all heal. Every one of us. Easily and in our sleep. I truly could not hear the baby's wails anymore. I went outside and I dozed in the sunlight. I found a bare tree and tacked a map to it. This map featured a long, thin, mountainous continent. A purple ocean with a hundred pin-dot islands. To my right, far off, the sky was hazy and gray, and I thought how glad I was that sort of sky would never touch me again.

As I was admiring my work, a woman staggered across the meadow. I didn't like her. She was hunched, sickly looking, and she wore rags. I looked down and realized I wore nothing at all. Around me, people were either naked or in sensible, untattered clothes. I thought this woman should make a choice.

She came right up to me, repeating a word I didn't recognize. When I started to turn from her, she took my wrist. I felt a heat—not the quiet warmth I was used to experiencing here but a tearing jolt, a sensation I might expect to be caused by a bullet. "Thera." Her gaze was angry, her nails sharp. "Thera, you're not supposed to be here."

I jerked my arm away. "I most certainly am. I live here. And I don't know what you are calling me, but it is not appropriate."

"Thera, listen to me." Her eyes were wide, frantic, the lashes strangely splayed and wet looking. She seemed almost familiar, but I didn't think she belonged here. I looked around for the woman with red hair, but I saw no one else on the plain. It was just me and the woman in rags, and that clot of dark sky drifting steadily closer. "You must leave."

"I like it here."

"You made a promise."

I stared at her. Opened my mouth to tell her the words meant nothing. But there was something in my skin like a splinter, the smallest of terrors. "Please," I begged the woman. "Please, I am happy here. Finally. I've never been happy before—not like this, not so easily."

"You promised." The woman crossed her arms and shivered. A wind whipped her hair, and clouds rolled in. "You promised you would slay the beast."

"I . . ." I did not remember my promises. Another gust of wind carried the faint sound of the infant crying. "No!" I clapped my hands over my ears. "No!"

The woman stared at me.

"She always cries," I explained. "That damn baby always cries. I just want to be away from her."

I saw a ball of thread go by in the wind.

I gazed into the woman's eyes. They seemed oddly blank to me. I didn't trust them, but I wanted whatever information she had. More clouds piled above us, and the woman before me seemed to swell too. The sky flickered.

I heard an enormous boom, and then the ground began to shake. I was off-balance, upset. It seemed unfair for the ground to be shaking just when I had grown used to feeling stable. I looked down and saw water bubbling up around my feet. The earth became spongy, fetid. My wrist. Something was supposed to be tied to my wrist, but my wrist was bare. I was seized by fear then.

"Thera." The woman in rags was beckoning me. "Come on!"

I began to run. And as I ran, my terror grew. My feet drew spouts of water from the land. The clouds were slashed open by a sideways streak of lightning, and water poured from them in sheets. There was too much water for me to see where I was going. It knocked my legs from under me and sent me sliding toward the building.

Before I could race inside and take shelter, the building came loose from its foundation with a *crack*. The wind whisked it away as though it were no more than wadded paper. Trees were wrenched from the ground and swept off over the horizon; maps flew through the air. The mud I struggled in seemed to anchor me to the earth. A moment later, the very sky and plains were blown away, and I found myself in a dark wooden hallway with a single dull lamp on the wall. The woman was nowhere in sight.

Asteria. The woman was Asteria. The fog seemed to have been shaken from my mind, and I knew where I was. And I was supposed to meet Asteria in the beast's lair.

I started to walk. I needed to find the wall covered in ivy.

There was a burbling sound behind me. Looking down at the floor, I saw, through the shadows, water seeping into the corridor.

I ran until I turned a corner and found myself in a hall of ice. Thick spikes of it hung from the ceiling and rose out of the floor. I began to shiver. I imagined I saw flashes of red in the ice around me. I heard a sound, a hushed, feminine moan, growing louder and louder still. It sounded like the sighs you'd make in the bedroom: "Huh-huh-huh-huh-huhhhh . . ." The last was drawn out, and then the panting began again. "Huh-huh-huh . . ." But this time more voices joined it, and the harmony was stunning. A choir singing, "Huh-huh-huh-huuuhhhhh," in ecstasy.

And I *did* see red in the ice—blushing skin, a swirl of copper hair, crimson nails. The chorus continued. I slipped on the ice in my struggle to escape the water, which flooded the crystal hall and slapped up the walls, and then . . . froze. In the most lovely glass waves, sharp and giving an illusion of motion, like a carved horse's mane. At last the ice ended, and I was in a wooden corridor again. Water was trickling behind me again, snakes of it. I opened the first door I saw and shut it behind me.

Glasses clinked, and there was a doomed sort of music, a last-waltz type of thing. I was in a beautiful room—all white tablecloths and gleaming silverware. Napkin rings shaped like ivy leaves. Thick, rose-colored drapes, and huge portraits on the walls of men with hunting dogs. People milled about and chatted—men in suits and women in gowns.

"Thera, there you are." My father clapped me on the shoulder. "We thought you weren't going to show."

I was too shocked to answer—shocked by the weight and solidity of his hand. He shouldn't have been here. But he was, and it was wonderful. He looked a little gray at the temples, but not too old. "I didn't know you wanted me."

"Yes, yes. It wouldn't be a party without you."

There was something odd about his mouth. A lizard. Every man in the room had a tiny lizard on his mouth. My father's was green and bitter looking. It snatched crumbs from his lips and spoke for him in a tiny, buzzy voice.

"A girl is a girl is a girl," my father was saying through his lizard, while a tall bald man nodded. My father took a sip of amber liquid, and the lizard flicked its tongue in too.

I looked around for my mother.

"We endure through mediocrity," my father went on. "One grand act and we're fine fodder for tales, but who in this world has a more unshakable sense of importance than those who do a passable job day after day? Whose output is functional and ungenius?"

The water found its way under the door, ruining men's shoes while they glanced down and lifted their feet, in a splashy, unison stamping.

I thought of a party aboard a sinking ship. But here it was the men who sank. The water rose and they tumbled into it, flailing and shouting. A waiter went down and a whole tray's worth of glasses soared into the air, forming a temporary constellation before they plunged into the flood.

I spied a door in the back of the room and slogged toward it, the cuffs of my trousers heavy with water. I struggled and finally pulled it open and slipped into the next room. The water didn't follow. When the door closed behind me, there was something final about the sound. *Phantoms*. I tried not to think about my father drowning in that room. *Phantoms. She has seen your dreams. She built him from that.*

I was in a narrow hallway. The only light came from around a corner—a dancing flame, casting shadows on the wall and illuminating ivy-leaf designs in the stone. I could hear faint music—the carnival song. And I walked carefully forward on a strip of red carpet until I turned another corner and found myself in a high-ceilinged room.

The center was open, and three flat, wide stone steps led up to a raised floor on which stood a huge white wooden bull. Large enough that I could have sheltered under its body. It stared at me with dark, painted eyes. It was indeed intricate—scars on its hide, one leg mangled, its tail wrapped around one flank. There was a softness to its muzzle, and a greenish patina like moss over its horns.

A fire burned in a large fireplace, and there were framed photographs of carousel animals on the walls. Beyond the table, on the raised part of the floor, stood a four-poster bed hung with thick green curtains. And spilling from the bed, leaking from between the curtains and surrounding the wooden posts, were jewels and gold coins, goblets and pearls.

I was in the Minotaur's lair. I wandered around, looking at the paintings, straining to hear music over the crackle of the fire. But I didn't go toward the bed. I understood that the treasure was a trap. That I must wait for the beast. I was still breathing hard, too wired to really be frightened. I knew I ought to look around for the blade, but I didn't wish to. I had things I wanted to say to the beast. Things I didn't intend to say with a sword in my hand.

I wished now more than ever that I held the end of the thread.

Eventually a shadow appeared on the wall, and I turned. Asteria stood in the entrance to the room, skin red-gold with firelight. Her rags had pieced themselves together into a white gown with bell sleeves; I could no longer see her breast, or the streaks of dirt. Her black hair fell in waves between her shoulders, and she stood straighter than she had before.

I knew then, and I suppose, had known all along.

I had already faced the beast many times. And this would be the last.

# CHAPTER 25

**M**iss Ridges used to go into quite a bit of detail about how people felt in the Dark Tales. If someone fell in love, there was always a lot of thinking and wishing and doubting involved. If someone was revealed to be wearing a second skin, the surprise was always palpable, the betrayal raw. I liked the Dark Tales because they were so much more complex than fairy tales—more truthful, I thought.

But there is some truth too in fairy tales where men turn to frogs or beetles and princes are blinded by thorns and women make deals with witches, and nothing more is said about it than that the prince was blinded or the deal was made. Sometimes the things that ought to shock us seem, under the circumstances, quite predictable.

"You?" I said softly.

She too seemed unwilling to indulge in a theatrical scene. "Thera." She walked along the wall and into the chamber. "I see you've found where you are meant to be."

"Are you going to kill me?" I asked.

"That depends." She moved toward the bed. "Will you try to take my treasure? What have you *really* come here for?"

I thought about all the reasons I had supposedly come here. The treasure. Because I didn't know where else to go. Because I wanted to be the one who slayed the beast. Because I needed to know why she and I dreamed together.

None of those worked as an explanation, and so I said nothing.

"Did you truly come here to kill me? Many have tried, you know." She reached the far end of the room and set her hand on one of the wall's stones. It flared for a moment with an orange glow. "Tall men and brave men and men who have been waiting for the praise, for the banner." She extended an arm slowly, then snapped her fingers. The fire died almost to embers and then rose again. "And girls. Such pretty girls, some with notes taped to them: *virgin* and *ripe* and *We've never cut her hair.* What could her hair possibly mean to me?"

I didn't answer.

"I'm not subtle," she said after a while, approaching me. "My magic is very . . ." She glanced at a painting of a carousel horse. Nodded, and the horse's mane grew and spilled out of the frame and down the wall—a pile of sturdy, coarse silver.

"It was you, though." I didn't back away, even though she was close enough to touch. "When I was in that place by the sea? You made the storm."

She glanced at me and smiled. "You were so beautiful. More so even than you were in your armor." She tapped just below my collarbone, where the edge of my chest plate ought to have been. "Perhaps you know that. Or why would you come to me without your armor?"

"You took it from me."

"You *lost it.*" She licked her lips. Across the room, the horse in the painting shifted. Its mane spiraled upward in a rope and was sucked back into the frame.

"Stop. Stop this performance. No more magic. Just talk to me."

She dipped her head. "What would you like to say?"

"I . . . I will help you get free."

"How?"

"I'll help you find the entrance. If you can take me back to where we were when you made the armor, I can find the thread again. We can follow it back to Alle, to the door." A journey to the labyrinth's entrance would buy me time. I could make her promise to find or fix Kenna. And once she had done that, once she had led me back to the thread, I could kill her and go to the entrance on my own.

Asteria looked longingly at me, and for a moment I thought I had her. That I was offering her what she truly wanted. Then she pursed her lips and gave a hum of laughter. "I'm afraid I've done something you won't like." She leaned close and whispered. "I've set her chasing a phantom."

"Who? Alle?"

"Hmm-hm-hm. I sent her somebody."

"Aaron McInroe?" I demanded.

"I don't remember names. But I know who she wants. And he will lead her on a chase that has no end."

I tried to keep breathing. *Be fearless. Love is a weakness.*

She continued walking past the white bull. "Why would I leave this place?" She stood before the bed and raised her arms, and her long white sleeves let just enough light pass through that I could see the shadows within the fabric—thin, slowly moving serpents that gathered to form a bull's head in profile. "I have such wonderful friends here—captives and heroes and pretty girls."

"I want to know how it felt. To terrorize Rock Hill."

Her body lifted off the ground, and she twisted in the air as though she were immersed in water, her mouth hanging open in a dull smile. "Why. Why why *whyyyyyy*? Everybody full of whys." She rolled again, slowly, and faced me. "Does it come as any surprise that cast-off daughters are angry, that destruction is art, that a person might do a thing simply because it is within her power to do it?"

"You're not *listening*." The last word echoed. "I didn't ask for an explanation. I asked how it felt."

She paused and turned. Set her feet back on the ground. "What if I don't remember how it felt?"

"You do."

She flung herself backward onto the pile of treasure and slid down it until she was sitting on the floor by the bed, limp like a doll, her legs splayed. She grabbed a handful of coins and let them fall one by one from her fist onto the stones. The gold flickered in the firelight, then vanished. She stared at the spot where it had been. "Good thing you didn't come here for that."

"Tell me," I said firmly.

She stood again and came toward me, stopping inches away. "I remember only this." She began to slap the left side of her chest, just under her collarbone, in a steady rhythm. "The heart beats *want-now, want-now, want, want, want, waaaaaaant* . . ." From somewhere came a harmony, joining her on the last three *wants*. "You must know something of that."

"Tell me," I said again.

"The darkness in each of us—it is simply *want*. And there is nothing inherently evil about wanting. We want and it makes us eat and it keeps us warm." She spun in the air again. "The evil, perhaps, is in the what-would-you-to-do-others? What would you do, Thera, to get what you want? Who would you hurt? Who would get a ragged skirt made of their belly, so that you might"—her tone turned mocking and singsong—"get a bit of food, buy yourself some time, live your pretty life?" She jabbed a finger at me. "Yes, you want a pretty life. Don't deny it. Even if it's pretty with oddities and with chaos, you want it pretty. You're a hound for that kind of beauty, you are."

"And what did *you* want?"

The corners of her mouth slunk upward. "The usual. A mommy who loved me. Friends, and to be extraordinary."

"You *made* yourself a prisoner. You hurt people. You ruined their homes. You broke families. And why? Because you didn't have a mommy?"

She flew past me, dress fluttering behind her like a kite tail. It was all I could do not to run.

"You had a father," I called to her. "He loved you."

She stopped and turned. "There is no one in this world who can love—truly love—a child whose blood is a stranger." Her voice was raw with fury.

"Did you know I was coming here?"

She nodded. "The dooooorrrrr." She let the word out on a breath. "I can feel it open, but I can never find it. I know every inch of this maze except. That. Dooooorrrr."

She panted and arched her back. Kicked her legs and thrust her hips, her eyes falling closed, her hair slung across her face and neck in damp tendrils.

"Enough!" I had spotted the sword above the fireplace, camouflaged in the stone. Sweat crept down my sides.

"I know this place," she said, resting in the air. "It was empty and I filled it. My playground; not my prison." She opened her eyes and gazed up at the ceiling. "I tell them to take me to the door. The heroes, the toys. I tell them I'll set them free, let them live, if they show me. But they cannot find it again." She glanced at my wrist. "You might have, with your clever thread. But you snapped that, didn't you?"

I ignored the sharp pain in my chest and stepped forward. "All that power"—I was unable to keep the mockery from my tone—"and you can't break out of here?"

Her grin broadened. "I suppose I waste my magic." She drifted toward the bull. "I left you gifts. Did you like what I made of the prisoner who stole your beauty's heart? Did you like my little dolly?"

"Tell me what happened to her. Where's Kenna?"

She circled behind me, her back to the door. She planted her feet and clasped her hands behind her back. "I could let them go. The dolly. Your pretty girl." She paused and seemed, for an instant, childishly uncertain. "And if you are looking for a place to belong, I can offer you that." She looked back at the spot where the treasure had been and shrugged. "It is a prison, but so are most places."

"I am here to stop you from ever hurting anyone again. And when I have done that, I will leave."

"Oh." She scrunched her brows together and clutched her chest dramatically. "No. We were something to each other. Didn't you trust me, Thera?"

"I would not have felt a moment's passion for you"—I inched toward the fireplace—"had I known what you are."

Her face grew red, and folds of skin rucked up around her mouth and eyes. She hissed, a long, slow sound. "You knew." She snapped her fingers, and the sword clattered to the floor near my feet. "You think you're ready? Pick it up. You think you're anything compared to me? You *infant*. The only thing fully grown is your sluttish mind."

"Me? An infant? Your war was a temper tantrum. And right now, you are doing nothing but playing with your toys."

She hopped onto the white bull and reclined on its broad back. Raised her legs so that her dress slid to her hips, then put a hand between her thighs and spread herself open. There was *fire* inside her; a roaring bellows of red and orange. The tips of the flames flicked out, licking her fingers and singeing hair, leaving black scorch marks on her inner thighs.

"You're not subtle," I agreed, picking up the sword. It was heavy. The closer I got to her, the less I could imagine plunging a blade into any living body. Even a beast's.

She drew her legs together and laughed, sitting up. "You're not impressed?"

"I'd prefer a lover, not a circus."

Her expression was, for a moment, genuinely poignant. No matter how much practice you have had, I would doubt even a sorceress's ability to re-create that blend of nerves, uncertainty, and readiness to be advised. "I do not know how to be any other thing."

Perhaps I should have pitied her in that moment. But she gave me no chance. She grabbed my wrist with such force and pulled me up beside her. Threw me onto my back and straddled me, her gown sweeping against me, coarse like mosquito netting. The sword fell. Across the room, the carousel animals stumbled out of their paintings. They bobbed in the air, their poles attached to nothing. Their mouths were twisted open and their eyes were wide, their limbs grossly contorted.

The carnival music grew louder, and musical notes appeared in the air, black as keyholes, large as my half my body. They stretched and sagged as figures climbed out of them. The figures gripped the edges of each note like half-drowned survivors at sea clinging to pieces of their dashed ship. I slid off the bull, and Asteria let me go.

I grabbed for the people I recognized—Denson's brother, Rocky Bottom—but when I tried to catch their hands they were swallowed back into the notes, which careened around the room, buzzing in the carousel animals' ears like flies and then vanishing, until the last note disappeared into the horse's hollow ear and the chamber was once again silent.

"Stop!" I shouted. "Let them go!"

"They are echoes and memories." Her voice seemed to come from all around me. "They are nothing."

I picked up the sword. Whirled again and caught hold of her arm. Dragged her off the bull, surprised by my own strength. The carousel animals bobbed out into the hall and vanished from sight, leaving behind empty frames on the walls. "A memory is not nothing."

She was still smiling. I pointed the sword at her.

"I am asking you to remember something good from your life." I was reaching, stealing words from Dark Tales. "Because all lives have good things, and if you can just—*remember*—"

She laughed. "Do you wish to hear that you are my one good thing? That I rejoice in the courage of a fool? That it shook me to the teeth to see you tug that thread, and see it move as she tugged back?"

"I don't care what your good thing is. I know my own. I'm trying to help *you*."

"Your pretty girl." Asteria patted the white bull. "Do you ever have trouble thinking of her as a person, not a prize? Is she a treasure because you can make her what you want? What if you peeled back the skin?" She lifted the bull's tattered hide, as though it really were flesh and not wood. She stuck her arm in the hole in its side and rummaged around. I heard slick, marshy sounds. "Can her beauty survive such an ... *interrogation*?" She pulled out something dark red and slimy. A liver. She tossed it on the floor, where it slid a few inches and then lay there dripping slime.

"I don't give a *shit* about beauty." I spat on the organ, which faded quickly, leaving just a small wet spot on the stone.

"Or are you afraid if you dig deep, you'll find she's really quite dull? Or do you resent her, because you'll never know?" She tapped her head with one finger. "Because everything up here is a secret, no matter how you try to let someone else in. Ah, always, even as you tell the story, you are rewriting it."

I pointed the sword at her once more. "I am giving you one chance. Find Alle. If you find her—alive—and if you take me to her, I will not kill you."

She stepped forward. I didn't think. There was none of the deliberateness with which Alle had killed the weasel, or with which I had once slain trees with my sticks. I plunged the blade clumsily into the center of her breast. It was heavy; I misjudged—I was nowhere near her heart.

She looked down, annoyed, as if I'd broken a glass or had some other trivial accident. I pulled the blade from her with an odd feeling of embarrassment, a sense that I'd been merely impolite rather than murderous. Blood spilled from the gash in thick, dark trails.

She grabbed the edges of her wound and yanked them together like the lapels of a jacket, watching as they sealed. Then she knocked me to the floor with a sweep of her arm. The sword clanged away from me.

She knelt by my side. She put her hands on my chest and belly, pressing until I felt sure my ribs would cave. My breath came out in crystals—diamond fountains spouting from my lungs, rattling across the floor. I choked on the sharp pieces, tried to scream but couldn't.

She stroked my cheek with fingers swollen and blistered from flames.

*She is trying to impress me. Hurt me, yes. But impress me.*

"Do you think I'm going to tell you how rough the world is?" she asked. "That the rich have their boots on the throats of the poor? That the wrong people die and the worst people live?" The fountains of diamonds stopped, and I breathed shallowly. She yanked my hair and shoved her mouth close enough to my ear that I could feel flecks of spit. "I don't need to tell you about injustice or revenge. But I'd like to tell you about mystery. For mystery, I have come to learn, is simply anything older than we are. Anything we did not discover, because we were born with it."

She pulled her head up slowly and gazed down at me.

"What we call mysteries—strange, wondrous—are often very common. Breath, the heartbeat, the slimy journey our food goes on." She traced from my throat down to my stomach. My throat clenched shut, and I flopped like a fish, trying to draw breath. "Have you ever played with a toy car, and made it stop and go? Imagine stopping a heartbeat. Imagine . . ." She passed a hand over my thigh, and she gave me a dangerous smile. She seemed to command the spirals of heat inside me the same way she commanded a storm. "Making it go faster."

I choked and pressed my legs together.

"Imagine we are all very simple beings, and that our greatest mysteries lie in the words we choose. Rendered speechless, like your dolly friend, all we will do is gasp and eat and fuck and sleep."

I heaved against the pressure of her touch. My eyes felt as if they were bulging out of my head. And then the invisible clamp eased, and I could breathe again. "We . . . do more than that. We m . . . make choices."

She waved her hand. "Predictable choices. You came here for the treasure, and yet I knew at once you'd end up in the center of the labyrinth. And didn't you know your pretty friend would go to town with you that night if you called her a coward?"

I gulped, not wanting to remember.

"People's words are often as trite as their actions, but there is no knowing *precisely* what someone is going to say. And I have spent many years thinking about words I long to hear, only to reach the conclusion that the words I long to hear are boring. That true joy will come from being surprised."

She made the frames of the paintings unwind and soften. They slithered down the walls and across the floor, their gilt catching the firelight, and they wrapped around my neck and waist. They didn't go tight. Instead they pulsed against my skin, as though awaiting a command. I swallowed. She tightened her hand into a fist, but the frames barely increased their pressure at all. It was if she wanted to crush the life out of me but could not. "So what will you say to me, Thera? Surprise me."

"Please," I whispered. "Please, if you want me, you can . . ."

"You are no seductress and never have been," she snapped. "If you are a warrior, be brave. If you are a whore, be skilled. And if you are something beyond either of those things—if you are difficult to describe, hard to win, and if your beauty comes not from symmetry and tits but from every strange, aching thing you are—" her eyes flashed and she leaned until her lips brushed my cheek— "then show me."

She grazed my stomach with her cold fingertips. I held my breath and then pushed it out bit by bit.

Her voice grew as soft as her touch. "You will always hide something from me. That's fair. I like mysteries and puzzles; I like liars. But the truth is a dance I want to see on command."

"You will never command me."

She smiled. "I will. But will you obey?"

I noticed a movement behind her. Alle had entered the room. My lungs froze, trapping my breath in ice. I felt sure I looked at a phantom. That Asteria had conjured Alle to torment me. I forced my gaze back to Asteria's. I could see by the slightest jerk of her shoulders that she knew—must know. Yet I couldn't take the chance. If Alle really had managed to sneak in unnoticed, I would not be the one to expose her.

"Try and see," I offered, trying to sound confident.

Behind her, Alle had crept over to the discarded sword. She picked it up and started toward Asteria, lifting the weapon.

Asteria turned and raised her arms like a dancer. The gesture was graceful, unhurried. Alle stopped. Her eyes went wide, and she extended her trembling arms, the blade now pointed toward her own stomach.

"Alle!" I cried.

Alle plunged the blade in. She shuddered, ribbons of red spilling over her lip and down her chin. She ripped the sword out, then stuck it in again. Blood tumbled from the wound, soaking her shawl, drizzling over the stones.

I didn't let myself scream. I fought, and the picture frames released me. I ran to Alle, who collapsed in my arms. Her shawl thwacked wetly on the floor. I eased her down and cradled her.

"Stop," I hissed at Asteria in the same quiet, furious way Miss Tophitt had sometimes scolded us children at Rock Point. I was beyond anger and beyond fear, on a cracked and desolate rock in a vast ocean. My voice was unrecognizable, a locust-plague buzz. "What have you done?"

"She meant to kill me." Asteria's face was wretched and red again, the veins in her neck standing out under the skin. I believed, then, that Alle was no phantom. That Asteria truly was furious. "She meant to kill *me*, and you grieve for *her*?"

"You *are* a beast!" I shouted. "You are everything they say you are."

She flinched. "Why should I be anything else?"

"Because it is *wrong*."

She grinned. Her skin had begun to sag, and her teeth looked bluish and bruised. "I taught a lesson to the town that shunned me. I have killed the fools who came here to kill me. I have witnessed the scum of the scum of your land—its murderers and its castoffs—become lost here forever, but I have not killed them. I have not killed anyone who came here unwillingly."

I was not sure whether to believe her, or whether I cared. My only concern was for Alle. She had gone very still, her eyes closed. I wanted to tell her what I'd always feared to say. That I would have gone with her to the end of anything—the end of a moment, an era, a lifetime.

The edge of any cliff or sensation or story. I would have fallen in much more than love. I was alone now, but that didn't mean I couldn't beg the aid of my memories. I thought of her hand in mine on the day it snowed. I remembered her face as she studied the drawings in the Minotaur book.

"Please," I said softly, as Alle's blood flowed over my arm. "She was only trying to save me. You're mightier; you've proven this." I looked down at Alle, whose head had fallen to one side, exposing her blood-streaked throat. "Don't let her die."

"What will you give me, to save her?"

I looked up again. Asteria appeared half-delighted, half-despairing. She stretched into a swaying, leering thing, like the winding sculpture in a dragon dance. Thunder sounded in the distance.

"Anything." It was a lazy answer, and Asteria only stared. I swallowed. "I will stay here with you."

"Done," she snapped. She thrust her arms forward as though inviting an embrace. I froze, confused, then watched in horror as Alle's spilled blood gathered, rising off the floor in a dripping sash and spinning its way into a thread made of ugly dark clots. The thread arched through the air and pierced Alle's skin at the edge of the wound, then stitched her up until across her belly was a black grin held together by a thread of her own blood.

Alle gasped, her eyes still closed. But she was breathing.

I turned to Asteria. Her expression was one of such anguish and fury that I couldn't speak.

She looked away, trembling. "I don't want you to stay."

I eased Alle down and stood, facing her, waiting until she met my gaze again. "What?"

"I thought," she whispered, "that once you held that blade, you would know what to do. But you are a fool like all the others."

"What do you want me to do?" I asked sharply.

She studied me for a long moment. "You could *free* me."

I didn't understand. I watched her skin grow more flushed and her trembling worsen. I tried to think how I was going to get Alle out of here, but I couldn't tear my gaze from the convulsive movements of Asteria's body.

The veins quivered in her throat, then burst through the skin one by one and hung, broken and limp, drizzling blood like kinked hoses. She stared at me—a manic smile wobbling on her lips, her guts churning like slop, so loudly I could hear them. Her eyes went blank, then the irises burst inward, leaving two black holes surrounded by jagged whites.

Her teeth exploded one by one, like they'd been shot out in a carnival game. Then the shards reconvened into long, flat molars. The bottom half of her face stretched down and forward, thin and sagging like putty, then hardened into a gnarled muzzle. She collapsed onto her hands and knees, and her spine broke in an upside down V at the base of the neck, forming a peak that was soon piled with muscle and covered in a dark hide. Her fists rounded—became black and glassy; became hooves. Her hind end hiked into the air and her knees snapped backward into hocks as muscle and fur covered her haunches. Her arms elongated and turned into a pair of front legs, and her head thickened, horns sprouting from the sides.

She towered, beautiful and terrible. Three times larger, at least, than a real bull, with her sleek coat rippling over her muscles and thick cords of drool hanging from her mouth. Her empty eye sockets bubbled like black oil; her tail was the lash of a whip. She tossed her great head and ropes of saliva struck the walls and dripped down the stones.

I staggered backward, positioning myself between the beast and Alle. I stumbled over something and glanced down.

I picked up the blood-soaked yellow shawl. Held it for a moment, feeling the weight of it. The blood was already drying, stiffening the fabric.

I extended my arms slowly and shook the garment out, spreading it between my hands until it was a wide, stained rectangle. Then I waved it at the beast.

Her mouth opened, and I saw broken bits of tooth bobbing on a slick pool of saliva, saw the thick, blue-black mass of her tongue. She lowered her head and pawed the ground. Her long horns pointed at my chest. And she charged.

Her hooves threw sparks as they met stone. A flash of lightning lit the entire ceiling, accompanied by a mighty *crack*. The rumbling in the floors and walls increased until it might have been a whole herd of beasts thundering toward me. The lightning outlined the Minotaur's broad black hump and bone-white horns. She caught Alle's shawl on the tip of one horn and yanked it from my grasp. I was sent spinning to the floor as she galloped past me and then skidded, unable to stop. She struck the wall, her horns lodging in the stone.

Lightning flashed again. Turning, I saw Alle crawling toward the discarded sword. I ran for it too, but Alle reached it first. She grasped the handle.

"Alle!" I called, holding my hand out so she could pass me the weapon. But Alle crawled back toward the white bull.

Asteria was still thrashing. "Alle!" I yelled again.

She ignored me. Reaching the wooden bull, she gripped its leg and pulled herself to her feet. She gasped and swayed, then drew back the sword and stabbed the carved creature through the chest.

Asteria let out a high-pitched, human-sounding scream as the labyrinth began to shake violently. An instant later, the clock tower collapsed onto the ceiling and sent cracks slinking through it. I looked up. The clock face stared down at me, white and luminescent, blood pouring from the clock hand into the web of faults. I reached Alle and dragged her underneath the white bull as the ceiling shattered and the tower plummeted into the chamber.

The clock hit the floor a few feet behind us in a spray of glass and stone. Alle and I were thrown upward against the wooden bull's belly. I caught a glimpse of Asteria, still trying frantically to dislodge her horns from the wall, and then suddenly the bulk of her vanished. I thought I spied movement on the ground where she had been standing, but I had no more time to think. The walls of the palace came shuddering down, spilling stones that fragmented and rolled across the floor. I shielded Alle with my body as the storm swept in. I heard glass striking the wooden bull's back, saw the shards bursting into salt-sized grains and skittering between the stones.

The wind toppled the white bull and it fell, not in a splintering of wood, but with a heavy, wet *slap* against the stone floor, as though it were truly made of flesh. I held Alle tighter as bits of glass and rock and ember swirled around us. The storm blew off suddenly, retreating out across the cliffs. I was surprised by how close we were to the precipice—stones from the palace were rolling over the edge, crashing into the sea or cracking against other rocks. The sky was a weak, watery gray, lightening rapidly as the worst of the dark clouds dissolved. It was several long moments before things went quiet but for the rough hush of Alle's breathing and my own.

A black mouse raced by my feet, climbing over and under rubble, darting onto the grass. It ran toward the cliff's edge, vanishing from my sight. A moment later, a fist-sized stone struck the grass, sending the mouse somersaulting through the air and over the ledge. Seconds crept by. *Is that it, then?* All at once, a gull swept up from beyond the cliff, soaring out over the sea until it became a black dot in the brightening sky, and then disappeared.

Alle's face was buried in my shoulder. Her body shook. The white bull lay beside us, and from the wound in its chest leaked a stream of blood. Yet when I touched the creature's body, all I felt was painted wood.

Alle inhaled sharply and looked up at me, her dark eyes wary, familiar. Everything softened then—her body and her gaze—and she reached up to touch my cheek. "I'm sorry," she whispered. "Thera. I'm so sorry."

"Me too." I pushed a curl back from her face.

As if love is ever a matter of forgiveness. We disappear in love. We hunger, regret, and resurface. Guilt and shame are how we decorate love when we are afraid to look at it directly. The core is something simpler. Bright, violent, and unadorned. I loved her; I always had. And now I held her, and I meant never to let her go.

# BOOK THREE

# TWENTY YEARS

# CHAPTER 26

It was the twentieth anniversary of the beast's fall. Twenty years ago today, Alle and I staggered over rocks and splintered boards, over glass and scraps of clock face, looking for other survivors. We found nothing. Not Denson's brother or Kenna or Rocky Bottom or strange corpses. No sharks or sheepdogs. No jungle vines, no great trees. Only rubble.

We had walked to Rock Hill. It took us hours, and our feet bled so badly that we were taken to the hospital once we arrived in town. We announced to anyone we saw that the beast was dead. Most people flinched from us like they were afraid, but finally a police officer heard us and rounded up a team to go to the promontory and check our claim. They found the ruins of the labyrinth and the body of the white bull. That always surprised me, how readily people accepted the carving as the body of the beast. When in fact it was her gift, her art, her shell, and her burden. They dragged it into town to taxidermy it for the museum, and as far as I know, no one has ever noticed it is made of wood.

They also found Kenna, alive but badly injured, buried under a heap of rubble.

Kenna we see sometimes. She lives in the heart of town, but she is considerably muted. Her left leg and back are no good; she limps and hates limping, so she tries not to move at all. In trying not to move, she has grown flaccid and a bit pathetic looking. She never talks about what happened to her in the labyrinth, but when we are together I sometimes catch her rubbing her nose with a compulsive fervor, or running her fingers over her lips in a zigzag pattern, as though tracing invisible stitches.

Alle and I were invited to a ball tonight, to be held at the grand hall the city built after the collapse of the labyrinth. They didn't build it on the promontory or anything so symbolic as that. The hall is on a hill overlooking Main Street's pubs and shops. I have heard it is splendid, but I've never been inside.

I had already skipped the afternoon's celebrations, but I'd been pressured into attending the ball. Alle had opted not to go. Twenty years ago, she arranged it so that, while we were both heralded as the bringers of the beast's doom, I emerged the hero. Alle told everyone that it was I who made the sacrifice. Who offered myself in exchange for Alle's life, an act so altruistic that—as the story now goes—the beast could not survive bearing witness to it. And in the Minotaur's moment of weakness, it is said I stabbed it through the heart.

I am still conflicted about this. I have indeed made a sacrifice, it seems. I sacrificed my chance to be human, complicated, weak and lovely both. I have seen so many people overlook what I was—an orphan, a crook, a tough in love with her own fists—in favor of the image of me as a warrior. The girl who set out to slay the Minotaur and succeeded.

I do not want the truth gone from me. I do not want only stories. What stories do to heroes is edge out the things that make them bravest—their insecurities and wrongdoings, their thrashing-tailed desire for self-preservation. The way they sharpen their love with a quiet, occasional contempt for the object of it. We paint heroes in broad strokes—nameable virtues and forgivable flaws. They brood, yes, but they are never paralyzed by self-loathing. They kill, but only monsters.

When I first read my tale in a book, I marveled at the stranger in those pages, like a starlet seeing a photo of herself with all her pimples painted out.

In twenty years there have been, to my knowledge, no sightings of Asteria. I do not take credit for this, but I do think often of what Asteria said when I asked why she did not kill the beast herself. *I am afraid.* In my fantasy she could have freed herself at any time, could have gone out into the world and lived a life where she was not hated or feared, if only she had not been so afraid.

If she lives, perhaps she has decided to do no more harm if she can help it.

Or perhaps she is biding her time.

Alle made a deal with me. If I stayed at the ball for one hour and did not enjoy myself, I could go home to her. She is good at gentle, loving decrees, and at being someone I long to come home to.

I am still not sure what we are. We have never untangled or tried to match our ideas about love, fidelity, and gratitude. I don't know if I am something she treasures or if I am simply a shelf above loneliness, where she sits and looks down at a void that dares her, coaxes her to lean forward. But I know she keeps me from feeling like I am meeting wall after wall. I think she is more beautiful than she has ever been, and that her beauty is featureless, magnificent, something beyond the body. I hope that if I was ever destined for anything, it was to lie beside her.

Rock Point Girls' Home closed five years ago, and now I am not sure where cast-off girls go. I suppose to other shelters in other towns. Alle and I have talked on occasion about driving to one of those places and adopting a daughter. But the idea frightens more than it pleases me, so I don't know. Parenthood seems like a journey I can't come home from, and I am only recently in love with the feeling that my maze has an end—that I have not one final destination, but many rooms and many returns.

I was too ashamed, too guilty, too exhausted to go back to Rock Point right away after the beast's fall. But I wanted to find Riley Denson. I wanted to apologize. When I finally did call the girls' home, pretending to be a young wife interested in adoption and asking if Denson was available, Rollins told me, curtly and politely, that Riley Denson had passed away several months prior.

The shock of the words held me motionless. "Passed away how?"

"She was ill." Rollins sounded hoarse, older. "She died in her sleep. Left everything to her daughter."

I sat there, frozen on the other end of the line, unable to speak.

"Riley Denson had no daughter," I said finally.

"No," Rollins agreed after a while.

It didn't occur to me to wonder why Rollins shared that last bit of information. But now I think it was because she knew who I was. I'd made no effort to disguise my voice after the initial shock of the news.

I thanked her and hung up.

I traveled to Rock Point two days later. Alle did not come with me. She had been staying at a shelter in town, and in truth I don't remember if I was glad or sorry she was not by my side. I asked the driver of the car to wait outside the main entrance, and I paid him from the money I'd been given by the town. A reward, one that would last me for years.

Inside the parlor, I waited for Rollins. I got distracted, remembering the day Alle had arrived at Rock Point, how she'd rested her chin on her folded arms and stared out the window. I tried to imitate the pose and was startled when Rollins said behind me, "Thera."

I whirled. She did not look much different—perhaps a little more gray in her hornets' nest of hair. It had been less than a year since I'd last seen her, and yet it felt longer. She took me to her office, to the room where I'd once picked the lock on the file cabinet. We sat at the desk where I'd found the adoption papers, signed by Denson and Rollins and awaiting my signature. It is strange, how there are numbnesses that seem sharper than pain, and when I sat, I had pushed all feeling so far to the side that its absence hurt terribly.

I didn't know what Rollins would say to me. If she would call me a hero, like everyone else. Part of me wanted to be recognized that way. Wanted Rollins to know that I, the girl everyone had thought so little of, had done something important. But she just chatted about the weather, commented on the new staff, and finally showed me Denson's will.

Denson had left everything to me. Not a large sum, but enough that, between this and my reward from Rock Hill, I'd be set for a long while. I also had Denson's cottage if I wanted it.

I waited for something to happen, something that would give me closure. Perhaps I would run into Miss Ridges, and she would say something wise and mysterious to me about what a true hero is. Perhaps I would see a sixteen-year-old girl who looked like me at that age, and whose glowering mistrust would pique my sympathy and nostalgia. Perhaps I would make up with Bessie Holmes. Or apologize to Van Narr for making fun of her lip hair.

"Is Tamna still here?" I asked suddenly. "I'd like to see her again."

Rollins glanced up. "Tamna is married. She lives in town with her husband."

This, for some reason, hit me as hard as the news of Denson's death. I could not banish the memory of Tamna grabbing fistfuls of her skirt that day in the kitchen, moaning and lost somewhere. And then I thought of weddings and of kicked turkeys, and I considered visiting my sister.

I did visit her, but I waited a couple of weeks. The visit with Rachel was more satisfying than my trip to Rock Point. She praised me over and over for my bravery and said she always knew I was courageous. Seeing Marc was odd—I was neither angry nor afraid. He opened a bottle of wine and asked me questions about the labyrinth, which I hated, because I had to edit so much of the story for the sake of my own modesty. Had to leave out kisses and phantoms. And that was when I realized I was the one who would keep the truth locked away. I would tell the story, and I would censor it, and soon people would be telling one another the easiest version.

There must have been so much more to the legend of the Minotaur than a cast-off daughter and her doomed child. More than a curse, more than a contest, more than a wooden bull. And yet if a girl is going to whisper that story to you while you pick apart clovers, it needs to be simple and it needs to be gruesome.

Alle had no family to visit, so she took to seeing Kenna regularly. They became closer in that first year after the labyrinth than they ever had been at Rock Point. I sometimes went along on these visits.

"Do you remember . . .?" Kenna asked us last time, her voice brittle, whirring, liked a dead leaf caught in the windshield of a moving car. She was propped at the table in her small, dirty kitchen, a shabby nurse named Mr. Himbrel cleaning a plate at the sink. "That time I was turned into a doll?" She chuckled. "I was all stitched together."

Neither Alle nor I knew what to say.

Kenna laughed again, and it sounded like she was guzzling lint, but it was a tremendous thing to see her smile. To remember that at Rock Point, she had smiled at cruelties, yes, but also at Christmas.

When I think now of the friends I have lost, when I think of what loneliness means, I feel like a fraud. Asteria told me that there is no loneliness so long as one has eyes. But I sometimes think it is what I see that makes me loneliest of all. Like shopping for clothes in a high-end store and finding everything you pull off the rack well beyond what you can afford—life seems a display of things that are yours to crave and dream on, but not to wrap yourself in.

This is all so maudlin, compared to what I thought when I was eighteen. My feelings then were mostly variations on rage. Everybody, it seemed, was a bullring clown, jabbing me, inciting me, and I charged until I was weak. I learned things in the labyrinth, yet I have remained much the same—a selfish girl with an open heart people toss spare change into like a beggar's hat. Epiphanies do not make me a better person. Seeing the light does not mean I will turn toward it. I can learn things in the whole maze and mess of myself and still make the most foolish choices.

Three months after my visit to Rock Point, I collected my inheritance. Alle and I moved into the cottage in Rock Hill, the cottage Denson had meant to share with her daughter, and we lived there and clung to each other fiercely, and we grew up.

# CHAPTER 27

The ball was loud. I wanted to leave at once, but I remembered my promise. One hour. I walked up a set of wide steps and between two fluted pillars and stepped into the grand hallway. Like most of Rock Hill, it was of an understated grandness. Blocky and open, with murals on the ceiling of trumpeting centaurs and thick-cheeked suns and moons. A long banquet table was loaded with food, and the mayor took my elbow as soon as he saw me and escorted me through the room. Introduced me to people who faded at once from my mind. Went on and on about the goose.

I stared at the goose as I loaded my plate with grapes, and I thought about kicking it.

An older man with combed-back silver hair approached me. He gripped his lapel with one hand. "May I have this dance?" He made a kissy noise.

I didn't turn away. I stared into his gray eyes in their slumping sockets. "No," I told him. "Not for anything in this world."

One thing I've found as I grow older is that untidiness has become distasteful to me. It used to be that anything raw and bad and filthy was exciting. Now I simply turn away, as though if I refuse to look at the world's ugliness, it doesn't exist. Or at least I can shield myself from it, like wearing rubber gloves or staying indoors. I miss the girl who stepped into the labyrinth. I miss the fool who welcomed brutality.

I search for her night after night, and sometimes I find her. I find her when Alle and I are together, when our legs are tangled, our fists in each other's hair, when I know she is more than a story. She has, over the years, unraveled her mysteries slowly. Trusted me with some of her secrets. She has told me about her experience in the labyrinth. She says she stood at the entrance for hours unspooling the thread. Occasionally she saw shadows, heard strange sounds. She could not always tell whether she was awake or asleep. When she felt the thread was no longer attached to me, she became frightened.

And then Aaron McInroe came to her. She followed him through the labyrinth, but always he was just out of reach. As she searched for her phantom, she realized there was only one way out, only one thing that mattered: to find me, if I still lived, and help me. It was her sacrifice that saved us both.

I still worry sometimes that I love an idea of her. That I'll never get far enough under her skin to satisfy my curiosity. But the truth grows upward from the seed of a fantasy. It is the magic beanstalk, towering madly and impossibly, so brilliant and absurd that it shields the listener from the knowledge that this is not a tale of magic but of greed. The truth is right there, tall and ugly but wrapped in enchantment.

Our story is very simple.

A girl who was scared loved one who was brave. A girl fool enough to try to play hero saw the underlying hornlessness of monsters. And in a sweet shock of ruin, two women found forgiveness, and they held each other in the wreckage left by one for whom forgiveness meant nothing. That is a tale ornery in its rejection of heroes, in its changeable villain, in its unwillingness to yield to invention.

Perhaps the broadest of all imaginations is the mind that truly sees what's in front of it.

There was a speech by the mayor, and a cavalcade of gowns in muted tones—even in the years since the Minotaur's disappearance, Rock Hill has not lost its love of gray. I heard so much laughter that evening. So many people came up to me to express gratitude for my bravery. I was asked again and again where Allendara was. I began again to get that feeling I'd gotten as a child—that there were secrets waiting for me just out of sight, that the here and now was going to drive me toward danger if it didn't stop being so dull and incomprehensible.

I picked at a plate of hors d'oeuvres and watched a dance that made me dizzy. And finally, I set the plate at a statue's stone feet and ran from the hall. I burst out the front entrance and down the steps and bolted toward the sea. I did not hear anyone calling after me. I arrived breathless at the hillside and stared down.

A *crash* like a falling clock, booming across the cliffs and the sea. I might have found a home in that prison. Or perhaps I was destined to explore the wider world, to find ravaged, cast-off places. To carve a path through those rich and bleeding lands mugged for their gifts, then left alone.

Instead I had a home in a town whose scars held it together like stitches. And I had someone to go home to. I sat on a cool patch of grass, and I watched the waves. I imagined commanding them, but was glad when I could not.

"Thera?"

I turned. Alle was walking toward me. The shock of seeing her gave way to gladness. She wore a dark-blue dress, and her hair was pinned up. She was not dressed for a ball, but she was tidy. I wished suddenly for another chance at our childhood. I would have taken her far beyond the gates of Rock Point. I would have looked out for her, and I would have healed her.

She sat beside me, tugging her dress over her knees. We watched the sea together. "How's the ball?" she asked.

"Crowded."

"I'm sorry I let you face it alone. I've been sitting at home thinking how selfish I am. I just hate this so much. These celebrations."

I nuzzled her shoulder. "You're not selfish."

"So you're less than enchanted with the festivities?"

"I just don't . . ." I gestured behind us toward the hall, "*understand* any of this."

She kissed my cheek. "Would you like to escape?"

"More than anything."

We stood and walked away from the glowing hall and its leaking music and drove home. We opened the door and stepped into the shadows of our cottage. I got myself a glass of water in the kitchen. She tilted her head at me. "Are you coming upstairs?"

"In a moment."

She smiled. "Don't be too long."

I wasn't sure how long I stayed in the kitchen, sipping water and listening to the house rasp and groan. Eventually I went upstairs and shed my ill-fitting dress outside the bedroom.

She was asleep, facing the door. One arm was draped over my pillow, and she was snoring softly. I crossed the room, careful of the creaking floorboards, and sat on the edge of the bed.

We think we know beauty when we see it. In a woman's face, in the curves of her body. In the sun sinking beyond the ocean or the flowers that pry themselves out of the softening ground each spring. But real beauty is a mystery. The minnows that dart away just before you glance into the shallows. The lightning that flashes in a desert somewhere across the world and destroys nothing—a victimless display of power. It's whatever makes us wish for happiness, even as the world offers us tragedy upon tragedy. It's not just in a woman's face, but in what she touches and how. The way the air and earth respond to her. It is in her fear as well as her courage. Courage without fear is simply recklessness.

I climbed under the covers, and as I did, Alle stirred and awoke. She rubbed the heel of her hand in circles on her forehead and yawned. "You're still awake." Her eyes drifted closed again.

"I can't sleep." I leaned in and kissed her cheek.

Her forehead furrowed slightly. She didn't open her eyes. "I missed you," she murmured, and tucked her head closer to my chest. After a moment her breathing deepened, and she was asleep once more. I shifted, cataloging the room's shadows.

*"Violence starts as a discovery—of power, of ambition. Of a force that rests with its head against your heart."*

I had, I hoped, chosen kindness over violence. Most of the time.

I heard a sound like skittering in the walls, and at once I was fully alert, my heart pounding.

This happens sometimes. I'm awakened by a persistent bird outside my window, singing out of tune. Or I'm in the kitchen and a mouse darts along the baseboard. I wonder if I am being haunted or watched over.

The beast and I, we are still dreaming.

Dear Reader,

Thank you for reading J.A. Rock's *Minotaur*!

We know your time is precious and you have many, many entertainment options, so it means a lot that you've chosen to spend your time reading. We really hope you enjoyed it.

We'd be honored if you'd consider posting a review—good or bad—on sites like **Amazon, Barnes & Noble, Kobo, Goodreads, Twitter, Facebook, Tumblr,** and your blog or website. We'd also be honored if you told your friends and family about this book. Word of mouth is a book's lifeblood!

For more information on upcoming releases, author interviews, blog tours, contests, giveaways, and more, please sign up for our weekly, spam-free newsletter and visit us around the web:

**Newsletter**: tinyurl.com/RiptideSignup
**Twitter**: twitter.com/RiptideBooks
**Facebook**: facebook.com/RiptidePublishing
**Goodreads**: tinyurl.com/RiptideOnGoodreads
**Tumblr**: riptidepublishing.tumblr.com

Thank you so much for Reading the Rainbow!

RiptidePublishing.com

# ACKNOWLEDGMENTS

Thanks to Del for being such a sharp, hilarious editor. And to my family and friends, for all the stories we've shared and for your continued love and support.

# ALSO BY J.A. ROCK

*Playing the Fool series, with Lisa Henry*
The Two Gentlemen of Altona
The Merchant of Death
Tempest

*Coming soon*
The Subs Club

*With Lisa Henry*
When All the World Sleeps
The Good Boy (The Boy #1)
The Naughty Boy (The Boy #1.5)
The Boy Who Belonged (The Boy #2)
Mark Cooper Versus America (Prescott College #1)
Brandon Mills Versus the V-Card (Prescott College #2)
Another Man's Treasure
Fall on Your Knees (*Rated XXXmas* Anthology)

By His Rules
Wacky Wednesday (Wacky Wednesday #1)
The Brat-tastic Jayk Parker (Wacky Wednesday #2)
Calling the Show
Take the Long Way Home
The Grand Ballast

# ABOUT THE AUTHOR

J.A. Rock is the author of queer romance and suspense novels, including *By His Rules*, *Take the Long Way Home*, and, with Lisa Henry, *The Good Boy* and *When All the World Sleeps*. She holds an MFA in creative writing from the University of Alabama and a BA in theater from Case Western Reserve University. J.A. also writes queer fiction and essays under the name Jill Smith. Raised in Ohio and West Virginia, she now lives in Chicago with her dog, Professor Anne Studebaker.

Website: www.jarockauthor.com
Blog: jarockauthor.blogspot.com
Twitter: twitter.com/jarockauthor
Facebook: facebook.com/ja.rock.39

# Enjoy more stories like
## *Minotaur* at
# RiptidePublishing.com!

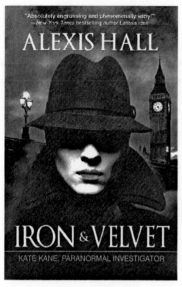
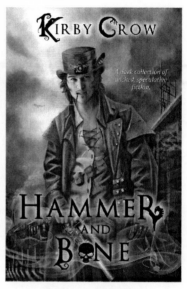

CPSIA information can be obtained at www.ICGtesting.com
Printed in the USA
LVOW10s1550231015

459498LV00005B/532/P